Dinuka McKenzie is an Australian writer and book addict. Her debut crime novel, *The Torrent*, won the HarperCollins Australia 2020 Banjo Prize. Her unpublished manuscript *Taken* was longlisted for the 2020 Richell Prize. When not writing, Dinuka works in the environmental sector and volunteers as part of the team behind the Writers Unleashed Festival. She lives in southern Sydney with her husband, two kids and their pet chicken.

Books by Dinuka McKenzie

The Torrent
Taken

THE TORRENT

DINUKA McKENZIE

HarperCollinsPublishers

HarperCollins_Publishers_

Australia • Brazil • Canada • France • Germany • Holland • India
Italy • Japan • Mexico • New Zealand • Poland • Spain • Sweden
Switzerland • United Kingdom • United States of America

HarperCollins acknowledges the Traditional Custodians
of the land upon which we live and work, and pays respect
to Elders past and present.

First published in Australia in 2022
This edition published in 2023
by HarperCollins_Publishers_ Australia Pty Limited
Gadigal Country
Level 19, 201 Elizabeth Street, Sydney NSW 2000
ABN 36 009 913 517
harpercollins.com.au

ISBN 978 1 4607 6534 0 (paperback)
ISBN 978 1 4607 1358 7 (ebook)
ISBN 978 1 4607 4041 5 (audiobook)

Cover design by Darren Holt, HarperCollins Design Studio
Cover images: Woman © Rekha Garton/Trevillion Images; all other images
by shutterstock.com
Author photograph by Emma Stergio
Typeset in Adobe Garamond Pro by Kelli Lonergan
Printed and bound in Australia by McPherson's Printing Group

MIX
Paper | Supporting
responsible forestry
FSC
www.fsc.org   FSC® C001695

To Scott, Harvey and Edie

THEN

Marty Drummond lowered himself into the flooded drainage culvert. The wet weather had begun again in earnest, the headlamp on his helmet illuminating the swift needles of rain against the gloom of the night. Clad in a wetsuit and lifejacket and strapped to a safety line tethered to the embankment, he began slowly treading across the churning waters of the open, concrete-lined channel. A slight tug of the line told him the second rescuer had entered behind him.

The headlights from one of the SES – State Emergency Service – trucks cast a sickly glow across the surge, revealing his destination some ten metres ahead to his right: a man perched precariously on debris, stranded in the middle of the drainage channel, his life raft consisting of nothing more than a tangle of tree branches, rubbish and silt that had built up against some kind of obstruction in the flow. Any second and the island of wedged-in materials could fall apart and wash away, taking its occupant with it. Despite the rain, a straggle of onlookers had gathered to witness the rescue operation, their phones out recording, pointing to the trapped man and shouting out directions, as if Marty needed instruction.

Mentally cursing, Marty pushed on. He had no idea how the man had ended up here, but after six years of volunteering for the SES, nothing the general public did surprised him anymore. It didn't matter that it had been raining for weeks or that the entire Northern Rivers region of the state was the subject of rising creeks and flood warnings. People still took no heed, risking their lives in floodwaters for all sorts of inadequate reasons, like being in a hurry. He had a feeling tonight was going to be one of those nights. Just a few hours ago, he had been enjoying a beer and a round of Xbox with his mates. Now, barely half an hour into his shift, he was already hip-deep in the drink.

The water was cold, but no more than Marty had experienced in previous rescue operations. What concerned him more were the unseen hazards swirling in its depths. He had no idea what muck was being carried by the dark turbid flow that eddied around him. If something large snagged him, he could easily lose his footing or get knocked into its silty current. Careful of where he was stepping, he slowly inched his way forward.

Peering ahead, Marty tried to get a better view of the trapped man. He could just make out the blue of the man's jacketed arm wedged into the mound. He was facing away, apparently unwilling to move for fear of losing his grip. He had been lucky to have been spotted by a jogger on the adjacent footpath. One of those diehard exercisers who pounded the pavement whatever the weather.

As Marty looked on, the fragile island seemed to shift, causing the man to slip further towards the waiting liquid. *I'm coming, mate. Just hang in there.* He needed to get to the bloke and secure a life vest on him before the debris mound disintegrated completely. Marty could then use the safety line to steer the man clear. Only a few metres away now.

'Mate, can you hear me? Are you okay to put on a lifejacket?'

There was no response. The man hadn't moved or given any indication that he had heard him. Marty felt a shadow of foreboding. *Shit!* He had no idea how long the bloke had been stuck there. He could be hurt or unconscious. Or worse.

He pressed on, heaving himself forward against the pressure of the water. Almost there. A few more steps and he would be within reach.

He heard a shout. Looking back, he registered his safety-line operator screaming something at him, seconds before he felt his knees buckle. Something large and bulky had knocked into him. He over-balanced and only just prevented himself from being pulled under by clinging onto the line. Correcting himself and taking a moment to signal back to the safety-line operator that he was right to proceed, he resumed, ignoring the savage flare of pain in his knee.

The rickety raft of rubbish was right in front of him now. Careful not to lean or put any weight on it in case it collapsed or moved, he manoeuvred himself around until he was facing the man. For a second, the face visible from the light of Marty's headlamp didn't register. Only the odd angle of his head. The cuts to his face and the mud and dirt plastered to his hair. Marty reached across and wiped a stray leaf from the man's lips.

Ice seared his nerves as recognition flickered. Instinctively, his fingers reached for the man's neck to feel for a pulse, even though he already knew the answer. Bile rose and he heaved into the water.

Joel. Jesus Christ. *It was Joel.*

His childhood friend. His footy mate. He had only seen Joel that afternoon. They had played Xbox together and mucked around. How the hell had Joel ended up here?

'You all right, mate? You need help?'

Rob, the second rescuer on the safety line, had reached him. His concerned face peered through the rain at Marty.

'He's a mate. I know him.' Marty gestured towards the limp body. 'I think he's dead.'

'Fuck! All right. Don't worry. Just help me get the vest on him and I can take him in.'

Marty nodded numbly. He grasped the lifeless body and held it steady, trying not to shudder at the unexpected weight of his dead friend, waiting for Rob to secure the life vest around Joel's chest.

He had little memory of treading back down the safety line, Joel's body being guided between Rob and him, a pathetic puppet on strings. The water felt like treacle, his limbs heavy against its shifting mass.

On the embankment, the spectators had turned silent, though some still held their phones aloft. A hushed audience bearing witness to the spectacle of death. Marty watched on as waiting ambulance personnel took charge of the battered body, going through the motions of checking for signs of life, before loading the body for transportation to the morgue.

He retched again behind a tree, but nothing came out. Gulping water from a bottle, he splashed the liquid onto his face to hide the hot barb of tears that flooded his eyes.

He looked up to find one of the gawkers, a teenage boy, had made his way towards him and was watching him through the gathering rain.

'You right there, mate?' Marty's tone was sharper than he had intended. He didn't need a witness to his grief.

The boy's answer when it came was jerky and agitated. 'Do you know who that was? Was it …? Do you know if it was Joel Marshall?'

Marty stared at him, suddenly alert. The kid's features were in shadow, obscured by his hoodie.

'Who are you? Why are you asking?'

The teenager turned away abruptly, but not before Marty had caught a glimpse of his face. A countenance marked by fear.

1

Thursday morning, first week of April

Dawn scratched the sky, pink-and-orange hues smudging into grey as Detective Sergeant Kathryn Aneesha Miles – Kate, to everyone who knew her – pulled into the carpark off Tweed Valley Way. An ambulance and a couple of patrol cars had arrived already. A disgruntled truckie was being moved on to get his morning McMuffin fix at the next fast-food restaurant along.

She collected herself in the unmarked Commodore, struggling into her jacket and straightening her bed hair as best she could in the visor mirror. She hadn't had time to get organised that morning, after being jolted awake by the dispatch call, cold recognition hardening into certainty as the call details came through. *A second one.*

She had slid carefully from beside the comforting warmth of her husband and their four-year-old son, Archie, moving his small, splayed arm from her chest, and creeping around the room in the dark to collect her clothes and shoes. Her fumbling had woken Geoff, and he had kissed her sleepily before she left.

'Pooh. Your breath smells.' She had stifled a laugh as she pressed her face to his.

'Have I told you you've put on weight, recently?' he had replied, ducking under the blanket as she swatted him.

She smiled at the memory, examining the puffiness around her eyes in the tiny square of glass. Sleep no longer came easy. Excess flesh padded the dusky curves of her face. Her body felt tight and strained, stretched uncomfortably under her swollen belly.

For a split second, an image of flushed crimson on cotton preyed on her mind; intimate and accusatory. *No.* She dismissed the unwanted memory, shrugging away the shard of guilt. She had talked to her doctor, she reminded herself. She would be fine. It was only one more week, anyway.

With a final hurried corralling of her hair into a pony tail, she hauled herself out of the car and into the brisk early morning. It was technically autumn, but the coolness lacked conviction and wouldn't survive the morning, burned away by the North Coast sun.

She glanced over at the fast-food eatery. It was one of the original restaurants of its kind to be built in the area back in the early nineties, and the building's brown brick façade had somehow come into style again as a retro throwback.

Making for the entrance marked by the iconic brazen yellow arches, she passed a ring of cockatoos, the bully boys of the bird world, raiding one of the external bins, picking through burger wrappers and discarded drink containers. They eyed her as she passed, standing their ground and protecting their haul, daring her to move them on.

The automatic doors sighed open and Kate stepped into a blast of recycled air heady with the smell of chip oil, burgers and sugar. Her gaze quickly swept the room.

Paramedics were attending to someone lying prone on the floor. Three young McDonald's employees in uniform – two boys and a girl – were huddled together watching on, the girl crying softly into a crumpled tissue. A female constable – Kate recognised the pert bob-cut of Vickie Harris – was with them, speaking quietly to the group. She clocked Constable Greg Darnley at the far end of the room, taking a statement from an agitated-looking young man in formal slacks and a pale-blue shirt with the McDonald's logo, a manager or supervisor of some kind.

Her eyes scanned the room for her partner, Josh Ellis, as yet a no-show. Swallowing her annoyance, she headed in the direction of the paramedics, walking slowly, one hand supporting her protruding belly, ignoring the discomfort of her straining body. A stirring within informed her that her baby was awake.

She caught the eye of Harris, who peeled away from the group. Kate didn't miss the young constable's quick glance at her belly. She knew what so many of them thought. That she was too late in her pregnancy to be effective. That she was a liability rather than an asset. The last time she checked though, her brains hadn't diminished despite the changes to her body. Ignoring the familiar niggle of irritation, she waited for Harris to bring her up to speed in a whispered conference.

'The victim's name is Josephine Allen, Sarge. Sixteen. She's been kicked and punched fairly heavily in the face and torso. Plus, she's got lacerations to her wrist and a stab wound to her stomach. The others are unhurt. Just scared. I've managed to contact all the parents except the Allens. The rest are on their way to pick up the kids.'

Kate nodded, taking in the pale, pinched faces and hunched shoulders of the group. 'Keep trying the Allens. If necessary, send an officer to the house and get them to go straight to the hospital. Have we got preliminary statements?'

'Yep. Everyone except Josephine. But nothing useful. None of them recognise the assailants.'

'Okay. Let's keep them together until the parents arrive and we can take it to the station.'

Seeking permission from the paramedics, she approached the girl – Josephine – on the floor, kneeling with difficulty beside her. She tried not to flinch at the sight of her facial injuries. Her left eye was swollen shut. Angry red bruising ballooned across the entire left side of her face. The girl appeared very young under the oxygen mask. A single darting, frightened eye locked onto Kate's face. She reached for the girl's hand and held it, pale and bleached against her own mellow brown.

'Josephine. My name is Detective Kate Miles. You're doing really well ... The paramedics are going to take care of you. They're going to take you to the hospital and your parents are going to meet you there. I'll come and visit you a bit later on and we can talk when you're feeling up to it, okay?'

There was no response. Kate had no idea if the girl had understood or even heard her. She squeezed the small hand in her palm, waiting for the girl to be lifted and strapped into the trolley that would wheel her into the ambulance outside, before letting go.

'Kate—'

She turned to find the imposing frame of Detective Ellis at the automatic doors. He reached her in long, unhurried steps, stopping only to make way for the exiting paramedics. Kate watched as he surveyed the room, his eyes pausing momentarily on the svelte figure of Constable Harris before moving on.

As usual, he was immaculately put together: a fitted suit, gel-moussed hair, and perfectly manicured stubble grazing his jawline. He looked fresh and rested, the perpetually sunny Tweed Shire apparently having no effect on his sweat glands. Next to him, Kate immediately felt dowdy in her stretched and dated maternity wear, saved over from her pregnancy with Archie.

Josh was a new transfer from down south, all the way from Sydney. He had been with Esserton Station less than a month and would be acting in her role when she left on maternity leave in just over a week. He was polite enough, she admitted, giving her the respect due to her seniority at least on the surface, but she was yet to get a proper handle on him. There was a slight insolence in his manner. Nothing obvious that she could put her finger on. Maybe it was because she was a woman. Possibly it was her colour, though she didn't think so. He didn't strike her as that kind of insecure. Most likely, it was the regional posting he had to endure to secure a promotion. Whatever it was, he was clearly biding his time.

She launched in without preamble. 'It's another holdup. Three boys, wearing superhero masks and armed with a knife. Just like the bakery job in town. Except this time, one of the staff got hurt. A Josephine Allen, sixteen. Stabbed in the stomach and bashed in the head. So they're escalating.'

Josh didn't reply, his eyes still flickering around the room with no indication that he had heard her. Impatience snagged at his lack of reaction. This was clearly just a piddly small-time job for him. He wasn't impressed or interested.

'Darnley's interviewed the manager,' she ploughed on. 'That's him over there.' She pointed to the gangly young man pacing laps at the back of the restaurant, his hands fiddling nervously with a mobile phone. He appeared defeated, like a cornered animal. Shoulders hunched and large sweat patches starting to bloom under his armpits. The man looked up, feeling their eyes on him, and blanched. Kate felt a sliver of sympathy for him. He seemed very young to be a manager in charge of the welfare of four teenagers. He struck her as being barely out of his teens himself.

When Kate turned back, Josh was signalling to Darnley at the other end of the room to join them. He nodded to Darnley for his report, assuming control. Kate willed herself silent.

Consulting his notes, Darnley directed his reply to Kate, the senior officer. She couldn't help but smile. Darnley was old-school and a stickler for the pecking order. He was showing the newcomer where his loyalties lay.

'Sarge, there were four employees plus a manager working the midnight-to-seven-am shift. Abigail Masters, Josephine Allen and Lucas Unwin, all sixteen, were on service together, manning the drive-through window and the front counter. Jack Goodwin, seventeen, was in the kitchen. There was meant to be one more employee helping out in the kitchen, another seventeen-year-old, Jarvis Ellwood, but he called in sick just before the start of the shift.

'The bloke in charge is Adrian Martello, twenty-four. Very nervous and jumpy. Like he's afraid of losing his job. And with good reason, I'd say, because it doesn't sound like he was much of a manager last night.'

Kate waited, knowing there was more to come.

'Yep,' continued Darnley, referring to his notes and settling into his stride. 'According to Jack Goodwin, Mr Martello was meant to be helping him in the kitchen to pick up the slack, but instead he spent all his time on his mobile, either in the staffroom or out the back. Jack thinks Mr Martello's fiancée is in the process of breaking it off with him and he was trying to talk her out of it.

'Apparently, he wasn't in the store when it all happened and missed the whole thing. He had gone out the back to haul the garbage into the dumpsters – a five-minute job at most – but he didn't reappear for a good twenty minutes. By that time, the assailants had come in, taken the cash and gone. According to the kids, even when he got back inside, he wasn't much help. He basically panicked when he realised Josephine was hurt and bleeding behind the counter. Fair to say, he's not the most popular boss at the moment.'

Darnley glanced over his shoulder in the direction of the beleaguered supervisor, and added with a grin, 'He's perked up a bit now, though. Suddenly remembered that he's meant to be in charge and is asking all sorts of questions. "How long will this take" and "how soon can the store reopen".'

Beside Kate, Josh was fiddling with his phone, clearly impatient for Darnley to finish.

'Okay, Greg.' Kate cut into Darnley's soliloquy, not unkindly. 'Let's leave Mr Martello for a second. Is there any CCTV footage?'

'Yep.' Darnley hurriedly flipped forward through his notes and resumed. 'That was something he was able to help us with. There's internal and external footage. Two cameras inside the store and one overlooking the store entrance—'

Josh interrupted. 'Anything of the carpark itself?'

'Unfortunately no. None of the cameras face the carpark—'

Josh swore as Darnley continued, undeterred. 'None of the staff on shift remember seeing or hearing a vehicle immediately before or after the incident, including Martello when he was out at the bins.' He motioned to the glass wall-panels set into the brown brick walls of the restaurant. 'The majority of the carpark is visible from the restaurant, apart from the southern end' – he pointed – which is blocked by the playland equipment. The bin area where Martello was holed up is on the opposite side of the store. In theory, a vehicle could have been parked at the southern end of the carpark and not have been spotted by anyone inside.'

'Right, Greg,' broke in Kate. 'Let's get the footage we do have and we'll review it at the station.'

'Not much use when they're wearing masks,' muttered Josh.

Ignoring him, she continued to instruct Darnley. 'Also, have someone check the Hungry Jack's next door, will you, and see if they have any external cameras that may have an angle on this carpark.'

Darnley nodded, scribbling into his notepad.

Kate glanced at her silent partner. 'We'll need to pull traffic footage off Tweed Valley Way going in both directions. They got lucky, no one seeing a vehicle. There's no chance they travelled here by foot … Plus, we should check on Mr Martello's fiancée. Make sure he was actually speaking to her all that time, and check the phone records to confirm.'

She waited to see if Josh had anything to add. Not a word.

'I'm going to speak to the kids again. See if they remember anything more. You coming?'

'You go ahead. I might just have a look around.'

Controlling her irritation, she turned away and headed towards the still-huddled group of employees.

Three faces peered up at her approach. The girl, Abigail Masters, had clearly been crying heavily, judging from her red eyes and blotchy face. Her two companions sat numb and silent, the adrenaline from the night starting to wear off. Despite their obvious distress, she instinctively recognised them as the popular kids. Blessed with good looks and confidence, they no doubt ran the joint on any normal day. They had that air of untouchability, a world unto themselves that she remembered from high school. It was no wonder the unfortunate manager of this group felt on the outer.

Mentally shaking herself, she addressed the teens, carefully taking them through the events of the early morning. Each of them agreed on the main points – the boys, the masks and the knife –

but couldn't add anything new to their original statements. None of the three had recognised the assailants. Their faces had been covered and their voices unfamiliar. The only thing of interest she gleaned was that evidently all three youths had worn skin-tight disposable gloves.

She was interrupted by Constable Harris, who pulled her away from the group's hearing.

'We have a problem, Sarge. Josephine Allen's father. It's Roman Allen, as in Councillor Allen. He's at the hospital now and wants to see the detective in charge.'

A pebble of memory dislodged and settled like an unwelcome guest. An added complication that would need careful handling. She nodded, dismissing the constable.

2

Roman Allen. Kate hadn't thought of him in close to fifteen years and now she was driving over to see him.

He must be in his early forties, she figured. She had heard that he had been voted to council in the last election and had become quite influential backed by the state Nationals, but their paths had never crossed since their early association. She hoped he wouldn't become a problem for the investigation. She didn't need him pulling strings to pressure the team.

Unbidden, an image of fairy floss and laughter flashed through her mind. The sweet and savoury tang of carnival food mingling with show animals and dust. She pushed it away. This was not the time.

She shifted in her seat, adjusting the pressure on her lower back, and forced her mind onto the problem of her partner. Josh had left the scene before her. She had no idea if he had headed back to the station or elsewhere. He hadn't bothered to inform her, which she would have to address. Sighing, she turned up the radio. The local station was advertising the season's latest cane-toad muster. A song she didn't recognise followed the news report, filling the car with melancholic chords.

Outside her car window, the outer reaches of Esserton flashed past in a blur. In the past decade, Esserton had expanded rapidly from a sleepy satellite suburb of South Murwillumbah to a flourishing regional township in its own right. Thanks to an influx of tree-changers and a burgeoning organic and artisanal food movement, the town had carved itself a place on the North Rivers gourmet-food trail and tourist scene. Comparatively low land prices had led to a mini-boom in housing development. Cresting a rise, she viewed the new subdivision spreading ahead of her like a perfectly constructed Lego town glinting in the mid-morning sun.

She took the river route through town, following its wide, meandering circuit, deliberately taking her time. The water glinted in the sun, oily and slick, a slow-moving beast, its power in check. Observing the houses perched on the bank, Kate marvelled anew how, not more than three months ago, at least a metre of water had been lapping at their foundations, the streetscape converted into a network of muddy canals and at least one local dead.

Many of the houses still showed signs of their ordeal, awaiting insurance money to fully exorcise the effects of the flood. A faint scum line from the water level could be discerned on the weatherboard exteriors and fences of some of the houses, though their yards seemed to be experiencing a new spurt of greenery, courtesy of the river silt deposited onto the garden beds.

Stopping at the lights, Kate watched as a sweat-soaked jogger, resplendent in neon Lycra, pounded the esplanade alongside the river. It was back in public use after a mini-facelift by council following the flood. Scoured of accumulated black river mud and debris, repainted and newly landscaped, it was once more the showpiece of the town.

Turning west, she drove until the dark-grey walls of Esserton Central Hospital rose into view.

After pulling into the hospital carpark and showing her ID, Kate was informed that Josephine was in the ward four levels up. She rode the lift alongside a man holding aloft a large blue balloon emblazoned with, *It's a Boy!* He exited at the maternity ward, grinning and motioning to her bloated figure. 'Not long to go now.'

She obliged with a cramped smile in return. The uninvited commentary from strangers on her pregnant form, she had discovered, was as tediously regular as it was unoriginal.

Travelling up a further two floors and following the signs embellished with cartoon animals, she located the children's ward. Following the directions of the duty nurse, she walked the brightly coloured corridors in search of Josephine's room. Ahead of her, a door swung open from the inside and two men stepped out. With a stab of shock, she realised it was Roman Allen in conversation with Detective Ellis.

She could do nothing but stare, rooted to the spot. Roman looked the same as he had fifteen years ago. Older, yes. His shock of black hair was distinguished with grey, his skin starting to show the effects of the sun, but it was still unmistakably him. Confident, powerful and well-built. A man's man, expecting the world to fall at his feet.

Allen held out his hand and Josh shook it, manoeuvring what appeared to be a plastic evidence bag out of the way. Kate assumed it enclosed Josephine's McDonald's uniform.

'It was very nice to meet you, Detective. Thank you for taking the time to visit and run me through what's being done. I can see the case is in good hands.'

Fury rose like steam, propelling Kate forward.

'Detective Sergeant Kate Miles, Mr Allen. It's nice to meet you.' She stuck out her hand. 'My apologies for running late. I was stuck at the scene. I see you've already met my partner.' The words were spoken without a glance in Josh's direction.

Roman Allen hesitated momentarily, no doubt silently correlating her 'Australian'-sounding name to her discernibly South-Asian heritage. She was used to the reaction. It hardly gave her pause anymore. In the genetic stakes, it was her mother, a Sri Lankan migrant from the UK who had placed her stamp on Kate's appearance, while her younger brother, Luke had taken after their Australian father, inheriting his deep grey eyes and light skin, freckles and all. Growing up she had lost count of the minuscule double takes and swift second glances that had been thrown their way when she had been out and about with her father.

She felt Allen's eyes flicker across her heavily pregnant form. She could almost hear the cogs whirring in his brain, trying to work out where she fit into the mix. Was she junior or senior to the detective he had just met? In the end, he simply accepted her hand and shook it briefly.

Kate met his eyes. Nothing. She didn't know why she had worried. Of course he wouldn't remember. She had only been a raw young thing at the time, too unimportant to register.

'I'm sure Detective Ellis has already enquired, but can you tell me how Josephine is doing?'

At the mention of his daughter, a spasm of pain seemed to jolt through him.

'The cuts around her stomach are only flesh wounds, thank God. The doctor in emergency reckoned the knife they used was blunt. Didn't penetrate very deep.' Allen swallowed hard. 'They've just brought her up after her scans. They say there's no sign of internal bleeding so far, but they'll need to observe her for a few days.'

'That's great news, Mr Allen. You must be very relieved.'

'It's a bloody miracle she escaped without any serious damage. Have you seen her face? Who knows what long-term effects there will be? Those absolute gutless bastards. Imagine kicking someone in the head? What kind of person does that?'

Her insides twisted at his words. All the things she could say. She settled for what was expected of her. 'Please rest assured, Mr Allen. We'll be doing our best to catch the offenders. We'll need to speak to Josephine at some point when she's able. See what she remembers. Any little detail that will help us identify the assailants means the quicker we can catch them—'

'She's resting now,' he interrupted. 'Josh's already seen her. I don't want anyone else disturbing her today. She needs to rest. That's what the doctor said.'

On first-name basis already, Kate noticed. 'That's fine, Mr Allen. We don't need to disturb her right this minute. We can come back later. Just give us a call when Josephine wakes up and feels up to talking.'

'Yes. All right. I've got Josh's number.'

'I'll give you mine as well,' Kate persisted, holding out her card. He accepted it placing it in his pocket without a glance.

They said their goodbyes and Kate strode ahead of Josh out of the ward.

At the lifts, he caught up with her. 'Kate. Hang on a second—'

She rounded on him, speaking through gritted teeth. 'For your information, I am the senior officer on this case and will be until I go on leave. Until that time, you will inform me before you wander off from the scene and consult me on any decisions you make about the case, and that includes meeting the families of the victims.'

Josh bit his lip. 'Fair enough,' he said. 'But for the record, I was told to get down here by the chief inspector. I didn't know you were going to be here as well.'

'Skinner asked you?'

Josh nodded. 'Roman Allen's been working the phone. The chief asked me to attend and smooth down ruffled feathers. He thought a … male detective would make a better impression on Mr Allen.'

Josh had paused infinitesimally before landing on the word 'male', and Kate had a fair idea what he had been about to say before changing tack. No doubt Skinner had not had any such qualms. 'He said that, did he?'

'Kate, this is not about you. This is about Allen. He's a fucking dinosaur in politician's clothing who still thinks women should be wearing aprons and staying at home cooking strudel or whatever. We don't want him hanging over us running interference and pulling strings. We need him on our side.'

She waited him out, her face set.

'The chief thought – and actually I agree – that sending me rather than you to talk to him would work better. Meet the clown's expectations of what a detective should look like or whatever … But you're right. You are the senior officer and I should have run it past you.'

He had the grace to appear shamefaced and she guessed that was the closest she was going to get to an apology. She jabbed the 'down' button for the lift.

'Why strudel?'

'Sorry?'

'You said Allen is a dinosaur who thinks women should be wearing aprons and cooking strudel … Strudel is very specific. Why strudel?'

He met her eyes and half grinned. 'I had a girlfriend who cooked strudel. She was bloody good at it, too. Crisp and cinnamony. She was Viennese,' he added unnecessarily.

Kate's lips twitched involuntarily and she felt something shift between them.

The lift arrived and they stepped in together.

'So, what's the plan?'

Kate reached into her jacket pocket and pulled out an evidence bag with two USBs. 'Security footage.'

3

The grey-white security footage flickered into life. The time stamp read 4.33 am.

Kate and Josh had reconvened in one of the meeting rooms at the station. A laptop and monitor had been set up and the security footage, tagged into evidence, had been uploaded.

On screen, they observed as three masked boys entered the fast-food restaurant. Nondescript jeans and dark, light-weight jackets. Their heads and faces entirely covered by rubber Avenger movie masks – Iron Man, Hulk and Captain America. They appeared to be goofing around, feigning punches and pretending to swipe off each other's masks. Relaxed and in control, they approached the counter, studying the menu board as if to order.

'They're trying to put the staff at ease,' observed Josh.

Kate nodded. Josh was right. On screen, the two girls at the counter, Abigail and Josephine, didn't look fazed. The masked boys were clearly young and had the swagger of high-schoolers clowning around. The girls were smiling at them, expecting to be brought in on the joke.

Kate had viewed each of the security recordings once already along with Josh, and they were now re-watching the footage from the camera on the corner wall that was angled to catch the restaurant floor and the counter. The youths were visible mainly from behind and in profile, but it was still the best play-by-play vision of the events.

Kate watched as the teen with the Iron Man mask spoke to Josephine, apparently ordering some food. She entered the order into the register. Kate could see Lucas in the background heading for the fries station and Abigail moving to the drinks machine. Jack Goodwin, out the back in the kitchen, was away from shot.

The teen Iron Man held out a twenty-dollar note to pay for the order. She noticed how he held the note back just enough to make Josephine reach for it. As she leaned over, he grabbed her outstretched arm and pulled her forward, pinning her arm down so she was perched awkwardly halfway across the counter. At the same time, the boy wearing the Hulk mask reached swiftly forward and helped to hold her down. From inside his jacket, the Hulk pulled out what looked like an ordinary kitchen paring knife and held it over Josephine's neck. It had all happened within seconds. Josephine hadn't had a chance to react or scream. Lucas and Abigail had both half turned at the kerfuffle and seemed frozen in place in shock.

Josephine's face was starting to show signs of fear and pain, her mouth twisted in panic. Iron Man now appeared to be speaking calmly to Josephine and Lucas. The security footage had no sound, but they saw Lucas come to life and approach the register.

Abigail had shrunk from view, crouching on the floor behind the drinks machine, trying to disappear.

From the back, a new figure came into frame: Jack Goodwin. For a second, it seemed as though he was going to walk around to the counter and confront the youths. The Hulk made a swift, stabbing motion with the knife, stopping just short of Josephine's ear. In the footage, Josephine's eyes widened in fear and her mouth gaped, an open wound of terror. She appeared to be screaming and Jack stopped where he was.

Kate watched as Iron Man said something and Lucas rushed to open the till. For the first time since the youths had entered the restaurant, the boy in the Captain America mask now joined in the drama. He had been waiting and watching from the sidelines and seemed to finally come to life, stepping up to the counter and holding out a canvas shopping bag. Kate and Josh watched as Lucas started to stuff money into it. In his haste, he dropped some coins on the floor and scrambled down to retrieve them, but jumped back up in a hurry when Iron Man seemed to shout at him. He concentrated on transferring the remainder of the money. Finally, task completed, he handed the bag back to Captain America. Without a word, the boy turned and ran out of the restaurant.

He'll be the one getting the car started, Kate surmised.

Iron Man was now addressing Jack, Lucas and Abigail, motioning to the latter from her position frozen on the floor. The Hulk, making a threatening gesture, moved the knife closer to Josephine, pointing it at her face, the tip centimetres from her eye. Message received, the two boys and Abigail backed away from the counter into the kitchen and out of the camera frame, closely followed by Iron Man. From interviewing the teenagers, Kate knew that the teenager masked as Iron Man had stopped just inside the kitchen and watched them until they had retired down the corridor to a storeroom at the very end of the store.

Momentarily alone with the Hulk, this was when Josephine had taken her chance, suddenly and violently jerking her body back to free her pinned arm. For an instant she was clear, and had rolled behind the counter out of sight. Seemingly enraged that he had even for a moment lost control, the Hulk was up and over the counter and after her within seconds, the knife flashing in the light. For four long seconds the footage was still, the counter hiding what was happening behind it. Until finally he was up. Even with only the top half of the Hulk's body visible, they could still make out his frenzied movements: he was kicking Josephine on the floor.

Kate recalled Josephine's broken and swollen face. All that damage had been inflicted in less than a minute.

Iron Man was now back in shot, screaming at the Hulk, trying to pull him off Josephine. This was clearly not part of the plan. Finally succeeding in grabbing his partner, the two boys sprinted for the exit, but not before the Hulk had made one final gesture. Breaking to a halt at the entrance doors, he turned to face the security camera housed on the opposite wall, raised his knife and pretended to drag it across his neck. The motion was crude and unnecessary. A boy playing at being a gangster.

On screen, Iron Man pulled his friend away and they were finally gone. Kate watched as a few moments later Jack and Lucas, along with Abigail, cautiously ventured back into the counter area and rushed to Josephine's aid.

Kate paused the footage, observing the time stamp: 4.38 am. The entire holdup had taken less than five minutes.

'They're getting bolder,' she remarked. Her mind was on the previous incident two weeks ago. After watching the footage, she had no doubt in her mind that the two jobs had been carried out by the same assailants.

The earlier holdup had been of a Vietnamese bakery just after opening at 7 am. The Nguyens, a husband and wife team who ran the business, had both been at the store. He had been busy out the back, cleaning bakery equipment, and she had been manning the store along with her younger sister. Mrs Nguyen had been kneeling at the drinks fridge near the front entrance of the bakery, stacking bottles, and had been an easy target for the boys with their knife. There had been only two of them in that first attack: one threatening Mrs Nguyen on the floor and the other demanding money from her terrified sister at the counter. Having just opened, there had been hardly any money in the till, a token amount to provide sufficient change for customers. The boys had gone off with just under forty dollars in notes and coins, which made Kate think it had been a practice run to get one under their belts.

The two Vietnamese women, recent migrants to the country, had been scared and distressed. They had been poor witnesses, made worse by the language barrier. They had given vague descriptions of the perpetrators, apart from the one intriguing detail about the masks. On that point, they had been adamant. '*Green Man, Red Robot*,' they had exclaimed repeatedly to the police officers in attendance. In frustration at their lack of understanding, one of the women had motioned the police constables to the drinks fridge and pointed fiercely at an Avengers-themed drink bottle, jabbing a finger insistently at a picture of the Hulk and Iron Man until they had finally got their message through.

There had been no other witnesses and the shop, located on a quiet side street, had no CCTV. The boys had been quiet and efficient, in and out of the shop in a couple of minutes. The husband had not heard anything. The Nguyens' six-month-old baby had slept through the whole incident on a blanket on the floor behind the counter.

Kate motioned to Constable Harris standing to the side. 'All right, Vickie. It's all yours. Let's get as many stills as we can for the media release. We should be in time for the evening news. Let's see if someone recognises them.'

'Actually, I'd like to run the footage again,' Josh broke in. 'Get a better view of Captain America, the new addition.'

Kate suppressed a sigh. She hadn't missed the swift look of appraisal he had given Harris when she had entered the room, or the rush of heat that had crept up the constable's neck. He was chasing skirt and showing off.

Without a word, she let him skip back the footage to the moment when Iron Man and the Hulk had gained control over Josephine. In silence, they viewed again the vision of the boys threatening Josephine. The footage moved on to Lucas at the till, filling the canvas bag with money. Now Captain America was reaching out to retrieve the canvas bag.

'Hang on,' Kate exclaimed. 'Replay that bit.' Heaving herself awkwardly off her seat, she leaned into the screen.

In reaching for the bag, the right-hand arm of Captain America's long-sleeved jacket had rolled back slightly. 'Pause it there.'

Kate pointed to the thin sliver of skin revealed by the loose sleeve just above the edge of the disposable glove. 'What's that? Is that a shadow or is it a mark on his skin? Is it a tattoo?'

Josh was up and beside her. 'Not sure,' he said, squinting. 'It could be.'

He reran the footage again. They watched the recordings another half a dozen times, checking and rechecking the footage from each of the camera angles to see if they could find a better view of Captain America's right hand just above his wrist. Nothing else could be gleaned. Kate had noticed a millisecond's worth of footage, visible and then gone in an instant. It was partially obscured by the teen's jacket-sleeve, but there was definitely something.

'We'll need the techies to examine it,' Kate noted. 'See if they can zoom in and enhance it somehow. Can you see to it, Vickie?'

'Will do, Sarge. That was a good catch.'

'All credit to the detective here for insisting we take another look. Good instincts, Josh.' She suppressed a smile as he turned away.

* * *

Kate rose from her chair with a groan. She stretched, feeling the muscles and sinews in her lower back and hips protest. She ran her knuckles down her spine to alleviate the tightness. Her bare feet felt good on the cushioned carpet. The boots she had started the day with lay discarded under her desk, her swollen feet at their worst at the day's end.

The office was largely empty and outside the day was slipping into dusk. Investigation running sheets from the day's activities sat piled on her desk. She just had to get through a final briefing with Josh and hopefully could make it home to Archie, before his bedtime.

'Ready?' Josh was beside her, laptop in hand, his shirtsleeves rolled up and his jaws working a wad of gum.

'Yep. Ready when you are.'

Josh eyed her feet, naked aside from the cracked nail polish that adorned her toes, and dragged a chair over without comment. He took his time scrolling through his notes on screen. She sat back down, stretching her toes under the desk, and waited him out.

'So, the forensics are a non-starter. No fingerprints this time due to the gloves, so nothing to compare with the prints lifted at the bakery. They're obviously learning. Plus, the place is a zoo of fibres. It's not going to be a quick job cross-checking between the two sites. I'm not holding my breath.'

'What about Josephine? Anything useful from this morning?'

Given the physical attack she had been subjected to by the boy in the Hulk mask, Josephine was the only victim that they had any hope of lifting DNA or trace evidence from. With her parents' consent, Josh had taken the opportunity to process Josephine for physical evidence when he had visited her that morning. She had been in and out of consciousness and unable to provide a witness statement, but he had been able to photograph her physical injuries, run swabs of her face and arms and remove fingernail clippings at the same time as he had collected her McDonald's uniform.

Josh made a face and shrugged. 'It's with forensics.' He left the remainder unsaid.

Kate held no illusions about it being a long shot. The gloves and the rubber masks the boys had worn would have minimised the chance of any DNA transfer, and there were countless potential sources of contamination – from the restaurant staff and ambulance and medical officers – who would all need to be eliminated should any trace evidence be isolated.

'Okay. What about the masks?'

'I think that's a dead end. They're sold everywhere: newsagents, two-dollar shops, Big W. Anywhere that sells party supplies. We've checked over a dozen stores since the bakery job, and so far, no one remembers selling a set of masks or individual masks to any specific teenage boy. That's not to say they didn't, but without a photo to jog their memories, no one can say for certain. I doubt we're going to get any headway there.'

'Agreed. Let's move on to the McDonald's staff. Have we talked to the staff member who called in sick? What's his name …?' She paused to check her notes.

'Jarvis Ellwood,' he supplied. 'Yeah, Harris spoke to the family. He was definitely sick last night. In fact, the whole family had some dodgy takeaway and were up all night. Apparently suffering from both ends,' he finished with a rare grin.

'Lovely,' Kate commented drily. 'What about the rest of them? None of them reckon they recognise the assailants. What do you think? Do you believe them?' She searched Josh's face, trying to get him to open up. To gain insight into what he was thinking beyond just answering her questions.

The sound of his jaw working filled the silence, the faint scent of spearmint pervading the space between them.

'Abigail. I think she deserves another chat.' He looked up and their eyes met. So, there was a brain underneath the hair gel.

Formal statements had been taken at the station from each of the employees, the teenage staff in the presence of their parents. In response to being asked if anything about the assailants had been familiar – their voice, mannerisms or body language – or if they could be a current or past employee of the McDonald's store, or someone from school, or anywhere else, Abigail had hesitated almost imperceptibly before answering in the negative. It was only a moment's hesitation, but it had been there. There had been no such reaction from the two boys or Mr Martello. At the time, Kate wasn't sure if Josh had picked up on it. His face had given nothing away.

'I think you're right,' she replied. 'Let's try and visit her tomorrow. She'll be more comfortable being interviewed at home. I doubt she'll be at school so soon after everything.' The frozen panic on Abigail's face came back to Kate, from the video footage. A frighted girl looking for a place to hide.

She drummed her fingers on her desk thinking. 'All right, what else? Martello? Anything useful from his fiancée?'

'His ex-fiancée, actually.' Josh smiled. 'I saw her this arvo.

The lovely Miss Arbericci. I can definitely see why he doesn't want to lose her.'

Kate waited without reacting and he continued with a smirk. 'Anyway, she backs up his story that they were on the phone all night. We've compared their phones and the call records match. A total of seven phone calls from Martello's mobile to Ms Arbericci's mobile between the hours of 2 am and 4.20 am in the morning, the last of which lasted for twenty-four minutes, covering the time he was out at the dumpsters.'

'Okay, then that just leaves the traffic footage. I assume we're still chasing Transport?'

'Darnley's on that.' From his emphasis on the constable's name, Kate could tell that Josh hadn't quite forgiven Darnley for their interaction that morning.

'That and the Hungry Jack's CCTV, but we'll be lucky to get anything there. I drove through the place this morning and none of their cameras face the right direction.'

'Okay, well, let's see when it comes in. Anything else?'

'No, that's about it.' Snapping his laptop shut, Josh rose without further pleasantries but found his path blocked by a suave figure in a crisp, charcoal suit better suited to a corporate law office, trailing the scent of expensive cologne. Their chief inspector: Andrew Skinner. He immediately stood up straighter. 'Sir.'

Skinner acknowledged Josh with a nod and turned to Kate. 'Miles, I need a word today before you leave. In my office in fifteen?'

She agreed, her spirits sinking. There went her plan to get home on time. She half wondered if this was to do with her encounter with Roman Allen that morning. Surely, he hadn't complained?

She could feel Josh's interest spark, a quick appraisal of her face, trying to work out why she had been singled out.

'Roman Allen seems to be on board, sir. We had a good chat to him this morning.'

Skinner's eyes swept back across to Josh, regarding him silently until he reddened. 'Good. That's good.' Skinner nodded briefly and left.

Kate almost felt sorry for Josh. Reading Skinner's moods was a full-time job in itself. Just because Skinner had favoured Josh that morning didn't mean anything ten hours later.

When it was time to make her way to Skinner's office, she could see Josh hovering, still harbouring hopes of being admitted into the conference. She felt his gaze follow her out – half curious and half calculating.

4

'One more story!'

'Not one more story. It's time for bed, monkey.'

'One more story, Daddy. Please, please, please!'

'All right, just one more, Mister, and then it's time for bed.'

'Yay! Yay! Yay! Cranky Bear! Cranky Bear!'

'All right, *The Very Cranky Bear* it is.'

Kate smiled to herself from the doorway of her son's bedroom. She had made it home in time to help Geoff with dinner and bath time, after all. However, her husband was without a doubt the bedtime-story expert, with a knack for over-the-top expression and funny voices. Leaving him to it, she headed back to the kitchen, where the dishwasher yawned, waiting to be stacked. It would keep.

She stopped at the fridge, surveying the possibilities. A bottle of Pinot Grigio was squeezed into the door between the milk and half a dozen condiment jars that had spilled over from the shelves above. The wine was Argentinean, she noted in passing, another one of Geoff's finds, no doubt. He was the wine buff. She would be hard-pressed to tell the difference between a chardonnay and champagne, if it wasn't for the bubbles.

She settled for a non-alcoholic cider, pouring herself a glass and sitting down with relief at the dining-room table, her feet up on the adjacent chair. Sipping her drink and savouring its sweet acidity, she flicked absently through the file she had brought home with her – the one she had acquired from Skinner that evening. Reflecting on their conversation less than an hour ago, she was still unclear exactly what she had agreed to.

* * *

Skinner had been on his mobile when she reached his office. With his back to the door, he stood at the open window, a grey square of aluminium that framed a view of the concrete carpark at the front of the station. One hand clutched his phone, while the other dragged through his once-luxurious, now fast-thinning hair – a sure sign of mounting frustration. Turning around at her entrance, he held up two fingers, silently mouthing 'two minutes' and waving her towards a chair, before returning to his call.

'Not Edgar,' she heard him growl into the phone through gritted teeth. 'I don't care what else, but you tell the bitch she's not having Edgar.' There was a long silence, followed by some choice expletives, before he hung up.

Skinner flung himself into his chair and blew out air through his mouth. 'Fucking women.'

'Present company excluded, of course,' Kate remarked drily. She had heard enough of the one-way conversation to guess at the subject. Skinner, the eternal and unrepentant womaniser, was going through yet another toxic divorce. This marriage had lasted nineteen months, a new low even for him. Two years ago, Jean had been the receptionist at a dental clinic when Andrew Skinner had walked through the doors with a broken filling. The rest, as they say, was history.

'Why the fuck does she want the dog?' he demanded. 'She hates the fucking dog.'

Kate refrained from answering the obvious.

'Fucking vindictive bitch,' he muttered to himself.

Again, Kate remained silent. Reminding her boss of the reason why his wife had filed for divorce – Skinner having slipped his dick into one of Jean's colleagues at her work Christmas party – would be less than useless.

'He pissed on her shoes once. She was fucking furious.' A sudden smile broke through Skinner's features at the memory of Edgar's misdemeanours, wiping away the malcontent and replacing it with the cheeky, little-boy good looks that still endured despite his age. Kate could see why they fell for him in droves.

Restored to a semblance of good humour, Skinner finally got down to business. Flicking a manila folder towards her, he said without preamble, 'Preston's office wants us to review this.'

Kate's eyebrows rose in an unspoken question as she reached for the file. John Preston meant the assistant commissioner, and involvement from the AC's office was never a good thing.

'It's one of the flood deaths. The Marshall case.' His eyes met hers, waiting for comprehension to dawn. Waiting for a reaction.

She felt her interest stir. Everybody knew the Marshall case. You couldn't bloody escape it if you tried. The young married couple, Joel and Gabby, swept away by the swollen waters of Red Cedar Creek, with only the distraught wife surviving to tell the tale. Gabby, a local swimming instructor and an ex-Iron Woman, had been picked up by the national media as the ill-fated poster girl of the flood, her beauty underscoring her pathos, her past sporting achievements now blown into heroic proportions. The loss of her parents in her early twenties completed the picture of a woman alone in the world. The husband, who had actually lost his life in the tragedy, had become a mere backstory in the meteoric rise of the tragic heroine.

Kate met Skinner's gaze and understood his unspoken warning. They would be dealing with celebrity here.

'This is one of the cases handled by Tweed?'

Skinner nodded. The question had been rhetorical, anyway. She already knew the answer.

At the height of the flood crisis, an operational decision had been made to direct all flood-related casualties from the local area through a single police station, in this case Tweed Heads. *To ensure that the cases are dealt with efficiently and to streamline family support*, the internal memo had read at the time. There had been a total of five deaths in their area command: an elderly man from Tumbulgum, Joel Marshall, and a young family of three near Chinderah. The officers from Esserton Station had had little direct involvement in the investigations, but she remembered all three circumstances had been remarkably similar: people trying to outrun swollen waters in their vehicles.

Kate frowned. 'All the deaths were classified as accidental by Tweed?'

Again, Skinner nodded calmly.

'There were no inquests?'

'Didn't need any. No suspicious circumstances. The identity, manner and cause of death were all satisfactory. None of the postmortems raised any questions. In two of the cases, there were multiple witnesses, and in the Marshall case, they had Gabby Marshall's account. The coroner decided no inquest was required in each case.'

'So, what's the AC's interest? Did Tweed stuff something up?' Kate's eyes narrowed.

Skinner took his time answering. 'This is not a formal review,' he said finally, a tiny grin playing on his face. 'The Honourable John Preston has asked me to look into this informally.' His grin widened at her expression. 'I thought you'd like that,' he continued cheerfully. 'He asked me to handle it personally. So I'm personally delegating the matter to you,' he finished with a flourish.

She stared at him, not sharing the joke.

Ignoring the fact that he had just palmed off a steaming pile of proverbial into her lap, she pursued him for details. 'But what am I supposed to be looking at? Have we received any new information? What's prompted the review?'

He held up his palms to stop her flow. 'There's nothing new. The investigation stands. We've got nothing to justify reopening the case. This is … I think this is just a favour for a friend.'

At her questioning gaze, Skinner continued. 'It turns out, the mother of the deceased is an old family friend of the Prestons.

Apparently she's been making noises, and I think the AC's just throwing her a bone to shut her up. He's agreed to re-examine the file to see if we missed anything.'

'What does she expect us to find? Her son was swept away in a flood, for Christ's sake. What does she think happened?'

'She's got a bee in her bonnet about Gabby Marshall. I'm guessing the constant media appearances aren't helping. Mrs Marshall is convinced that her daughter-in-law was somehow responsible for her son's death. Maybe poisoned his tea on the fatal day, who knows.'

Kate rolled her eyes and Skinner grinned, clearly enjoying himself.

'The point is, she believes that the funnelling of all of the flood victims through a single station led to tunnel vision and the officers in charge didn't scrutinise the specific circumstances of her son's death or consider any alternative options as to how he might have died.' His voice had taken on a mock-monotone as if reading from a news report.

Kate had been about to speak, but stopped herself.

'Yeah, it's a thought, isn't it?' observed Skinner. 'It's all bullshit, of course. The woman's clearly out of control. But there's just enough plausibility in her that the AC's got his wind up. It wouldn't look good in print, and the last thing we need is another bloody press story casting us as incompetent.'

'So, he wants us to review the file to make sure that Tweed did everything by the book. To make sure there's no case to answer?'

'Got it in one, Miles,' Skinner replied. 'I knew there was a reason you're my favourite.'

'Is Superintendent Wright aware of this?' Lucas Wright was the commander of the Tweed–Byron police district that covered Tweed Heads as well as Esserton, Murwillumbah and others.

'He's aware and on board and very supportive of my choice for undertaking the review.'

'Who in Tweed was the officer in charge?'

'Murchison,' Skinner replied. They both knew what that meant. Leading Senior Constable Murchison had worked at Esserton for over thirty-five years before transferring to Tweed Heads just over eighteen months ago to be closer to his aging parents. He was an unimaginative officer, a couple years off retirement, who was devoted to procedure and paperwork. So whatever had been done would have been done to the letter of the law. The only problem was if the wrong path had been taken early on, Murchison was unlikely to have noticed or deviated.

'Murchison,' Skinner continued, 'or anyone else at Tweed, for that matter, apart from Superintendent Wright, is definitely not in the know. So keep it quiet. No fraternising with the Tweed blokes until you're done.'

'Also, nothing to Ellis just yet,' Skinner added. 'He's got enough on with the holdups. You should be done with this before you leave, anyway.'

There was no fear of that, she thought. Her relationship with Josh may have thawed, but it was nowhere near sunny.

'Is Mrs Marshall angling for the case to be reopened? For an inquest to be held?' she enquired.

'It hasn't got to that stage yet. It sounds like she just wants someone to listen to her.'

'And that's where I come in,' Kate remarked, realisation dawning. She knew how much Skinner disliked dealing with victims' families.

He smiled broadly in reply. 'You've got an appointment with the Marshalls tomorrow at two. The AC's office has set it up.' Skinner was up on his feet, grabbing his jacket off the back of his chair, a none-too-subtle sign that the meeting was coming to a close. 'A few days of light reading, Miles. A report on my desk by next week and you're done and dusted, and you can ride off into the sunset,' he quipped without a hint of irony.

'Unless I find something, of course.' She had been joking, but it stopped Skinner in the middle of sliding on his jacket.

'Don't be a fucking hero, Miles,' he told her. 'Just read the file and write me a report. Then we are both out of it. There's nothing to bloody find.'

On her way out, he followed up with a comment designed to needle, just because he could.

'By the way, I saw Gray in town the other day, at Bunnings. He's looking good. The country life suits him.'

She wavered momentarily, but resisted taking the bait, leaving without responding.

That had been that. For better or worse, the Marshall case was now hers.

* * *

Draining her glass, Kate continued to flick randomly through the file she had inherited, engrossed in thought and not really focusing on any of the documents. She was joined by Geoff with a full glass of the Argentinean white she had spied in the fridge, swirling and sipping the blond liquid. 'This is good. Hints of passionfruit and citrus,' he noted, glancing at her. 'It was on special.'

Kate smiled and made a non-committal murmur. 'Did he go down all right?' she asked.

'Yep. All tucked in. He started to nod off by the fifth reading.'

Kate chuckled. She gazed at her husband with a sudden rush of fierce, protective affection. She took in the scraggly beard, rumpled clothes and the once-slim figure that was slipping slowly to dough. She loved this man: love handles, wine pretensions and all. She was lucky to have him. Very few men she knew would have been as accommodating as Geoff. He had swapped a highly successful job as the principal architect of an established North Coast firm to become a stay-at-home dad, working part-time from home when Archie was at preschool, content to take the small jobs thrown his way by his old firm.

Thank God it worked out that way, she thought. Geoff was an excellent dad. He had the knack for getting down to Archie's level and playing with him for hours on end. Kate loved her son, but knew she couldn't have coped with the Duplo, fire trucks and Batman thing all day long, day in, day out. She would be climbing the walls. With Geoff taking care of Archie, she had been free to pursue her career and chase her promotion to sergeant. She was intensely grateful that Geoff seemed to be genuinely content with his role. A slight pang of anxiety dipped in her stomach. Would he continue to feel the same way when the next one arrived?

'Who's that woman?'

'What woman?' asked Kate, startled out of her reverie.

'The photo in your file.'

Kate glanced to where Geoff was pointing and took in a beach photo of Gabby Marshall wearing a soft, gauzy summer shift. She appeared to have been caught unawares in the photo and was staring slightly to the left of the camera. The image captured a startlingly beautiful woman with long, textured, black hair and laughing grey eyes. For a moment, Kate considered the ego of the woman who had passed on such an attractive and presumably personal photo of herself to the police.

'That's Gabby Marshall. She's pretty, isn't she?'

'I was actually thinking she looks a bit like you.'

Kate screwed up her face. 'No, she doesn't. I look nothing like her.'

'Well, not her skin, obviously. Or her face … No, what I mean is …' Geoff hurried on as Kate started to laugh, '… she has the same body type as you. You know, tall, and the same colour hair and everything …' He trailed off.

'Good save, Husband. Well done.' Kate laughed, hauling herself off the chair. 'C'mon, I'll help you stack the dishes.'

'Who is she, anyway?' asked Geoff, following her.

Kate rolled her eyes, constantly amazed at her husband's complete lack of awareness of current events. She grabbed his arm and circled it around her waist. 'Come with me and I'll explain.'

5

Stills of the Hulk, Iron Man and Captain America flashed across the screen. Kate had missed the six o'clock newscast but had waited up for the late bulletin. They were good shots. Clear and in focus. Harris had done a good job with the images. And yet, she wondered if it was all in vain. Would anyone recognise these teens in their Avengers masks when the key features that could trigger recognition were covered?

At least the Allens' name hadn't been mentioned, she reflected, though she had no idea how long that particular detail would remain hidden. It was only a matter of time.

The news cast switched to the 'celebrity story of the year' – the Carmichaels, Mr and Mrs, stars of an American reality TV series who had decided to holiday in northern New South Wales for a few days ahead of their paid appearance at a Sydney award ceremony. Various footage of the couple's activities followed: sunbaking on their private yacht, swimming at a hitherto secluded beach and dining at a hatted beach-front restaurant. She muted the TV.

Settling into the couch, a half-empty packet of Maltesers and an empty bottle of mineral water by her side, she adjusted her swollen body to find a more comfortable position. Geoff had already called it a night, but she would be seeing the Marshalls tomorrow and had yet to properly read the file. The case notes and her laptop lay waiting. She was procrastinating, and that wasn't like her.

Her mobile beeped. A series of WhatsApp messages from her younger brother, Luke, down in Sydney, showing off his new acquisition: a Kawasaki 'Ninja' series motorcycle. She grimaced. She had no interest in motorbikes, as her brother well knew. The photos were aimed at their father. Luke knew she could be relied on to pass them on. She wished for the thousandth time that Luke and her dad would sort out their differences and stop using her as a conduit for communication. She switched off her phone. She would message Luke back tomorrow.

She yawned and rubbed a twinge in her belly. She felt the baby kick and concentrated on the feeling. This pregnancy felt different, her body more overstretched and sluggish in the third trimester than she remembered feeling with Archie. For weeks she had felt parts of her body creak and groan, occasional stabs of pain and phantom aches. She put it down to age and tiredness. She was inching up to forty – only two more years until that particular milestone – and right at present she felt every minute of her thirty-eight years. She wasn't as focused on the baby as she had been with Archie. The second time around, life was busier, the sensations of pregnancy less a source of wonderment than a daily discomfort to work around.

Maybe it would have been easier if she had resorted to desk duties, as Skinner had pushed for, when she had neared the midpoint of her pregnancy. But the thought of being forced off operational duties so soon after her promotion had been too much to accept. She had stood her ground and negotiated until they had agreed on duty parameters, which they could both live with and which strayed on the right side of work-health requirements. It meant she had less autonomy and had to run 'at-risk' duties past Skinner constantly, but it was better than nothing. Still, her upcoming leave and the chance to rest for a few weeks before the new baby arrived was not unwelcome. She had managed to almost entirely dismiss from her mind the spotting from a few weeks ago. It was a one-off, she told herself, unwilling to consider any other possibility. Shaking away the memory, she concentrated on the task at hand.

The reports, typed out by Murchison, were as she had expected – thorough but long-winded. If it could be said in three words, why not use twenty? Nevertheless, Kate infinitely preferred Murchison's pedantic style to a sloppy case file with sparse case notes and half the information missing. In Murchison's case, everything had been minutely documented and everything she expected to see was present and accounted for.

The Marshall death had occurred at the height of summer three months back. The evening of the sixth of January, a Saturday, following days of record-breaking rain and warnings of rising river levels. Nevertheless, Joel and Gabby had tried their luck at crossing Red Cedar Creek, an offshoot of the Tweed River at a low causeway. She gathered from the accounts of several locals whom Murchison had questioned that the causeway had apparently been still passable by vehicles just the day before.

Kate went through the folder of witness statements. There were full written transcripts along with recordings of the interviews on media files. She found the file she wanted and inserted her earphones into her laptop to listen. It was Gabby's account of the events from her hospital bed, taken a day after the incident. After some background noise and the preliminaries, stating the names of those present and the date and time of the interview, Gabby's voice could be heard, quiet but composed, responding to Murchison's prompting.

'We were on our way to Joel's parents' for dinner. Joel was driving and we were running late. I think we were meant to be at their place by seven and it was already half past. It was wet and the traffic was really slow because of an accident earlier. Joel turned into Callandra Street because it's the quickest way. But the road dips and you have to cross Red Cedar Creek.

'It was raining and getting dark, and we could see that the creek was full, but Joel was sure the ute would make it and he just drove in. He didn't hesitate or anything. He drove like it was part of the road, and it was like hitting a wall or something.

'The water was moving so fast. You couldn't tell from the road that it would be so strong. The ute got washed off right away. We went sideways. Then it sort of dipped and got stuck, and the water started rushing up the sides. We managed to pull ourselves out of the windows and into the back tray. Joel... He helped me. We thought it would be safer back there, but the water kept rising. And then something slammed into the side. I don't know what. Maybe a log or

something, and the whole thing just sort of tilted and we were both in the water.

'Joel had a hold of my arm when we fell in, but we got separated almost immediately. The water was so strong. We were together one minute and then he was just gone ...'

A silence followed, then Gabby's voice resumed, quieter still.

'I don't know how long I got swept away for. I couldn't see anything clearly. It was raining and there was so much stuff in the water. Branches and rocks and mud and I don't know what. Something hit me in the face and almost took my eye out, and I swallowed water and went under a couple of times.

'After a while, I'm not really sure how long, the creek sort of widened and the strength of the water lessened a bit and I got washed near the bank. I managed to grab onto some rocks on the creek bank. I didn't know where I was. I just hung there and screamed and screamed hoping someone would hear me ...'

Kate pressed 'stop'. Gabby, she reflected, had been extremely lucky to survive. The section of creek she had washed up on happened to back onto a residential property and the owners, a family named Pavić, had been on the spot at the right time to rescue her. According to the file notes, the daughter had been searching the back garden for the family's normally house-bound cat, afraid that it had come to harm in the rain, and had heard Gabby's faint cries from the water. She had raised the alarm and her father had managed to haul Gabby up, despite the dangers of the swirling waters below. Kate admired the tenacity of the family. They had been incredibly courageous and resourceful in the circumstances, taking the initiative to rescue Gabby, rather than waiting for emergency services that may not have arrived in time.

Going through the witness statements of the Pavićs, the husband and wife, Kate was struck by the quiet humility of the family. They had not considered what they had done to be remarkable and had not sought any recognition for their collective act of heroism. Given the amount of publicity Gabby was enjoying, Kate was surprised not much coverage had been given to the Pavićs and their role in the rescue. She wondered what their feelings towards Gabby were now.

She pulled out the autopsy report. Joel's body had been recovered within an hour of Gabby's rescue, trapped in a flood-control drain, a few kilometres from the Callandra Street causeway and the Pavić property. A forensic pathologist attached to the Northern District Base Hospital at Tweed Heads had performed the autopsy.

The official cause of death was given as asphyxia due to respiratory impairment from submersion: in other words, drowning. The cause of death had been confirmed by the presence of water-filled lungs, blood-tinged, frothy liquid in sections of lung tissue, and the presence of silt and plant matter in the stomach and air passages as a result of involuntary water ingestion and aspiration during submersion. The body had exhibited a range of abrasions and contusions, consistent with ante- and postmortem injuries from being struck by passing debris during submersion and transport in floodwaters. A dislocated right shoulder was identified as a postmortem injury due to the position in which the body was wedged in the drainage channel.

The body was found to be otherwise healthy for the victim's age of twenty-seven.

From previous enquiries into drowning deaths, Kate knew loss of consciousness could occur in as little as two minutes after submersion, particularly in cold water. It would have felt like a lifetime for Joel, though, being swept away in the dark, with God knows what rushing past and banging into him, as he struggled to breathe and to stay afloat. He would have been terrified, the poor bugger.

She noted the ute had been recovered some days later, a few hundred metres from the Callandra Street causeway, and was found to be in excellent mechanical condition apart from a flooded engine, ruined electricals and innumerable dents and scratches to the body work. As far as forensic services could determine, the car was in perfectly good working condition before being submerged in floodwaters.

She pulled Joel's toxicology results. No drugs. A blood alcohol level of 0.048, just under the legal driving limit.

Statements from the family identified Joel to have been a strong swimmer in his youth, but no longer swimming regularly. He would have been no match for the strength of the floodwaters.

Based on the brief of evidence prepared, the coroner was satisfied with the findings of the police investigation, concluding the manner and cause of death to be the result of an accident and dispensing with the need for an inquest.

She pushed the files and laptop away from her and stretched awkwardly. It was well past midnight and the house was quiet, the baby likewise still inside her body. She drew circles across her stretched skin, thinking over the facts that she had just reviewed.

The case seemed straightforward and had been handled as such. The case notes reflected the work of an experienced police officer. All procedures had been followed to a tee; she would expect nothing less from Murchison. Based on her reading of the file, it would seem that Skinner was right. She could write this up quickly and it would be off their hands. There was nothing to find. Case closed.

So, why did she feel like she was missing something? Her interview with Skinner had unsettled her. She had felt manoeuvred and managed and she didn't like that. She wondered again why she had been chosen for the review and not one of the officers at Tweed, or even Brunswick, with more seniority. Could it be her position as a female officer? Or was it her skin colour? Skinner pulling out the diversity card to shore up his credit. The man had form. It wasn't the first time her mixed heritage, that distinctive shading she had inherited from her South Asian mother, had been used by Skinner for optics and internal politics. Her skin itched just thinking about it.

She fixed her eyes on the ceiling, taking in the tendrils of an old spiderweb stretching across a corner cornice, considering her options and coming to a decision. If she was going to put her name to something, she would make damn sure she could stand by it. She would only write up what Skinner wanted once she was quite certain there was nothing else to say.

THEN

Last period, double history. Fourteen minutes and twenty-three seconds to go until the final bell. Eamon stared at the wall clock above the white board, watching the hands ticking out the final minutes of the school day, willing it to go faster. Fourteen minutes until freedom and Anika.

Outside, the sun bore down on the uninsulated metal roof of the demountable, creating a sauna-like heat inside the classroom. The open windows did little to dissipate the heavy stillness of the air within. Eamon could feel the sweat from his thighs sticking to the moulded plastic of his chair. Strands of tinsel hung limply along the window and door seals, the school's annual attempt at getting into the spirit ahead of the Christmas holidays.

The frenzied chorus of cicadas outside had long drowned out the sing-song voice of Mr Nargalingham (or 'Nargey', as he was generally referred to among the pupils of Esserton High). Nargey, their Year Ten maths teacher, was today substituting at short notice for Mrs Ainsley, whose third baby had decided to make an early entrance into the world that morning. Trying to be heard above the crescendo of insects, Nargey was reading out Mrs Ainsley's notes on the 1854 Eureka Stockade to an uninterested classroom, with little success. A few minutes before the end of the school day and a week before the end of school term and the summer holidays, the Eureka Stockade and its significance to modern Australian democracy was of little interest to Eamon and the majority of his classmates.

Apart from a few swotter types up the front taking notes, no one was paying much attention, although many were staring directly at Nargey, which gave the impression of interest. As per usual, a wager was underway among the more enterprising of the pupils regarding how many times Nargey would wipe, with his perfectly folded and ironed blue-and-white handkerchief, the spittle that collected at the sides of his mouth as he spoke. Today, Nargey was alternating between his lips and his sweating brow.

The business of correctly noting down each wipe was being handled, like always, by Eamon's best friend, Matt, class clown and general originator of all things juvenile and disruptive in their year. Each swab had to be diligently recorded to ensure fair distribution of the day's winnings, comprising however many pilfered ciggies had been bet on that day. Today's extra class with Nargey was an unexpected bonus.

Eamon could see Matt, his unruly blond hair that all the girls went potty for falling across his forehead, as he pretended to bend over his history textbook. Matt caught him watching and gave him a wink.

Eamon grinned back. Usually an active participant, Eamon wasn't betting today. All he wanted was for the class to end so he could get to Anika. He didn't have time to muck around after class arguing about winnings. Anika would be coming home from the end of school camp and he wanted to be there when her bus rolled in. She had texted him the time they were due in: around 3.40 pm. He would have ten minutes to sprint to the bus stop in front of St Therese High, the exclusive girls-only private school she attended a block away. If he timed it right, he should get there before her mum drove in to pick her up and they would have time to share a quick hello.

He couldn't believe how much he had missed her. The past five days of not seeing her in person had been torture. Talking and texting on their mobiles had been good, but not nearly enough. Especially after what they had shared the day before she had headed off to camp. He got a shiver down his back just thinking about it. She had called him over so they could hang out before she went away. When he got to her house, he realised that they were all alone and she had planned it that way. Her parents had taken her younger brother to the movies and her grandmother was having lunch with her friends at the Croatian Club. He still couldn't quite believe what had followed.

The feel of her body was still fresh in his mind. That Sunday, holed up in her room, was the first time she had allowed him to touch her underneath her clothes. Up until then, they had just fumbled around fully clothed, making out. He had felt her breasts through her school jumper and uniform before. Nothing, though, had prepared him for their naked, milky softness, her nipples erect like plump sultanas between his fingers.

Her breasts were nothing like what he had seen on the internet when he and Matt had accessed porn sites on their phones. They weren't bulbous and bloated and in your face. Anika's were small and slightly turned out. Her body was soft and yielding, her arms covered in fine peach down and her tummy a delicate curve of puppy fat. She didn't look hard and aggressively perfect like the women on the websites and he liked her better for it. He had seen it in her face when she had first taken off her top, and then her bra: that she was afraid he wouldn't think her sexy enough. Just like his own hang-ups about his gangly chest and secret fears about the size and shape of his dick. He certainly knew he didn't resemble any of the men he had seen on the net frantically working those large-breasted women.

The vulnerability on her face had made him feel a tenderness and protectiveness towards her. Their tentative exploration of each other's bodies, a first for both, had felt different somehow. Less a frantic groping session, a race to see how far they could get, than a slow realisation that this could be something special for both of them. Images of that day flickered in his mind and filled him with anticipation.

He glanced up at the clock again. He had to get out of here – and fast. He needed to start running and have blood pumping to other parts of his body. Otherwise, he was in serious danger of getting a semi right here in front of everyone.

The bell screamed its last call. *Finally!* He was up and off, shouting a quick 'See ya' to Matt over his shoulder. He skirted the quadrangle, dodging the students streaming out of the classrooms, and veered along the edge of the sporting fields, taking a shortcut to Aimes Road. His shirt stuck to him as he ran through the heat and he was soaked with sweat by the time he skidded into the covered bus interchange opposite St Therese's. Under the shade of the interchange, he fanned his face with his cap, trying to cool down. Glancing up the road, he nervously mussed his hair, waiting for the bus to appear.

The school day had just ended at St Therese's. From his spot behind the bollard, he could see the girls streaming out in giggly, tight-knit groups of twos and threes in their precise, buttoned-up uniforms, all knee-length pleated skirts, monogrammed shirts and boater hats. They ducked into waiting Mercedes, BMWs and SUVs lining the imposing front entrance of the school.

Before meeting Anika, Eamon had shared the general opinion held by the male population of Esserton High, that the girls of St Therese's were all stuck-up bitches who looked down their snooty noses at anyone who didn't share the same high-end car or house size. St Therese's was an old and highly prestigious girls' school that attracted rich students from up and down the North Coast of New South Wales. It had started life in the late 1800s as a Catholic seminary for nuns and remained the educational destination of choice for adolescent girls whose families could afford the privilege. Apart from a few girls who liked to slum it from time to time, Eamon knew the vast majority of students at the school would have nothing to do with the likes of him, living well and truly outside the required income bracket.

Since meeting Anika, though, Eamon had found out there was another side to St Therese's, made up of girls who didn't come from silver-spoon families. Girls who were there thanks to hard-won scholarships, especially from surrounding rural areas. Anika was there because she had scored one of the six full academic scholarships made available each year. Even so, her parents worked tirelessly so they could pay for all the extras that came with the privilege, from multiple school uniforms to school camps and excursions.

Eamon knew for a fact that Anika's family weren't well off. Her dad owned a car mechanic business and her mum worked two jobs, including at the local Woollies. They lived in a worn-out double-storey and drove a beat-up Holden station wagon and an equally battered Toyota Celica. Anika hated her school and buttoned-up uniform, and had few friends.

Up ahead, a large coach with the St Therese school emblem lumbered into the interchange and opened its doors with a loud hiss. Eamon stepped out of sight for a second to watch the girls exit. He wanted to catch the first glimpse of Anika before she spotted him. He loved to observe her when she wasn't aware of it, even though she always got embarrassed and self-conscious when she caught him looking. He couldn't help it. She was just so damn beautiful.

There she was, climbing down the steps behind one of her friends. She was in jeans and a school T-shirt, slightly crumpled from the long bus ride. As she moved down the steps, he could make out the soft curves underneath her clothing. Her long, honey-blonde hair was tied up in a high ponytail, and her open, smiling face instantly started scanning the bus interchange, searching for signs of him. He stepped out from behind the bollard so she would see him and know that he hadn't missed their appointment. Instantly, she caught sight of him and her face lit up. Eamon wondered again with amazement that he could be the reason for that smile.

He grinned back as Anika turned to hug her friend goodbye. Her friend's eyes caught his over Anika's shoulder, half playful, half mocking and all knowing. He blinked and glanced away, self-conscious.

'You're all sweaty.' Anika was at his side, taking in his damp school shirt and laughing.

'I know. I ran here from school,' he replied. He was suddenly shy and nervous, not knowing what to do or whether to touch her, acutely aware of the proximity of her body.

She giggled and reached for his hands. She stood on her tippy-toes and kissed him lightly on his lips.

'Hey,' she whispered softly.

'Hey,' he whispered back, kissing her deeply and holding her close. She slowly withdrew, checking for any signs of her mother. Her family knew about Eamon, of course, and he had been accepted into the household, but not without reservations. He was aware that Anika's Croatian parents, and especially her grandmother, had traditional views, and accepting that their teenage daughter had a boyfriend was still a big step for them. He knew Anika was nervous about her mum catching them kissing out in the open.

'Hey, guess what?' cried Anika. 'I texted Mum and asked her if you can stay for dinner tonight and she said that's fine, as long as you check with your mum.'

Eamon's grin widened. His mum wouldn't care. One less thing for her to worry about. He usually fixed his own meals, anyway, his mum not being the best around the kitchen or the house in general. Dinner at his place more often than not consisted of something canned slopped on toast, or something nuked in the microwave. Going to Anika's meant an actual homemade meal, dessert even. His mouth watered just thinking about it.

'Should be fine. I'll text her later.' He squeezed Anika's hand and pressed his lips to her temple. 'Come on. Let's get your bags.'

6

Friday

Friday

Kate's mobile rang its familiar tone just as she climbed into the police vehicle parked at her driveway. She was on call and had retained use of the Commodore.

'Miles. Glad I caught you.' Skinner's voice, chipper and over-loud.

'Sir. I'm about ten minutes out,' she replied, struggling with the seatbelt as she balanced her phone between her face and shoulder.

'No need. I want you in Murwillumbah this morning.'

'Sir?'

'The volunteer thing. I can't go. Called away to the lawyers. You need to replace me.'

'Sir.'

'I'll send you the details. It'll be the usual. Just shake hands and smile a bit. You're due there at nine-thirty.'

'Sir.'

'Cheer up, Miles. I just got you out of the office for the day.'

Kate smiled sourly and hung up. The 'volunteer thing' was an annual morning tea hosted by the Lions Club in support of a range of local charities, including domestic abuse, drug-and-alcohol-related support services and at-risk youth programs. The charities and their volunteer staff were well known to the police in the area through community policing initiatives, and it was a matter of courtesy, but also a given, that a representative of the local area command would make an appearance.

It wasn't that she objected to going. She supported the cause and had worked with many of the staff who would be honoured today. It was just that she was never very good at these kinds of affairs. The morning tea was an important community event. The local media would be out in force and the place would be bleeding councillors, local MPs and other notables. That meant colleagues of Councillor Allen who would all want to grill her about the holdup case. No wonder Skinner had discovered a non-existent appointment in his calendar.

She swore under her breath, running through all the things she had meant to follow up today, which she would now have to delegate to Josh. Frowning, she punched in his number.

* * *

It had been less painful than she had expected. The speeches had been on the short side and she had been able to sit through most of it, saving her feet. She had caught up with several of the volunteers and managed to avoid most of the journos and politicians – including Councillor Manning, Roman Allen's right-hand man.

There was an abundance of food and the selection of tea bags was more than one, which was something.

Another half an hour, she reckoned, and she could get away. She had to go soon, anyway. She was meeting Josh at the hospital. Josephine was alert and ready to talk.

'Detective, I didn't realise you would be here. Not sure if you can remember me. I used to work at Esserton Station. Constable Murchison.'

Kate shook the offered hand, taking in the middle-aged man who stood at her elbow: neatly trimmed crew cut, suit and tie, Crown Lager in hand. The suit was an older style of cut, worn for function rather than fashion. The body it hung off was that of an ex-footballer gone to seed. The wide shoulders giving a hint of the former sportsman, while the tightening of suit buttons around the middle alluded to a thickening of flesh elsewhere.

'Constable, it's good to see you. Yes, here replacing the chief inspector. He was called away at the last moment,' she replied with a slight roll of her eyes.

He nodded into his beer, his expression unchanged.

'Call me Kate. It's Darryl, isn't it?'

There was the briefest pause before he nodded confirmation.

'You're not on duty today, Darryl?' Kate motioned to his suit.

'No. My niece Christine is one of the volunteers.' He pointed to a short, slight figure with a head of tight, blonde curls, among a group of laughing women. 'She's studying to be a counsellor. Been volunteering at the Mercy Heart women's shelter. My sister's daughter. They live too far west for the drive. So I'm representing the family, you could say.'

'That's great, Constable,' Kate said warmly. 'Pass on my congratulations. It's not an easy job. She's brave to take it on.'

He didn't reply straightaway, throwing a speculative gaze across at his niece. 'It'll be interesting to see how long she lasts. The burn-out rate is high.'

'Well, at least she's giving it a go. She seems happy with her decision, anyway,' said Kate, observing the group of women.

Murchison glanced at Kate and turned away, taking a deep draught of his beer. The silence stretched as they both surveyed the crowd. Kate wondered what had prompted him to make a point of talking to her. They were hardly friends. When she had moved to Esserton over two years ago, he had been on long-service leave. On his return to the station, he had gone back to general duties before transferring to Tweed a couple of months later. They had exchanged no more than polite conversation during that time. She observed him with curiosity. Before she had been given the Marshall file, she'd had no reason to be interested in Constable Murchison. Now, as fate would have it, she had the chance to form her own impressions. So far, they appeared to align with his repute. He was buttoned-up and a bit awkward around women. She had heard that he had missed out on a promotion several times before finally making leading senior constable ranking three years ago. She could understand why. He was an easy personality to overlook.

Murchison seemed to have made up his mind about something. 'Detective—'

'Kate,' she interrupted.

'Kate, I mean.' He hesitated again and then blurted out, 'Am I being investigated? Superintendent Wright mentioned something about the Marshall case undergoing an internal review. The file's been sequestered. I had to hand over my case notes. Is it true? You've been asked to review the case and see if there are any holes in my work?'

Kate groaned inwardly. So much for keeping it under wraps. She had thought the superintendent had more subtlety than this.

'Constable … Darryl. It's nothing like that. The victim's mother has been making noises and she's a family friend of the assistant commissioner. The AC's office has just promised her a second look at the file to keep her happy. It's not a formal review. I've only been brought on board to make sure it's all kept at arm's length from Tweed Station. There's no new evidence. The case findings still stand.'

He digested this in silence.

'Constable, I know your reputation. You're a good officer. I wouldn't lose any sleep about this.'

He nodded shortly.

There was a tap on her shoulder and they were interrupted by a red-faced man, wheezing heavily, his bulging beer belly overhanging pants that were held in place by straining braces. A limp suit jacket hung slack either side. 'Detective Miles. I'm glad I caught you. I hear you're on this McDonald's case. It's just a bloody disgrace what those bastards did to Josephine.'

Kate turned resignedly. 'Councillor Manning. How are you?'

Murchison, who had been about to say something, stopped at the intrusion. Excusing herself momentarily from the councillor, Kate turned back to Murchison. She put a hand on his shoulder but let it drop as she felt him stiffen.

'Constable. Like I said, I really wouldn't worry about this.'

He nodded tightly before striding off, depositing his empty beer bottle at the nearest table.

Kate watched him go, wondering if it had been wise to tell him not to worry. It was true she had found nothing obvious in the files, but she hadn't really looked closely into anything yet. For a moment, she felt a pang of unease. It was done now.

7

'Take your time, Josephine. There's no rush.'

'I'm sorry, I just can't remember. I know I should, but I can't.'

Josephine's bruised face, red raw, her left eye an inflamed slit, looked up at her, wanting to please yet unable. Kate smiled to hide her disappointment. 'It's okay, Josephine. You're doing great.'

Josephine was suffering from amnesia. She had no memory of the incident from the time the masked teens had first entered the store, which she only recalled as three vague, dark, featureless figures. Either as a result of the head trauma she had suffered or as a physiological self-protective reaction to it, her brain was unable or unwilling to access the memory. Only time would tell if the memories would come back.

Kate glanced at Josh and he nodded. They had debated showing the security footage to Josephine. The Allens had vetoed it, fearing the memories it could trigger. If Josephine couldn't recall her attackers, they didn't want the footage implanting their image in her mind. Josephine's doctor had also advised extreme caution. Kate understood their concerns, but she knew Josephine would have to face the images of her attackers at some stage. After all, pictures of the masked boys were everywhere, on the news and on social media. They had reached a compromise in the end: to show Josephine only a snippet of the footage at the start to try to clear up her memories of the youths when they had first entered the store. It would be up to Josephine if she wanted to view any more.

Kate placed the tablet gently on Josephine's lap. They were gathered in a group around her hospital bed – Josh, herself, the Allens and Josephine's doctor. A monitor behind Josephine's bedhead whirred and beeped, counting out the seconds. Beside her, Kate felt Josephine's mother stiffen, her thin, bejewelled fingers reaching out for her daughter's hand as the footage turned on.

As the now-familiar images of the masked boys goofing around appeared on screen, Kate observed Josephine closely for any reaction. Apart from a slight intake of breath, there was nothing. Maybe, because of the multiple eyes on her, she was making an effort to control her emotions? Pausing the video file, Kate waited in silence for Josephine to speak.

'It feels weird, you know? Like watching a movie. I know I was there, but I just can't put myself in there.'

Josephine's mother slowly exhaled and Kate could sense her relief.

'Don't worry if you can't remember them, Josephine. But seeing them now, does anything seem familiar to you? Their mannerisms? The way they're walking? Maybe someone who worked at the store previously or someone from school?'

Josephine frowned at the frozen image on the tablet and slowly shook her head. 'I don't know. I mean, I don't think so. I'm really sorry, but it's just hard with the masks. It could be anyone.'

'That's okay. And you're sure there's nothing else you remember from the night? Maybe how they sounded. Their voices?'

'No. I'm sorry. It's just all a blank.'

'Look, she's already told you she can't remember, all right? There's no need to badger her. She'd tell you if she could.'

Kate met Roman Allen's angry, belligerent eyes, and nodded. 'I think you're right, Mr Allen. That's probably fine for today.' She turned to Josephine and smiled. 'Thanks for talking to us, Josephine. If you do remember anything more, doesn't matter how small, just give us a call, okay? We'll drop in and see how you're doing in a few days.'

'Is everyone else okay? Mum said Abigail and Lucas were on shift with me and they took care of me after … you know. Do you know if they're okay?'

'They're fine. But they were really worried about you and I'm sure they'd like to visit when you're feeling up to it.'

'Abigail thought they were so pathetic.'

Kate's head whipped back and Josephine's hand flew to her mouth.

'Oh my God! I do remember something. It just popped into my head. Abigail spoke to me at the counter. It must have been when the boys had just come into the store. "God, they're such dicks." That's what she said.' A small smile played on her lips. She glanced at Kate, her eyes wide. 'Does that mean Abigail knows who they are?'

* * *

'So, what do you reckon? Think she's faking it?' Josh glanced at her as they made their way through the hospital corridors, weaving through people, back to the carpark.

Kate hesitated. 'It's possible, but that would mean she's protecting her attackers.'

'Or,' he countered, 'she wants them found out, but for whatever reason, not by her. Hence the segue into Abigail.'

Kate made a sceptical face, unconvinced. To her mind, Josephine's reaction had felt truthful. Given what she had suffered, Kate didn't believe that the girl would hold any sympathy for her attackers. If she had recognised the youths, Kate was certain they would have observed a response in her. Shock. Anger. Anxiety. Something. Given her diagnosis, Josephine's reactions felt credible, more so than deliberate deceit.

Josh had fallen silent. She glanced over at him and relented a fraction. He was playing around with ideas, which meant he was engaged. She didn't want to curb his enthusiasm.

'Anyway, as you said, it's just another reason we need to speak to Abigail. What's happening with that? Are we seeing her today?'

'No can do. Her mum's taken her to Surfer's shopping for the day. To take her mind off everything. I've scheduled an appointment for tomorrow.'

They had reached Kate's car. She hadn't managed to find a park in the shade and she could tell it was going to be boiling inside its steel-grey exterior. The sun-baked metal felt scorching to her touch. She opened the door and wrestled her bulk inside.

She ran the air-con, leaving the door open. A blast of hot air seared her face.

'You heading back to the station?'

'No. I've got a couple of errands to run,' Kate replied without elaborating. 'I'll see you back there later.'

There was that look again. Full of unasked questions. He wasn't stupid. Josh knew she was holding out on him.

He turned to walk back to his own car. 'Or she could be telling the truth,' he called out over his shoulder.

'Sorry?'

'Josephine. Maybe it is memory loss just like the doctor says. An honest witness. What are the odds?'

He met her gaze before turning on his heels.

8

Two o'clock on the dot, Kate pulled up opposite the stately, pale-brick façade of the Marshall residence.

Getting out of her car, she waited for a dark-blue Ford Falcon ute and oversized SUV to pass her before running awkwardly across the street to the opposite pavement. She cast her eyes up at the house. It was a model home, what used to be billed as an 'executive home'. It stood, imposing and distinctive, among the weatherboard cottages and single-storey bungalows on the street. A gnarled jacaranda tree dominated the front garden, its limbs heavy with dark-green foliage, the characteristic lavender blooms still several months off.

Kate made her way across an unswept stone pathway, through once-luxurious garden beds that had gone to seed, to the grand front entrance flanked by tall brick columns and a covered archway. An oversized timber door was framed by elaborate glasswork on either side, which rose up to the ceiling, mirroring the curve of the entrance way.

She rang the doorbell and waited. There seemed to be no movement in the house. For a moment, she wondered if she had been given the wrong date by Skinner. She rang the doorbell again, checking the windows for any sign of life. They were all shut up, curtains drawn. There were no cars in the driveway, but the two-car garage was shut, so that didn't mean anything.

She hesitated, unsure how to proceed. Weren't they expecting her? Had there been some kind of miscommunication with the AC's office? Maybe they hadn't set up the appointment at all? Maybe she should have called first? She had made time for this meeting, omitting to tell Josh where she was going – even though she had berated him for exactly that only a day ago – and now they weren't even home.

She tried the bell twice more and was ready to give up when she heard a faint fumbling of the doorhandle and the door was cracked open.

A thin woman in a misshapen, overlarge jumper and wrinkled black leggings stood at the entrance, her body half hidden from view behind the thick timber door. The woman's face, curtained by long lengths of dark hair threaded with silver, would have been striking but for being drawn and blunted by misery. She glanced at Kate, her expression questioning and faintly fearful, her eyes screwed up against the light of the day. She noticed Kate's protruding belly and stared.

Before Kate could introduce herself, she heard quick, firm footsteps and a grey-haired man in old, paint-splattered work clothes came into view, pulling the door open wide. 'Who is it, Annette?'

'Afternoon. I'm Detective Kate Miles from the Esserton Police Station,' she said, holding out her ID. 'Are you the parents of Joel Marshall?'

'Yes, that's right,' the man answered, his brows furrowed. 'Sorry. I was out the back. Didn't hear the door. I'm Neil Marshall. This is my wife, Annette. What's this about?'

No, he was definitely not expecting her. 'Do you think we could speak inside?'

Neil Marshall took in her pregnant form and stepped back from the doorway, ushering her in. 'Yes, of course. Come in. Come in.'

His wife was slower to move away, her eyes remaining fixed on Kate's belly.

Kate followed them through the spacious, airy entrance hall, light-filled from all the glass. Their feet tapped on amber stone-tiled floors into a carpeted, formal living room. An ornate fireplace with built-in shelves filled to bursting with books of all types dominated the far wall. A quick perusal saw Austen mixed with Virginia Woolf and tomes on modern history amid a pile of out-of-date *New Scientist* magazines, and political memoirs alongside chunky cookbooks, all arranged in haphazard abandon or artful consciousness, depending on how you viewed it.

A window seat with cushions was set into a generous bay window, which would have provided panoramic views of the street if it wasn't for the drawn curtains that shrouded the room in deep shadow. Original artwork on the walls, two oversized couches with matching easy chairs, throw rugs and scatter cushions completed the picture of expensive, lived-in elegance. However, the room had a closed-in, abandoned feel. It was dark and cool, belying the muggy heat outside, and faintly musty, with a fine thread of dust covering the furnishings.

Neil ushered Kate to a couch. Annette curled herself into an armchair, drawing her limbs into a tight ball and pulling the jumper close around herself. Neil made to draw back the curtains, but a look from his wife stopped him and he sat down instead on the couch opposite Kate. She noticed they didn't sit together.

Neil turned to Kate. 'Okay,' he began. 'So, what's all this about? You said something about Joel?'

'I understand you've been speaking to the assistant commissioner's office about having your son's case reopened?'

Neil appeared mystified. 'Sorry, what?'

Kate turned tentatively to Annette. Neil followed her glance. Annette sat absorbed, picking the thread off her jumper sleeve, not looking up at either of them.

'A few days ago, we received a request from the assistant commissioner's office to review the file on Joel's death. We were told it was at the request of the family.'

Neil stared at his wife. 'Annette? Do you know anything about this?'

She remained quiet for a long time. 'I called John a week ago. He remembered Joel. I knew he would understand and would try and help me.' Her voice was scratchy and hardly louder than a whisper, like she hadn't used it in weeks.

'John?' For a second, Neil's expression was pure bafflement before it cleared and was replaced by incredulity. 'John Preston? Uni John?'

'Yes, Uni John.' Her voice was tight with supressed emotion. 'He was promoted to assistant commissioner last year. If anyone could get the case reopened and get the bitch charged, it would be him.'

'Oh, Jesus! I don't believe this.' Neil stood up and ran his hands through his hair in frustration.

Annette turned to Kate and addressed her directly for the first time. 'Don't mind my husband. He's just upset because I used to go out with John before I met Neil and he doesn't like it that we still speak.'

Neil stared at her in disbelief. 'Are you serious? I don't give a shit about Johnny fucking Preston! I care about Joel's case being reopened. Why in God's name do you want that?'

'You know why!' Suddenly, Annette was off her chair and screaming at her husband. 'Because she killed him, she killed our son! And she got off. Scot-free. Free to fuck everything that moves and free to spend all his money. She's a lying little bitch and you don't care.' She collapsed onto the floor in a paroxysm of crying.

Neil stared at her, repulsed and unmoved.

Kate knelt down on the floor, as best she could, to console Annette. She rested her hand on Annette's sparrow-thin shoulders, which shook with ugly, heaving sobs. Shamed into action by seeing Kate struggle to manoeuvre, Neil finally came over and together they helped Annette back onto her chair. She curled into the armrest, moaning softly.

Placing a box of tissues on the coffee table in front of her, Neil left the room, saying abruptly, 'I'll get some tea.'

Kate returned to her seat on the couch and waited for Annette's tears to subside. Slowly, the hacking sobs dwindled to hiccupping gulps. Neil came back with a tray of three steaming mugs. He hadn't bothered to ask Kate's preference. All three mugs came with a limp tea bag, too much hot water and a smudge of milk. For a few minutes, they all drank their watery teas in silence.

Finally placing his mug on the floor beside him, Neil resumed their conversation. 'So, what exactly is going on? Why are you here? What's Preston got you doing?'

Kate put down her mug and addressed Neil. 'So far, there's nothing to warrant reopening the case. There's no new evidence and the case findings still stand.' She raised her hand to forestall Annette's cry of outrage. 'However, the AC's office has noted your concerns, Mrs Marshall.'

Neil rolled his eyes.

'That's why I'm here. I want to hear what you have to say. I want to know why you think the findings are incorrect, why you believe Gabby Marshall is responsible for your son's death. If there's something we've missed, then I'm happy to look into it. If I find anything, anything concrete that warrants further investigation, then yes, we can look into reopening the case.'

She directed her words to Annette. 'Mrs Marshall, I need you to understand that there are absolutely no guarantees that we will find anything new. I have gone through the file, and so far there is nothing to suggest anything other than an accidental death. You need to be prepared that there may not be anything new to find.'

Annette's eyes were shining, her face triumphant. Neil's expression was uncertain.

Kate felt a prickle of doubt. Had she promised too much? Had she gone further than Skinner had authorised? Had Annette even heard her reservations? It was too late now. She would have to run with it.

* * *

Forty minutes later, she was back in the car, having finally extricated herself from the Marshall residence. She sank down in her seat. It had been a draining encounter. She felt infected by Annette's anger and sadness. Dealing with victims' families always had this effect. Their pain and devastation placed a physical weight of expectation on her, to make things right. She knew her sense of responsibility would not ease until she had done everything she could. For better or worse, she felt tethered to the Marshalls.

A tap on the glass. She looked up to find Neil Marshall alongside. *Now what?* She wound down her window.

'I need to talk to you. But I can't at the moment.' He gestured in frustration back at the house, where Annette no doubt required his attention. 'Can we meet tomorrow. In the morning?'

Neil thrust a crumpled post-it note through the window. 'Not at the house. Can you meet me here?' He pointed to the scribbled address on the note. 'Say around nine?'

Kate glanced briefly at the address, registering the location, and nodded.

'Thank you,' he said with obvious relief.

Watching him hurry back to the house, she wondered what he wanted to tell her that he couldn't say in front of his wife.

9

Returning to the station, Darnley was the first person Kate noticed as she entered the office. He was standing by the kettle, an untouched cup of instant coffee cooling on the counter beside him. He stared past her, unseeing.

From the corner of her eye, Kate could see Josh at his cubicle, his hair wet and slick, apparently fresh from a shower. An afternoon gym session, she assumed. His devotion to fitness was another thing that faintly irritated her about him. He was on the phone, clearly unhappy about something. He spotted her and she acknowledged him with a nod. Whatever the problem was, she figured it could wait a few minutes. She turned towards the kitchenette.

Busying herself with the hot water and instant decaf, she spoke lightly to Darnley. 'How'd it go today, Greg?'

She was referring to the Adderton Coronial inquest, which Darnley had been attending all week. She knew he had headed to court straight from the scene yesterday. Today was the final day of the hearing, when the coroner's findings were due to be read out.

Startled out of his reverie, Darnley spoke with a slight hesitation. 'As expected, Sarge. Finding of murder-suicide.'

'How's Rosalyn?'

He sighed, not answering straightaway.

Ten weeks ago, Stephen Adderton – Rosalyn's son – had killed his wife of six years and two daughters, eighteen months and three years, before taking his own life. A dairy farmer, Stephen had been crippled by debt and weeks away from losing his farm. For months, he had been stockpiling prescription sleeping tablets and had crushed a fistful of pills into his wife and daughters' dinner, waiting until they were sufficiently sedated to carry them to bed, carefully arranging them under their blankets, before smothering and asphyxiating each in turn using a pillow. He had prowled the empty farmstead for hours afterwards, recording a tearful confession and a rambling angry tirade against banks and politicians who cared little for the rural sector, into his phone. Past midnight and after several hours of drinking, he had whispered his final thoughts before taking his own life using a .22 calibre rifle in the packing shed.

His mobile was left lying on top of a notice of repossession from the bank. Mrs Adderton had discovered the family a day later when visiting the farm to drop off her elder granddaughter's dance costume, which she had been sewing. She had found the petite, doll-like frame of her daughter-in-law and the equally elfin bodies of her grandkids swaddled in bed, fully clothed, seemingly asleep. The house was spotless. Stephen had meticulously washed and put away the dishes from his family's final meal, carefully preserving the leftover pumpkin soup in the fridge as evidence for the police and placing his empty bottles of beer in the recycling. The only sound from the house was the frantic barking of the family kelpie chained to the back verandah. Around a hundred and fifty head of dairy cows had been in the fields, bellowing pitifully, their udders painfully stretched and overfull, waiting to be milked, several already suffering from mastitis.

In a single day, Rosalyn Adderton, already a widow, had lost her only remaining family.

Kate remembered walking into the scene. The farm was forever etched in her mind, a combination of unrelenting mud from days of rain, the pungent smell of cow pat, and the distressing cries of cows in the background. A deep well of anger had cracked open within her in that moment against Stephen Adderton, a husband and father who had performed the ultimate violence against his family to escape his own mental anguish. The bruised faces of the children amid their scrupulously clean and tidy house still haunted her. It had been a case that she had happily surrendered to Darnley. He had been first on the scene. With two grown daughters of his own, she felt he was more affected than he cared to admit.

Darnley spoke quietly. 'She's not coping, Sarge. They played the iPhone footage this week. You know, Stephen's confession, and I thought she might faint, she went so white. She left straight after the findings. Didn't want to speak to anyone. I tried, but you know how she is.'

Kate remained silent. She did know and she also knew that right now there was nothing she or Darnley could say or do to make things better for Rosalyn Adderton. She was in her own private hell and wasn't ready yet to reach out.

'We just need to keep tabs on her.'

'I know.' Darnley nodded. 'I've been visiting her every few days to make sure she's okay. I don't think she's going to do anything stupid. But just in case, I'll run past again today after knock-off.'

She squeezed his shoulder lightly. 'You're a good man, Greg.'

He looked away, the edges of his neck turning pink.

Out in the corridor, Josh was waiting for her, fidgeting impatiently.

'Problem?' she asked mildly.

'That was digital forensics on the phone. They can't zoom in on the footage of Captain America's wrist with any detail. The resolution is too poor.' He thrust a black-and-white image in front of her. 'That's the best they could do.'

Kate regarded the image in silence. It showed a more close-up version of the moment they had noticed on the security footage. The youth they had dubbed Captain America reaching for the canvas bag of cash. The computer analyst had managed to adjust the contrast and brightness of the image so that the mark they had noticed on the assailant's wrist was now more noticeable as a darker shadow just below the cuff line. But Josh was right, the resolution wasn't great. The restaurant didn't employ HD cameras and the footage quality reflected it. The distance and angle of the capture meant that even their best stills only showed a partial view of the wrist.

'It's not perfect, but still worth getting out to the press.' She held the image closer. 'I reckon it could be part of a tattoo.' She passed the print back to Josh. 'Can we get it on the evening news?'

'On it. Harris is forwarding it through to the media unit now.

I'm heading over to the store. Show this around and see if it prompts anything from the staff.'

He paused briefly, before turning away, making a point that he was informing her of his movements. She was grateful he hadn't asked her to accompany him. Her feet ached and she wanted nothing more than to sit for a few moments without the need to talk to anybody.

Collapsing at her desk, Kate reached for her laptop and opened the image file that the techies had saved onto the server. Zooming in on the image had no effect, except to enlarge the pixilation and distort the picture. She zoomed out again. She firmly believed that something had been captured by the image. Was it the tail-end of a tattoo? Could it be a scar from an old injury? A skin discolouration? In theory, the image should trigger someone's memory. Unless it was just a trick of the light and she was clutching at straws and making a mountain out of a shadow. The more she viewed the image, the less certain she felt. She clicked out of the file in frustration.

'That the image from the holdup, is it?'

Kate turned to find Skinner paused behind her chair. She nodded. 'It'll be on the news tonight. Hopefully, we'll get a hit.'

'Good. Excellent. And Roman Allen is happy?'

'As far as I know. Josephine's name hasn't made it to the press, so that's helped.'

'And the girl's doing okay?'

'She's suffering from amnesia. Can't remember much of what happened, but in this case it's probably a blessing. Otherwise, she seems to be recovering.'

He nodded, still hovering by her desk and not moving away. The longer he waited, the more fidgety she felt. The baby kicked and her belly rippled. She felt the press of movement on her bladder, strong and urgent. She wished Skinner would get on with it. She knew what was coming and wasn't surprised when he finally enquired about the Marshall case.

'I met with the Marshalls today, and I've started going through the file,' she replied without elaborating. She could have told him the truth; that she had looked at everything in the file, multiple times, in fact, and found nothing. That her meeting with the Marshalls had mostly encountered a wall of rumour and conjecture. Instead she held it all in, a mulish reaction to being asked. She would report back when she was ready.

He didn't press her and dropped the subject. 'And everything else is okay? Gray's doing well?'

She held her tongue, knowing he was trying to wind her up, his amused eyes watching her, waiting for a reaction. Her mobile whirred and she reached for it, glad for the excuse.

A hoarse voice growled in her ear, 'I can give you ten minutes this afternoon. You need to get here before five.' There was a sound of phlegm-filled coughing before the line went dead. She glanced at the caller ID, but there was no mistaking who had been on the other end.

10

'Cut the bullshit, Miles. What the hell is really going on?'

Kate waited for Graham Barlow's hacking, spluttering smoker's cough to subside before answering.

'I told you, Graham. I'm doing an informal review of the case.'

Barlow harrumphed, took a deep drag of his cigarette and blew the smoke directly into her face. She held her breath and did a circuit of the concrete courtyard, waiting for the smoke to disperse before rejoining him. They were holed up in the tiny outdoor courtyard that led out of Barlow's office. She had made it to Tweed Heads by the deadline stipulated.

Enclosed on three sides by brick walls and opening out to the alleyway that led to the hospital's refuse collection point, this was the Northern District Base Hospital's concession to Barlow's chain-smoking and flagrant disregard of all conventions against smoking indoors. Cigarette butts littered the dirty paving of the eight-square-metre space, and a handful of dying pot plants sat slumped in the corner, scattered with cigarette ash.

The hospital's senior forensic pathologist was a dinosaur. Difficult, caustic, eternally ill-tempered and never shy with his opinions, he was a constant thorn in the side of the hospital administration. Graham Barlow had survived five separate administrations and had determinedly defied each of their efforts to get rid of him, shunt him sideways, or bestow him on another area health service. He was skeletally thin, the exception an unseemly paunch that extruded above his belt, with red-rimmed eyes and the patchy, broken-capillary skin of a lifelong smoker. He was the poster boy for ill-health, chain-smoking two packets a day and wandering the hospital corridors looking like death revived.

Kate wondered why he continued to abuse his body when he saw the daily results of ill use in the disease-riddled bodies wheeled into his morgue. Or maybe that was the reason he smoked, because more than most, he understood that none of it made any difference; the young and healthy died just the same as the old and diseased and it all came to naught in the end.

Barlow continued to smoke without meeting her gaze.

She tried again. 'Graham, I wouldn't ask if I didn't need to know. Are there any holes? Is there anything you would have done that Donaldson didn't?' Adrian Donaldson. The pathologist on the Marshall case. A junior pathologist from Lismore, he had been on a four-month rotation at the Northern District Base Hospital when the floods had hit. He had been filling in for Graham, who had been forced by the hospital to run down some of his ample store of annual leave.

Kate watched the tendrils of smoke from Barlow's cigarette swirl past his grizzled face. The seconds ticked past.

'I'm asking you as a friend of Dad's, Graham.' She didn't want to play the dad card, but if it made him talk …

The mention of her father roused him, but not in a good way. 'Well, as a fucking friend of your dad's, Miles, it's *Dr Barlow* to you.' He looked her up and down, a sneer on his face, the snub of the cigarette hanging off the side of his mouth. 'You're not your father: remember that.'

She suppressed her anger with difficulty, opened her mouth to try again, but he got in before her.

'Donaldson's findings are solid. There's nothing to question.'

It was the smallest of concessions. The merest softening of his tone. She would take it.

'But he's new, isn't he? That was, what, the third body he was the lead on?'

'Being new doesn't equate to not knowing his job.'

'I'm not accusing him of anything but inexperience, Dr Barlow. I have to be sure in my own mind that you don't have any reservations about his findings … The bruising and abrasions to the body, to the right arm and shoulder? They all seemed fine to you? Could it indicate anything else at all?' She ignored the sneer of disdain he gave her and pressed on. 'Like being pushed into the water, or the use of force in any way? He looked pretty beaten up.'

Barlow was silent for a long time. When he spoke, his tone was quiet, but she could hear the suppressed irritation beneath it.

'Miles, I don't know what you're trying to find. Pathologists I know don't muck up their autopsies for the hell of it. Of course he was beaten up. The poor bastard had just been sloshed around in a bloody great washing machine with tree branches and rocks.' He took a deep drag and blew out smoke through his teeth. 'The injuries are consistent with being swept away in a fucking great flood. That was Donaldson's conclusion and there's nothing to suggest that he got it wrong.'

Paying no heed to his increasing annoyance, she kept going. 'You don't think the injuries from the debris covered up any separate ante-mortem injuries?'

He eyed her with dislike. 'What is it you're after, Miles? Why are you questioning Donaldson's findings? Trying to ruin a young kid's career before it even starts?'

'No, of course not—' she began.

He held up his hand to stave off her protest. 'I read the report before you got here. Everything I saw was consistent with injuries sustained by a man swept through flood waters. Can I categorically say that every single cut and bruise on the body was the result of injuries sustained in the water, rather than before he entered the creek? Of course I can't. Neither can Donaldson. No one can. For all we know, the bloke may have bumped his head or scratched his face ten minutes before ending up in the creek. But the question is whether it's relevant.

'Our job,' he went on, speaking louder so she wouldn't interrupt, 'is to detect any anomalies. Any injuries that look out of place, given the circumstances. And I'm telling you there wasn't anything. Donaldson may be new, but he's thorough. The autopsy was done by the book.' He glowered at her, daring her to challenge him.

She met his eyes evenly. 'Thank you, Dr Barlow. I just needed to hear that.' She turned to go. 'I know I don't need to say this, but I would appreciate it if you could keep this conversation to yourself.'

'Fuck off!'

11

Kate lay on the couch in front of the television, the sound turned down low. It was evening and Archie lay asleep on her lap. She needed to pee, but she didn't want to disturb him.

He had taken ill that afternoon, running a temperature of 38.5. A 24-hour virus, the GP had assured Geoff, prescribing paracetamol for the fever.

Kate had headed home straight from Barlow's to help her husband with the inevitable disaster of trying to get Archie to swallow the liquid-filled syringe of children's Panadol: a distressing few minutes of one parent holding Archie down and the other squirting the hated liquid down his throat, all the while dealing with his frenzied screaming, thrashing and crying. Today, he had managed to spit out the first lot, which had extended the ordeal through another round.

It was traumatic for all concerned and as close as she ever got to wanting to strike her child. In those moments, she could feel the anger boiling up beneath her skin, seconds from losing control. *Just drink the fucking thing!* her mind would scream.

No amount of coaxing, bribery, or mixing the medicine in juice ever seemed to work. After twenty minutes of negotiating, with no result and his temperature continuing to rise, they'd had to bite the bullet. She wondered if her childless colleagues at the station would have understood if they had witnessed the scene, or whether they would have labelled this as child abuse. Oh, for the pre-child days when parenting had seemed so straightforward and clear-cut.

She sighed and stroked her son's sweaty, tousled head. The poor little man had finally collapsed in her arms, exhausted and tear-stained. Her heart went out to him and she pulled him in closer.

Geoff popped his head into the room to check on them. 'How's he going?'

'Good, I think,' replied Kate. 'His temperature is coming down.' Gesturing to the digital thermometer beside her, she added, 'Thirty-seven-point-two.'

'Good. Good.' He reached down and softly felt Archie's forehead and cheek. 'Yeah, he's much cooler now. Do you want me to take him to bed or are you right with him?'

'What's the time?'

'Just after eight,' he answered.

She suppressed a yawn. 'Leave him for a bit. I don't want to wake him up.'

Geoff settled beside her, taking in the tiredness around her eyes. 'Maybe you should think about turning in, too?'

'After this ends,' she said, referring to the show on TV. It was some kind of historical doco that she was only half paying attention to. She leaned into Geoff's shoulder, reaching for her phone and checking for messages.

She noted a brief text from Josh reporting that so far none of the McDonald's staff had recognised the security image or recalled any current or former employee as having any kind of marking on their wrists. She hoped they would have better luck with the public broadcast of the image. She had missed the evening news, busy with Archie, but as she scrolled through the online news sites, she could see that the report was getting wide coverage.

Her email icon blinked and she registered a new message from an address she didn't recognise: *AM23@gmail.com*. She opened the message, curious.

A string of images of a laughing, blond-headed boy opened up on her screen. The photos were of the child at all different ages, from a pudgy toddler in a rashie, plastered with zinc cream running under a garden sprinkler, to photos from the high-school football team. Only after scanning the latter photos did she recognise the subject: Joel Marshall.

So, that meant *AM23* was Annette, she guessed. There was no text in the body of the email, but there was no mistaking the message. Annette was giving life and shape to the name on the file. Just a few months ago, Joel had been a living, breathing person. A much-loved son and friend. She was making sure Kate didn't forget who the case was about.

Her mind swept back to her interview with the Marshalls that afternoon. Skinner had been right about Mrs Marshall senior. She was toxic with grief, ready to blame anyone and anything to relieve for one moment the pain that consumed her. So what if she had chosen her daughter-in-law, the beautiful and sophisticated interloper from the south who had usurped her importance in her son's life, as the target for her wrath? Could Kate really judge? Did she know how she would cope with losing a child? Grief did funny things to people. She looked down at the sleeping form of her son. How would she cope if she lost Archie? She flinched, squeezing her son's small frame.

She pictured again Annette's face twisted by grief and bitterness as she spoke of her daughter-in-law. If Mrs Marshall was to be believed, Gabby had motives aplenty. Despite the rosy picture Gabby had painted to the press, according to Annette, her son's marriage hadn't been working out. In Annette's telling, Gabby wasn't happy with her life in Esserton. It didn't match the urbane buzz of Sydney. She wanted to move back south, but Joel had resisted, afraid of the hefty house prices and the likely colossal mortgage they would have to take on. Apparently, Joel had wanted to raise their children in Esserton surrounded by the family and friends he had known all his life. With no family on Gabby's side, he hadn't wanted to move to Sydney where they would have little support. 'And rightly so,' Annette had declared, her lips set rigid with disdain.

Kate couldn't decide how much of what she had heard was the truth or just wishful thinking on Annette's part. How many of Joel's marital problems would he have really confided in his mother? The one thing Annette was convinced of was that Gabby was having an affair. She had no concrete proof, but evidently she 'just knew' from certain things Joel had let slip, and from her own observations.

Then there was the life-insurance money. That, Kate felt, was the crux of the matter, the real source of Annette's bitterness; the fact that Gabby had got access to Joel's money. It had come through three weeks ago and Gabby was the sole beneficiary. Annette was adamant, now Gabby had access to the insurance money, it would only be a matter of time before she moved down south again, or overseas, preventing any chance of bringing her to justice. Kate had not missed the flicker of impatience that had crossed Neil's face at the mention of the insurance money. Clearly, he had a different perspective and she would be enquiring into that when she saw him next.

In contrast, the urgency of Annette's convictions had been palpable. The problem was, it was all supposition and innuendo. Nothing concrete. Plenty of people Kate knew had bad marriages that didn't end in murder. On the other hand, some relationships did exactly that. Annette had no theories on how Gabby had actually gone about it, or why she would have put her own life at risk by being in the water with Joel. She had just kept repeating that it was for the police to find out, if they did their job properly. In other words, a circumstantial straw house Annette wanted the police to shore up.

Kate sighed. It would help if she could speak to Gabby herself, get her side of the story and form her own impressions of the Marshalls' daughter-in-law. But she knew there was no way that Skinner would go for it. He wanted this finished quickly and quietly. Unless she could go to him with something tangible, he would never authorise an interview with Gabby Marshall, the celebrity.

Again, Kate felt the faint unease that she had experienced earlier. Had she raised Annette's expectations too high? If her review came to nothing, would Annette be able to cope with her findings?

She glanced back to the email, her finger hovering over the 'reply' icon. She pressed it, typing simply: *Thanks, Annette. I will keep these safe.*

THEN

'Eamon, the water's still coming in!' His mother's screeching reached him from the kitchen.

'Hang on!' Eamon yelled back through gritted teeth. *Just shut the fuck up.*

He wrenched open the hall closet, rummaging inside for spare towels, suitable for sopping up dirty water. The linen shelves were bare apart from a couple of old winter parkas. *Fuck.* He would have to wade through the mound of unwashed clothes in the laundry to pull out some towels. He wrestled a loose vacuum cord back inside the cupboard and slammed the door shut.

His mother had hauled him out of bed that morning, shouting incoherently about the kitchen floor being backed up with muddy water. Her whining voice had reached him even underneath his pillow, her sour wine breath and cigarette stench assaulting his nose the moment he had emerged from under the covers.

'Get up, baby. Mum needs your help. The kitchen's flooded. And it wasn't me this time.' She had laughed and swayed dangerously, her feet still squeezed into high heels from the night

before. He realised that she had only just got home. Sharing an
Uber with her loser friends, or more likely dropped off by some
man she had met last night.

In the dim light of the morning, he had taken in her smudged
makeup and clothes that left nothing to the imagination and an
image had sprung into his mind, unbidden. A porno that was
doing the rounds by phone, at school. A brash, older woman
with the same bouncy hair and sculpted makeup that his mother
favoured, being taken by two thrusting men who appeared half
her age. *Old cheese* had been the title of the video. He blushed at
the memory, repulsed and embarrassed.

'Give us a hug, hon.' His mum had half fallen, half sprawled
on his bed and he had shrugged her off roughly.

Stumbling downstairs still half asleep into an overcast and
slate-grey morning, he had inspected the damage. The gutters
had overrun from the previous night's almost ceaseless rain. The
water was draining into the house, seeping in under the frayed
seal of the back door. He had examined the mess with a sinking
feeling. He would have to take care of the clean-up, while she
nursed her head in bed with coffee and painkillers. No doubt she
would expect him to stick a ladder up to the roof and clear out the
gutters before the clouds gave way again.

It was in times like these when his vague yearning for a father
or a responsible adult of any kind seemed to flare. For a second, his
mind brought up the quiet, calm face of Anika's dad; dependable
and capable. Eamon could hardly remember his own dad, who
had walked out on them before he had reached the age of two.
All photographic evidence of the man had long been scoured

from their lives, and his mother only spoke of him to perpetually bemoan her lack of child support. Eamon had a vague impression of a larger-than-life character with a raucous, booming laugh. That could have been something he had made up or seen on TV. When he was younger, he had spent countless hours imagining what his dad may have looked like or what he did for a living. It was always something exciting, of course, befitting a six-year-old boy's imagination: an astronaut, or policeman, or fireman. His mother had laughed outright when he had confided his imaginings to her. These days, Eamon no more wondered about the whereabouts of his father than of Santa Claus.

He stalked into the laundry and started to riffle through the dirty linen. The back pocket of his jeans pinged. Instantly, his heart skipped a beat. *Anika.*

He removed his phone and glanced at the screen. He hoped Anika was messaging him about meeting up. He needed to get away from here and he hadn't seen her in over two weeks. She had been down the coast with her family visiting relatives over the Christmas and new year break and had only got back a few days ago. He read her text and smiled.

Hey, Mum & Dad are going out tomorrow night. Want 2 come over?

He typed back quickly:

Definitely! Have u asked them?

He hated arriving at Anika's house when he wasn't expected. Especially when her dad answered the door.

> Yes! Don't worry. They know! 😜
> Just checking!
> Do u want Dad to give u a lift if it's still raining?
> It's OK I'll ride over. I don't mind getting wet.
> Mmm. I quite like getting wet too! 😏😏
> 😏 OMG!!! U R killing me here! 😏
> C U TMRW 😘😘

'Eamon, it's started raining again.'

Fuck's sake. 'Coming. I'm coming.'

12

Kate followed her GPS directions towards the scribbled address on Neil's post-it note through the outskirts of town. Older fibro and brick-veneer homes blended into rural pastures separated by unexpected swathes of remnant bush. The pastures were a patchwork of alternating shades of green and brown occupied by languid dairy cattle and an occasional horse. Low streaks of early-morning clouds scudded across the sky, one minute cloudy and the next piercingly bright.

Her body ached. It had been a bad night. She had sore hips from sleeping on her sides, lying on her back no longer being a viable option. Her pregnancy was at a stage where no amount of pillows shoved, moulded or pummelled into place could provide a position of comfort for longer than ten minutes. Plus, she had got up several times in the night to check on Archie. She needn't have bothered. Dosed up on Panadol, he had slept deeply and peacefully all night, waking up at the crack of dawn, full of beans and demanding pancakes for breakfast.

Though her eyes felt gritty with fatigue, she had been happy to oblige, rarely getting uninterrupted alone time with Archie. They had pottered contentedly while Geoff slept, Archie taking full advantage of his uncommon freedom in the kitchen and leaving a trail of spilled batter, Nutella and pieces of banana in his wake. They had eaten together on the balcony, the TV and morning cartoons forgotten for once, watching the rainbow lorikeets dive and dart among the bottlebrush. She had caught a momentary glimpse of life during maternity leave, sitting with Archie and listening to his prattle while another little life nuzzled against her breast.

Yawning widely, she switched her attention to the road as the GPS warned of her destination ahead. She slowed down and felt the Commodore dip in and out of a wide causeway. Just beyond, she spotted Neil's Subaru sedan stopped at the verge. She parked behind it and joined him where he stood waiting by a white timber sign: *Red Cedar Creek*.

They both glanced at the sign, Neil with some self-consciousness. He had insisted on bringing her to the spot where his son and daughter-in-law had been washed away. Kate made no comment. There was nothing to say.

She looked around. The verge on which they had parked formed a scrubby bank that slumped into the creek channel. Named after the native cedars, prized by loggers, which had once lined its horizons, today, Red Cedar Creek comprised a placid channel of water that flowed under the road causeway via box culverts. Gnarled gum trees, roots exposed, clung on to the deeply incised weed-smothered banks. A few mounds of debris were the only reminder that, just a few months back, the water level had been high enough to surge across this road and devour a young life.

Neil started for the causeway and she began to follow. A four-wheel drive beeped, startling her. Waiting for the car to pass, and making sure there were no other vehicles about, she scrambled awkwardly down the bank to the creek bed, where Neil was waiting for her on the eastern side, the direction in which Joel and Gabby's ute had been washed way. Without a word, they began to walk.

'I started coming here about two months ago. I'm not sure why. I mean, it's not like there's anything left to see.' He glanced sideways at her and smiled feebly. 'But it makes me feel better to walk along here, you know? Makes me feel closer to him, like I'm here with him at the end.'

Kate nodded, images of the fair-haired boy with a lopsided grin from Annette's email filling her mind. She understood. The pain and irrational guilt that only a parent could feel, that somehow they could have done something to prevent their child from being harmed. The need to visit and honour the last place where your child was alive. The need to say goodbye in whatever way was left, when the actual opportunity had been snatched away.

'I thought if I could just walk far enough up the creek, I could reach the spot where he died. But no one knows that, do they? Not even Gabby. I could walk right past without a clue. I'll never be sure where he left us.' Neil's voice cracked and he swallowed hard.

Kate let him speak, to say his piece without interruption. The time for questions would come.

'I was hoping to walk to the place where Gabby was rescued, where the creek backs onto those people's property who saved her.'

'The Pavićs,' Kate offered quietly.

'That's it. The Pavićs. I met them briefly at the police station. They looked like nice people.' He fell silent, seeming to lose his train of thought, then gave a short laugh. 'I've never made it that far yet. Maybe I will one day. Something to aim for.' He gave her a rueful smile.

They walked on, Kate doing her best to keep pace, her hand moving to support the bulk of her belly and stepping with care along the muddy creek bed. She noticed several thick tree branches, rocks of all sizes, and even the odd shopping trolley. Flood debris, lying where the waters had dropped them, inert and innocent. She imagined Neil's son being struck by these objects, being dragged away in a torrent, unable to see, unable to defend himself in the murky water. The fear he must have felt, knowing this was the end. She shuddered despite the bright morning sun.

She stepped next to Neil and felt a warning hand on her arm. She turned to him questioningly. He held a finger to his lips, motioned her to keep still and gestured to her right side.

A movement on the ground and she felt herself go rigid, frozen in mid-motion. Less than a metre away from her foot, a thin, black sliver of life was making its way along the creek bed, its flushed pink underbelly visible as its body coiled through the undergrowth. Its movements were slow and laboured. As the snake gained the bank, they had a view of its entire length. The back third appeared to be limp, a dead weight, possibly crushed by something: a vehicle maybe. The red-bellied black was making its way into the bush to die.

They watched the snake disappear into the scrub and Kate exhaled, feeling the sickening pulse of adrenaline drain through her body.

'Maybe we've walked enough?'

Neil was all apologies, as if only just realising that he had made a heavily pregnant woman trudge after him along a rutted creek bed. They found a rocky outcrop along the side of the creek, smoothed down by years of flowing water. Kate carefully examined its surrounds for any signs of wildlife before gingerly sitting down.

They sat together in silence, Kate's heart rate slowly returning to normal. After a while, the bush cast its own spell and their silence lengthened without awkwardness. The scrub was thick on either side of them, casting shadows on the water. She could hear birds darting among the leaves. She watched a train of ants moving nimbly among the sand grains and grit.

Neil seemed at peace, staring at the trees and listening to the occasional bird calls, the worry lines along his forehead smoothed out. She hated having to break the spell.

'Neil, was there anything you wanted to add to what Annette said yesterday?'

The mood shattered. Neil started back to the present and his face took on the puckered, slightly worried expression he had worn the previous day. He glanced at Kate and away.

'Have you spoken to Gabby yet? I mean, will you be speaking to her about everything Annette said?'

'I haven't spoken to Gabby yet, no. We would only speak to her if anything new came up. Some material new evidence.' She hesitated. 'So far, everything Annette told me is unsubstantiated.

I will be looking into it. But at the moment, there's nothing that would warrant me calling Gabby in.'

Relief played on his face. 'I wanted to say that you need to take everything Annette tells you with a grain of salt. She's not been herself since Joel died. I've tried getting her to see a counsellor ...' He sighed in frustration and didn't finish the sentence. 'This thing with Gabby. It's all in her head. I mean, it's all gossip and bullshit she's made up.'

'So, you don't agree with your wife's assessment of your son's marriage. You don't believe things were strained between them? That things had changed in any way?'

'There may have been problems. I don't honestly know. Sometimes they were a bit touchy with each other. But that's just normal marriage stuff, isn't it? You can't expect them to stay exactly the same as when they first met. Did they have issues? Probably, but does that mean Gabby killed Joel? Of course not.

'I mean, it's just absurd, what Annette's suggesting. She's obsessed with Gabby. She never liked her, you know? Just took an instant dislike the minute Joel brought her back from Sydney and introduced us. It was the speed of their relationship and the fact that she was—' He stopped himself, embarrassed.

Kate raised her eyebrows and waited.

'It's because she wasn't well off,' he said eventually. 'Had nothing to her name, unlike ... well, unlike us. We've always had enough to get by.'

A clear understatement, thought Kate.

Neil smiled without a trace of humour. 'It's not nice, is it? But that's how Annette is. She didn't think Gabby was good enough for Joel.' His lips curved in disgust. 'But to accuse her of murder? That's a new low, even for Annette. I mean, we know Gabby. This is our daughter-in-law. She's practically lived in our house for the past four years and she has no one to defend her. No family. We should be her family. Blaming Gabby won't bring Joel back. It's muddying her name and putting doubt in people's minds for no reason; destroying Gabby's life purely because she survived, and Joel didn't.'

He stopped his flow abruptly, suddenly exhausted.

'What do you think of your wife's theory that Gabby was having an affair?' Kate asked quietly.

'I think it's bullshit,' Neil replied fiercely, flaring up again. 'But even if she was, it's none of our business. That was between Joel and Gabby. It doesn't add up to murder.'

Kate agreed. She had learned nothing new from this interview apart from a more balanced view of Joel's marriage. She needed to wrap this up. She opened her mouth to speak, but Neil got in first.

'I thought she was getting over it, you know. Well, not getting over it, but learning to accept it. After the funeral, and after we received the coroner's findings, I thought she had settled down. But this life-insurance thing, it seems to have set her right off again. That's what's brought this on. I wish I never bloody mentioned it to her when Gabby told me.'

'Are you aware of the sum of money involved?' Kate asked, glad that the conversation had finally turned in the right direction.

'It's not a ridiculous sum. I think it's something like a hundred and thirty grand including Joel's super, what little there was. Not nothing, but not some kind of million-dollar windfall like Annette's making out, either. It was one of those nominal policies that get attached to your super account. The premiums were coming out of Joel's super. Gabby had no idea he had even agreed to the policy. Joel probably didn't either. He was hopeless with that stuff,' Neil added with a sad smile. 'Probably ticked the wrong box in the form or didn't realise he had to opt out.'

'How can you be sure Gabby wasn't aware of the policy, Neil? Did she mention something to you?' Kate probed.

'I was with her at the house when the letter came.' He didn't look at her as he answered, his voice sounding tired, weary of explaining. 'We were going through all of Joel's stuff. Deciding what to do with it all. Didn't get very far in the end.' He laughed shortly. A rough bark that sounded strangled.

Neil cleared his throat loudly and continued. 'Anyway, she gave most of it away. Eighty thousand to the RFS. Something to remember Joel by, because he used to volunteer.' He spoke bitterly. 'I've told Annette, but she won't believe me.' He gritted his teeth, his face brimming with frustration. 'Gabby didn't kill my son for his life insurance, Detective. It just didn't happen.'

Kate remained silent. She now had two very different versions of Gabby. She could be just as Neil had portrayed her: a grieving wife, entirely innocent of what Annette accused, wanting nothing more than to honour Joel's memory. And yet the money grated at Kate. Eighty thousand dollars wasn't a sum to be sneezed at, regardless of what other money Gabby was earning from her TV and magazine endorsements and what she had inherited from Joel's estate. For Gabby to have given away such a sum to the Rural Fire Service, meant that she was either a self-sacrificing saint or had a very guilty conscience to assuage.

Some of her doubt must have shown on her face because Neil once more began to speak, trying to convince her. 'They were a normal couple, Detective. Maybe their feelings were waning a bit, but they weren't at each other's throats, all right? I don't care what Annette thinks, there was no reason for Gabby to do anything to Joel. I mean, she was a swimming instructor. She taught people to swim up and down a pool, for Christ's sake! Does that sound like a murderer to you?'

Kate regarded him thoughtfully. She wondered at his utter conviction. Was it merely because Gabby was female? She had discovered in her job that a surprising number of people found it almost impossible to believe that a woman would commit a crime, especially a violent one, whereas the opposite was true when the accused was a man, sometimes well after the poor sod was found to be innocent. She wondered also if this was a case of misplaced chivalry; a need to protect a young woman, who was otherwise without parental support, from slander and disgrace; a young woman who Neil had come to think of as a daughter, even a substitute for his dead son. Or did it all stem from his deep antipathy towards his wife? Was he willing to oppose Annette on principle, unable to consider any truth in her perspective?

Kate couldn't make up her mind. After a few more follow-up questions she took her leave, promising to stay in touch. She left him seated on the rock, his gaze trained on the bushland opposite and his face in shadow.

13

'So, that's a dead end as well ...'

Josh was standing at the head of the incident room, reviewing the case status. The assembled team included Kate, Darnley and Harris. Two additional officers, constables Roby and Grant, had been pulled off general duties to assist the team and man the information line, which had been made public on the news the previous night.

Josh's voice droned on, summarising the various threads of their investigation to date. So far, the results had been resoundingly negative. Kate watched a lone fly trapped in between the panes of the casement window hammering its body feverishly at the glass, trying to access the afternoon sun outside. Josh's constant highlighting of their lack of progress was starting to grate on her nerves. She crushed a half-eaten sandwich inside its wrapper, swallowing against the familiar sting of heartburn, the effect of the baby pressing on her stomach. She could feel a headache coming on.

Her mind reverted to the Marshall file, unable to stop herself.

She needed to make a decision on it soon. She wouldn't be able to dodge Skinner for much longer. Her chat with Neil Marshall had raised a flicker of doubt in her mind about Gabby. Instinctively, she felt that there was something behind the insurance-money donation. Long years of dealing with every kind of person both inside and out of an interview room, told her that something was off about that particular detail. And yet, was it enough to warrant further enquiry? Barlow's opinion on the autopsy had been so definite that she knew she had to tread lightly. Was it simpler to nip the whole thing in the bud, just like Skinner had wanted, and be done with it?

She thought wearily of the second email she had received that morning from Annette, with another string of photos of Joel attached. Kate hadn't replied to the email yet. She didn't want to encourage Annette further. Pushing the problem to the back of her mind, Kate forced her attention to return to the present.

Josh was recounting the interviews with the McDonald's and neighbouring Hungry Jack's employees from the previous afternoon, none of which had produced the desired result: recognition of the wrist marking. The screening of the image on the news and in the newspapers was also yet to produce anything concrete on the information line. So far, all of the calls had been unrelated to the investigation. A not entirely unexpected outcome. There were just too many lonely people around. All wanting someone to talk to, someone to unload their grievances on, a moment of importance; every single extraneous call sucking up valuable time.

The fact that no one recognised the image was worrying. Esserton was a close community. There were only a limited number of schools. Most of the teenagers from the area should be known to each other, or have come across one another in some way. If not in the classroom or school yard, then at a party, in a sports team, or a part-time job. Surely, such a distinctive feature on a person's wrist wouldn't go unnoticed. Unless, of course, they had got it wrong, misinterpreting a trick of the light for something that wasn't there? The splinter of misgiving that she had felt yesterday burrowed in further, but she shook it away. It was early days, she told herself. Someone would recognise the footage.

Josh's frustration was palpable, and she could tell from the slumped shoulders and set faces that the negativity was starting to seep into the rest of the team. Now was not the time to sow more doubts.

'Okay, thanks, Josh,' she broke in as he took a breather. 'So, our priority today is to finish off the remaining Macca's and Hungry Jack's interviews. Darnley and Harris, you're on that. Roby and Grant will continue to man the info line. Darnley, have Transport got back to us with the road footage?'

'Yes, Sarge. It came through yesterday arvo. I started going through the files this morning.'

'Okay. Once you and Harris get back from the interviews, you can both keep going on the footage. Divide and conquer.' She turned to her partner. 'Josh, what's happening with Abigail? Are we seeing her today?'

Josh raised his eyebrows. 'No. It seems Miss Masters is busy again. Her mother informed me, when I called this morning, that

Abigail and her dad are on their way to Yamba today to visit her grandparents.' He met Kate's eyes.

'Hmm. Methinks someone is trying to avoid us.'

Josh nodded. 'I've made it clear to Mrs Masters that we will be coming to see Abigail first thing in the morning and if she is not there, the interview will be transferred to the police station. I think she got the message.'

Kate nodded, taking a moment to collect her thoughts . 'About the wrist footage. If we don't get a hit on it this weekend, we need to take it to the high schools. I think we need to schedule in visits to Esserton High and Esserton West next week. I want to show the image around. See if it jogs the memories of the principals or the teachers.'

She paused again, gathering her thoughts. 'We need stills of the wrist marking and the assailants circulated to the schools. The security footage needs to be front and centre for these kids. One of them will come forward, surely. The Avengers must attend one of the local schools.'

Darnley's slow, measured voice joined in. 'Wouldn't hurt to get St Therese's to put up the images, too. The boys could be known to the St Therese girls. A boyfriend or a relative or something. You never know.'

Something had shifted in the room. A small shiver of optimism had penetrated the earlier mood. 'Good idea,' said Kate, getting to her feet. 'Josh, you and Harris can get onto that on Monday.' She didn't miss the quick exchange of glances between them. 'Thanks, everyone, I think that's it for now.'

Kate waited for the team to leave, and she was alone with Josh before addressing him. 'Josh, I know the results have been slow, but it isn't anyone's fault. A little bit of encouragement would not go astray, yeah?'

She could see the battle playing out in his features. He wasn't used to taking criticism, certainly not from a woman, but she was his superior and he had little recourse. He acknowledged the rebuke with a short nod, waiting for her to walk ahead of him, before following her out.

Out in the corridor, they heard a door slam and the screech of a woman's voice. Darnley and Harris, who had left the room ahead of them, were hurriedly making their way back down the corridor. Constable Harris was barely containing her laughter.

'It's Jean, Sarge,' Darnley said significantly. 'She's with the chief.'

Josh raised his eyebrows as Kate mouthed, 'Skinner's ex.'

She made a quick decision. With Abigail's cancellation, their afternoon had opened up. She turned to Josh. It was time to mend some fences.

'Right. We need to get out of here.' For a second she thought he'd refuse, but he followed her without a word.

* * *

'So, where exactly are we going?'

They were in the unmarked, Kate at the wheel. They had travelled west out of town some ten kilometres, driving past lush green pastures with grazing sheep and cattle, along dirt roads with verdant vegetation on either side that sometimes created an almost complete tunnel for the car to drive through. Apart from the occasional farm vehicle and a ute that dropped in and out of view, they had been alone on the road for kilometres.

'We're going to see my dad.'

'Right.' He was clearly unimpressed.

'You know the oil painting in the conference room?' Kate kept her eyes on the road, waiting for the inevitable reaction.

'The what?' She had finally piqued his curiosity.

'The painting. The one of Arthur Grayling.'

'What? The ex-chief inspector?'

'Yep. That's who we're driving to see.'

'So … hang on. Arthur Grayling is your dad?'

'One and the same.'

'Right.'

Kate smiled to herself, giving him a moment to digest the information. She had no doubt Josh had heard of Arthur Grayling. He would have done his research before his transfer to Esserton. Gray's reputation spoke for itself: forty years on the police force, chief inspector of Esserton Station for over fifteen years before retiring three years ago, making way for Skinner. An exemplary senior officer and something of a local legend.

Being the daughter of the great Arthur Grayling carried its own baggage and it wasn't something Kate advertised. She wanted to stand on her own merits.

'Did you work at the station under your dad?' Josh finally enquired.

'God, no. I worked in Grafton, mostly. Geoff and I only decided to move back after Dad retired three years ago. I'm a firm believer in maintaining a healthy distance between work and family.'

'Amen to that.'

Kate smiled. She had heard that he was the youngest of four brothers, all of them police officers in Sydney. Suddenly, the transfer this far up north made more sense. Like her, he was trying to escape the long shadow of family and build his own path.

'Why exactly are we visiting him?'

Kate didn't answer him straightaway, focusing on the road. 'He always had good local knowledge. I thought we might show him the footage, see if the boys look familiar. It's amazing how many people he knows in town.'

Josh remained silent. She could tell he was trying to decide whether or not to believe her.

'Plus, I haven't seen him in a couple of weeks. I'm due for a visit,' she added.

Josh shrugged. 'Well, it can't hurt. I'm willing to try anything at this point.'

'Don't worry. You'll like him.' Kate smiled.

Within a few minutes, they had pulled up to a property, a timber sign erected on the fence reading, *Hill Top View*. A lush bougainvillea, ablaze with purple blooms, wound around the fence, sending heavy sprays over the sign and almost obscuring a small metal mailbox attached to the fencepost. They drove in and followed a rutted dirt track uphill. The track curved its way around scrubby paddocks manned by a few desultory sheep and occasional towering gum trees. A few hundred metres up, they passed two dirt driveways, one after the other, marked by separate signs, *Lodge 1* and *Lodge 2*.

'Holiday accommodation,' Kate explained as Josh eyed the signs. 'Dad got a couple of cabins built on the property last year to rent out.'

After a further minute of climbing, the track levelled off and widened, ending in a gravelled area just outside a neat miner's cottage complete with picket fence and wisteria. Although tiny, the cottage was perfectly situated at the top of the hill to command sweeping views of the valley below. An aging ute was parked on the gravel underneath an oversized lemon-scented myrtle. Kate pulled up next to it.

Josh peered out of the window at the picture-perfect cottage.

'So, you grew up here?'

'What?' Kate laughed. 'No. Dad bought this place about five years ago. We used to live in town. After Mum died, he got sick of taking care of the old house and moved up here.'

Kate got out of the car, then reached up and pulled a leaf from the bulging branches of the lemon-scented myrtle, in the process showering herself with yellow-green confetti from the flowers gone to seed. She crushed the leaf between her fingers and passed it to Josh to smell. He inhaled deeply: an instant, technicolour, lemon-lolly scent, more lemony than lemon. He smiled in surprise. She reached up and broke off an entire branch of leaves and threw it onto the back seat. 'Great with tea,' she said with a smile.

'Oi! Stop that. You've made a hole in the crown.'

A tall man, broad-shouldered and sunburnt, had walked into view, a little thinner than his painting at the station, but still recognisably its subject in the flesh. In faded jeans, a flannelette shirt rolled at the sleeves and an old NSW Police cap, he resembled a grizzled farmer more than a retired police chief.

Kate rolled her eyes. 'Afternoon, Dad,' she called out.

Gray held the gate open for them, an ornate picket creation matching the fence, and kissed his daughter lightly as she stepped through.

'God! You're looking like a whale, woman. How long have you got to go? You should be at home resting.'

He ducked as she swatted him. He held out his hand to Josh. 'And you must be the new detective.'

'Josh Ellis, sir. It's very nice to meet you.'

Kate hid her smile. Josh was clearly on his best behaviour.

'Come in. Come in. You're actually just in time to help me.' He started walking, not to the front door, but around the side of the house towards the back garden.

'Oh, yeah?' Kate asked cautiously.

Gray opened the latch on the side gate and let them through. 'Yes. I forgot to put the chooks away before going out this morning. So you can guess what happened.'

They turned the corner of the house and Josh let out an involuntary expletive. 'Shit!'

'Yes, exactly. People don't really understand how much of it is actually involved when you've got free-range chickens.'

The three of them surveyed the innumerable small mounds of bird droppings littered all over the timber verandah and the lawn; some with the crusted permanence of an entire day baking in the sun.

Gray headed for the garden hose. Four chickens – two black bantams and a couple of ISA browns – scurried out of his way. Gray held out the hose to Josh. 'You get a head-start while I put the chickens away.'

'Right. Well. I might just go and put the kettle on.' Studiously avoiding Josh's eyes, Kate made her way to the back door, careful to step around each crusted mound.

Ten minutes later, Gray joined Kate in the kitchen. She had the tea things ready and was waiting for the kettle to boil. Gray's well-fed, orange-and-white tabby, Bunty, was on the kitchen table, demanding to be scratched, and Kate was obliging.

Kate eyed him. 'You haven't left Josh out there by himself, have you?'

'He's going well. He's still finding his technique, but he's getting there.'

Through the kitchen window, they both caught a glimpse of Josh spraying a dropping on the verandah with the hose on full blast. Pieces of shit were blasted everywhere. They heard him swear.

'Classic rookie mistake,' said Gray, watching. 'You need the water on slow and steady to melt the shit between the timber slats.'

Kate shuddered. 'Maybe you should be telling him that?'

'He'll work it out.' His face broadened into a grin. 'Anyhow, I'm here to help him.' He headed towards the kettle that was just coming to a boil. 'Need boiling water to melt the hardened poo.'

She protested the pinching of her hot water and he waved her off.

'Don't worry, I'll put a new one on. Probably need a full kettle to get through that lot, anyway.' He poured steaming water into each of the waiting mugs and headed to the sink to refill the kettle. With his back to Kate, he addressed her. 'So, Josh tells me you're here to show me the footage from the Macca's holdup.' He turned around to face her. 'You know I've already seen the stills in the paper. If I recognised anything, I would have told you already. Is this some new footage?'

Kate shook her head, fiddling with her mug of tea, not meeting his eyes.

'C'mon, Kit,' he tried again gently, 'what's going on?'

'Skinner's got me reviewing a case,' she said at last.

Immediately, she could see that his guard was up. 'Oh, yes?' he said slowly.

'It's one of the flood deaths. The mother of the victim has been making noises to the AC's office and Skinner's got me reviewing the file to make sure no one missed anything.' She quickly and succinctly filled him in on the task she had been given and on her interviews with the Marshalls.

'And?'

'And nothing. I've read the bloody thing from end to end and everything seems fine. Murchison was the officer in charge and he's done everything by the book. Mrs Marshall's allegations are just that, allegations. Unsubstantiated by any physical evidence at all. Even assuming she's right and Joel's marriage was failing, there's nothing in the postmortem or forensics to support wilful

murder. I even double-checked the autopsy results with Barlow.'
She caught Gray's amused glance. 'Yeah, and that was a bloody
laugh.' She shook her head and stopped.

'What, you doubt Barlow? He's made a couple of mistakes in
the past, but he's always admitted to them. If something was off
with the autopsy, he'd tell you.'

'No. It's not Barlow. It's … On the surface, it all looks okay.'

'But you have a problem because …'

'I have a problem because it's Skinner.' Kate brought her mug
down harder than she intended, sloshing tea on the table.

She didn't glance at her father but could imagine his expression.
The kettle boiled and switched off automatically. He tossed a tea
towel at her. 'Kit, Skinner and I have history, but it's not yours
to take on. He's an ambitious, arse-licking dickhead, but he's a
solid policeman. There's no reason for him to cover anything up.
His arse is not on the line. He wasn't in charge of the original
investigation. It wouldn't be in his interest to throw you to the
dogs over this.'

She faced him, smiling wanly.

Gray walked over to her and pecked her lightly on her crown.
'If Skinner's the only reason you have doubts, then I think you
may need to reconsider. Go home. Have a good night's rest. Read
through the file with a clear head tomorrow, and if you still can't
find anything, then I think you should be right to sign it off.'

Gray turned from her back to the window. 'Right. I think
I should rejoin your partner. Otherwise, he might start taking
things personally.'

14

Sunday

'We just want to be absolutely certain you didn't recognise anyone from that night.'

'I told you already. I didn't recognise anyone. They were wearing masks.'

Abigail Masters' tone was patient and accommodating, calculated to persuade. Her impish, perfectly oval face framed by spikey, close-cropped hair was fixed and watchful. Observing her, Kate felt that Abigail's was a face made for laughing. Seriousness didn't suit her.

It was Sunday morning and Josh and Kate sat with Abigail on the back verandah of her parents' house. Josh had made the effort to pick Kate up and they had driven together to the interview. Both of Abigail's parents, sporting immaculate casual wear, had been present to meet them at the door, the father all smiles and over-hearty, the mother silent and alert. After initial pleasantries, they had been led across a vast, ultra-modern living space, all concrete, bronze and timber, past a sleek chef's kitchen to the back verandah overlooking lush, dense greenery, where Abigail was already seated at a large outdoor table. A plunger of freshly brewed coffee, a carafe of ice-cold water with slices of lemon, and a plate of chocolate croissants sat waiting. Abigail's parents didn't join them, but left the sliding door open, a clear signal they were just around the corner if their daughter needed them, if the police started becoming difficult.

Sipping her iced water, Kate studied Abigail's face, waiting for the silence to lengthen. She brushed flakes of pastry off the rise of her belly, the remnants of a single perfect puff of butter and chocolate. With difficulty, she had refrained from indulging in a second. Josh, with no such compunctions, was already onto his third, chased down with a fresh cup of black coffee. Abigail had touched nothing.

She was disciplined, Kate conceded, only addressing the police officers when they asked her a question, otherwise staring determinedly down at the garden. Apart from asking after Josephine, she had let the police officers do the talking. Kate glanced at Josh. He obviously had his hands full concentrating on his second breakfast. She took the lead.

'Abigail, thanks for agreeing to speak with us again. We just wanted to clear up something we noticed in your statement when you were interviewed at the station on Thursday.' Receiving no acknowledgement from Abigail, Kate went on. 'I was hoping to play you a section of the recording so you can see what we mean.'

Taking her silence as concurrence, Kate pulled out her laptop from her satchel and brought up the snippet of Abigail's police interview that she wanted her to view. She turned the laptop to face Abigail and pressed 'play'.

The recording was of Abigail's follow-up interview the afternoon of the holdup. Her father sat beside her, silent and protective, and Kate and Josh had sat opposite across the interview table. The footage resumed just as Josh was starting to speak.

'Did anything seem familiar to you about the boys, Abigail? Anything at all? The reason we are asking is that the boys are most likely from the area, going to one of the local high schools. They may be regulars at McDonald's or even have worked there previously. Did anything strike you as familiar? Anything in their mannerisms, maybe? Their voices or the way they walked or stood or held themselves? Anything that you didn't remember before?'

There was a long silence. The recording showed Abigail staring down at her hands on her lap rather than at the officers.

'Abigail?' The prompting was from her father.

A tiny hesitation and Abigail had spoken quietly. *'No. I don't think so.'* She had cleared her throat and continued in a stronger voice. *'No. There was nothing familiar about any of them.'*

The hesitation could have been interpreted as nerves or something else. At the time, Josh had not pushed the issue and had moved on.

Kate pressed 'pause' on the recording and faced Abigail. 'Do you see why we feel we need to ask you again, Abigail? Neither Lucas nor Jack hesitated on any of their answers. This footage makes us think that maybe there was something you noticed that you didn't want to mention before.'

Abigail avoided her eyes. She picked up a croissant and started breaking it apart on her plate. She had yet to taste a morsel.

Kate was patient. 'There's also another reason why we wanted to talk to you, Abigail. When we spoke to Josephine on Friday, she remembered something you said when the boys first entered the store. It was something like, "They are such dicks." Again, that makes us think you may have recognised something about the boys. Did you?'

At long last Josh joined in. 'Do you know any of the boys, Abigail? It's okay to tell us. You won't get into trouble.'

'I don't. Really. I don't.' Abigail looked up now, her eyes imploring Kate. 'I can't remember saying that to Josephine. Maybe I did, but all I meant was that they looked so ridiculous when they first came in with their masks and everything. Immature, like little kids.'

Kate placed her hand on Abigail's arm, stilling her obliteration of the croissant. 'Abigail. We understand that you might not want to get someone you know into trouble. But these boys chose to do what they did. They could have seriously hurt Josephine that night. It was pure luck that she escaped without terrible head injuries or stab wounds. If you know something, you need to tell us so we can find them before they do it again.'

Abigail continued to stare at her plate of shredded croissant, chewing her lip.

Josh stepped in. 'You're not doing yourself any favours, Abigail. If we decide you're holding back important information, you could be charged with hindering an investigation.'

Abigail glanced up at Josh's pronouncement, her face watchful. That had got her attention.

Kate decided to take a punt. 'It's Captain America, isn't it, Abigail? You think you know who Captain America is, but you're not sure and you don't want to get him into trouble?'

Abigail stiffened at Kate's words. Both officers saw it.

Gotcha, thought Kate.

'It's okay, Abigail,' she continued. 'You can tell us who you think it is. Obviously if it's not him, then that'll be the end of it.'

At a nod from Kate, Josh pulled out the blown-up image of Captain America's wrist. He placed it in front of Abigail. 'This is from security-camera footage of the night. We managed to catch a view of Captain America's wrist when he was reaching out to Lucas for the money. This image has been showing on the news since Friday.'

'I don't watch the news.'

'Abigail,' Kate took over, 'in your statement, you said you couldn't remember seeing any distinguishing features or marks on any of the boys.'

'I didn't!'

'I believe you, Abigail. It was pure luck that we caught this image. He was wearing long sleeves and the gloves, and it was only visible for a second. I'm not surprised that no one saw it on the night. I want you to look at the photo now. See if you recognise it. This marking – we think it's a tattoo or possibly a scar. Does this tally with the person you're thinking of?'

* * *

'That's when we lost her.'

'I know.' They were in the squad car driving back from Abigail's, Josh at the wheel. Kate could have screamed with frustration. They had thought they had her. In fact, Kate was sure they'd had her. The photo was to be the final confirmation. Instead, it had been the reverse. Abigail had studied the photo and all of the tension had seemed to drain from her features. She had turned to them, relieved, relaxed even, and declared that she knew no one with a marking on their wrists like the one that had been captured on the footage. From that point, she had been adamant she had no idea who any of the three masked assailants were and could not be shaken from that view.

'It was almost like she knew the person and then the image convinced her otherwise.' Josh struck the steering wheel in annoyance.

Kate didn't bother responding. The failure of the interview hung over her like a haze. She had pushed too hard. She should have let Abigail get there on her own without forcing her hand with the security footage, and now they wouldn't be able to gain her corroboration, even if the footage proved irrelevant.

'So, here's my thinking,' Josh observed, glancing her way. 'Either she's genuinely mistaken about who she thought she recognised and the photo proved to her that Captain America is not the person she was thinking of. Or … the wrist marking is new. Like a new tattoo or something that she knows nothing about. So the footage makes her think it's not her guy.'

Kate mulled over the possibilities. The car had slowed down. Josh huffed and drummed his fingers impatiently as a P-plater in a Nissan Micra performed an awkward parallel park ahead of them.

A horn beeped and Kate's eyes automatically took in the waiting traffic behind in the side mirror: a white minivan, a couple of sedans and a dark-coloured ute. Josh swore and drove on.

'You could be right,' she conceded. She sat up, giving more thought to what he had said. 'Okay, so maybe someone she knew who she hasn't seen in a while? Like an old friend or a boyfriend, maybe?'

Their eyes met. 'That's a line to pursue. Tomorrow, when you're at the schools, ask the principal and teachers at Abigail's school about any boyfriends, past or present. See if they'll let you speak to some of her friends about it. It's worth trying the parents again too, though I doubt we'll get any more from them, after today.'

'Will do.'

She could feel him studying her as she checked her phone for messages.

'Are you coming back to the station?' he asked.

'No, can you drop me off at the aquatic centre? I said I'd try and catch Archie's swimming lesson. I'll head back in later. I want to pop in on Josephine again. Make sure she's okay.'

He didn't answer, his eyes back on the road. She looked his way. Maybe she should loosen the reins a bit? Let him manage things. After all, he would be responsible for the team in less than a week.

'Actually, on second thoughts, can you deal with the Allens? I might just have the afternoon with the family. I'll be on the phone if you need me.'

'Yep. Fine. Whatever works.'

His tone was neutral, but she didn't miss the lightening of his expression. It was the right decision.

15

The Esserton Aquatic Centre was crammed with the usual Sunday family crowd of kids enduring swimming lessons, seniors aqua aerobics, young families in the waist-deep kids' pool and weekend swimmers. The centre was steaming with warm air from the heated pools and unnecessary indoor heating. Kate walked into the warm fug and immediately felt overdressed and uncomfortable.

She dodged her way around toddlers in *Star Wars* towels waiting in line for lolly bags at the centre café, lithe women in blazing Lycra heading to Pilates and circuit classes, and grizzled old men in Speedos completely at ease in their stout, leathery, sun-worn bodies.

She reached the end pool, where the swimming classes were in full swing. Predictably, she had missed Archie's swimming lesson. She was just in time to see her son give his instructor a lively high-five and climb out of the pool into the waiting, towel-laden arms of his father.

She joined her family and was rewarded with a smile from Geoff and cries of delight from Archie.

'Mummy, Mummy, Mummy! Can I have an icy pole? Please! Please! Please!'

'Of course you can, monkey.' Kate hugged her son's towel-encased body, ignoring the wetness on her suit jacket. She caught Geoff's disapproving look. 'What?' she mouthed.

He rolled his eyes and shook his head resignedly. Clearly, she had just undermined whatever after-swimming-treat rule Geoff had established with Archie. *Oh well*, she thought, *another day, another fail.*

'Archie. Do you want to have a play in the kids' pool first? We can get the icy pole after.'

Archie turned around at his father's suggestion, his face undecided, clearly torn.

'We can go under the frog fountain.'

Archie's eyes lit up. 'And the crocodile water jet?'

'Of course.'

'Yay! Yay! Yay!'

Geoff laughed and started rounding up their things. 'And,' he continued, 'while we are in the fun pool, Mummy can go for a swim in the big pool.' At Kate's surprised glance, he gestured to their hold-all. 'I brought your swimmers, just in case. I know how sore you've been.'

Kate hugged him tightly without a word.

Later, in her swimmers, with an old T-shirt Geoff had also remembered to pack covering the parts of her bloated body that her overstretched bikini couldn't quite manage, she stepped into the pool with relief. There was nothing quite like the weightlessness of water to relieve the aches and pains of pregnancy. She had swum regularly when she had been pregnant with Archie. This time around, she could never seem to find the time.

Kate pushed off into the water, immediately cocooned in its insulating silence, the background cacophony of the centre hushed in an instant and the weight of her pregnancy taken over by the water. It felt good to stretch her muscles, feeling her body work as she cut through the water. The tensions of the week washed away with the tempo of her strokes, the busyness of her mind quietening as the warm water enveloped her and muffled all external stimuli. She concentrated on her breathing and maintaining a steady pace.

After fifteen laps, she emerged with a gasp, out of breath but feeling more energised than she had in weeks. She removed her goggles and took in her surrounds as she caught her breath. She had one of the medium-paced lap lanes all to herself. To her right, two fit, young men were pacing each other up and down the fast lane. The left two lanes were occupied by a couple of women treading water lazily and chatting across the rope divide.

Kate surveyed the neighbouring pool area to see if she could spot Archie. The adjacent pool was made up on one side by a shallow kids' section, complete with various water jets and fountains, and on the other side by a large closed-off area reserved for aqua-aerobics classes, injury rehabilitation and one-on-one classes. Kate could just make out Geoff, at the far end of the kids' section, playing with Archie near the water jets. They were looking in her direction and she tried waving, but she was pretty sure they hadn't spotted her.

A sudden high-pitched wailing made her turn her attention to the reserved area of the pool. A female swimming instructor was trying to coax a boy of about nine or ten, suited up in a rashie, from the pool steps into the water. Something seemed to have gone awry with the lesson. The boy was shrieking, both hands to his ears, his fists balled up, dark lengths of hair falling across his face. His instructor was talking to him slowly, trying to calm him, but it didn't appear to be working. Kate saw a tiny, wiry woman, her blonde hair pulled into a tight plait, rush to the edge of the pool and attempt to comfort the boy.

Careful not to touch him, she appeared to be repeating something with practised calm, a particular word or expression to focus the boy's attention. With his mother at his side, the boy's wailing slowly subsided into a low whimper. The swimming lesson now abandoned, Kate watched as the woman addressed a few words to the instructor and coaxed her son into the stands to get changed. The young instructor watched them go, clearly rattled. Glancing around quickly to see who had witnessed the scene, she hurriedly pulled herself out of the water and headed off to the staff change rooms.

Kate heard a snort of impatience to her left and a voice rose above the background noise. It was one of the women in the neighbouring lane.

'God, did you see that? If my Conner refused to get in the pool, I would just make him. You can't just let them get away with that stuff. He knows if I'm paying for the lesson, he needs to go through with it.'

'Exactly. And why wasn't he wearing a swim cap? That's so unhygienic.'

The woman's companion said something in reply, which Kate

didn't catch. They both laughed and Kate felt a whip of anger at the easy judgement of another parent. Their conversation put her in mind of her mother's group days when Archie had been a newborn. The cliquey, competitive, humble-bragging ways of some of the mothers she had encountered. Their subtle criticisms disguised as experience and advice. She hadn't lasted long at the group. The urge to retort flared and then faded as the moment passed without the right words materialising.

'Finished?'

She looked up to find Geoff at the head of the pool with Archie covered in an oversized towel. She had been planning on another ten laps, but she could see Archie was hanging out for his icy pole.

She smiled. 'Yep. Just about to get out.'

* * *

Later, Kate sat with Geoff and Archie on the stretch of grass that overlooked the outdoor play area. Geoff had treated them to fish and chips from the centre café, the perfect antidote to all the calories she had just burned in the water, and they had decided on a makeshift picnic outside. She watched as Archie made a meal of spearing a piece of battered flake onto his fork, the majority of it ending up on his clothes or on the ground. She exchanged amused glances with her husband. Neither of them offered to help, knowing the reaction it would elicit.

Most of the swimming classes had now ended and the crowds of parents and children packing the centre had thinned. A few families had, like them, ended up outside enjoying the autumn sunshine on the grass or at the scattering of outdoor tables.

'Are you right with him for a bit?'

'Why, where are you going?'

'I just want to ask around about Gabby Marshall. See if I can find someone who knew her when she worked here. I might as well, since we're here already.'

Geoff nodded tightly, not replying. Kate knew what he was thinking. She had once more inserted work into family time.

'Half an hour,' Kate promised, struggling to her feet. She felt bad, but she knew that if she didn't take the opportunity now, she would only have to come back. Kate squeezed Geoff's shoulder lightly, a silent apology, winked at Archie still entirely absorbed in his meal, and headed back inside the artificial warmth of the centre.

Inside, she surveyed the possibilities. There were still a couple of instructors in the pool finishing up lessons for the day. Another instructor was on lifeguard duty, sitting high above the kids' pool. A couple of office staff were visible behind a glass screen, one on the phone and the other attending to a customer at the counter. She had promised Geoff she would be quick. Archie would want to head home soon and she didn't want to eat into their whole afternoon.

A bored-looking cashier was swiping listlessly on her mobile at the café. Kate headed for the eatery and ordered a pot of chamomile tea, trying not to wince at the price – $4.50 for a teabag plopped into a pot of boiling water. The woman at the servery put away her phone and smiled broadly, seemingly glad for the company.

Kate tagged her as being in her thirties, a tank top and three-quarter-length denim pants revealing taut, tanned limbs, and bleached-blonde hair cascading in waves around her face. Picking her as someone who enjoyed a chat with her customers, Kate sat at the counter, hoping to engage the woman in conversation.

She needn't have worried. Placing the tea in front of Kate, the attendant – her name tag read Carlie – leaned in, seemingly only too willing to oblige.

'Wow, hon. I love your skin. Where are you from?'

Controlling the familiar bite of impatience, Kate voiced the words that came by rote after years of being asked the same question. 'My mother's originally from Sri Lanka. I was born here.'

'Oooh, I love Sri Lanka All those beaches. And the elephants.'

Kate smiled and nodded, burying her head in her tea. *I wouldn't know. I've never visited.* Her hand went to her belly as movement rippled across her skin. The woman's eyes followed the motion.

'Oh! I saw that. It looks like you're ready to pop. How far along are you now?'

'Coming up to thirty-six weeks on Tuesday,' Kate replied, glad the conversation had moved on.

'Getting to the end. Is this your first?'

'No. I've got a boy. Just turned four.'

'Ah, yes. They're lovely at that age and then they grow up.' She laughed and tapped her phone, holding a photo out to Kate. 'That's my one. He's older now, but I still love that photo.' The screen showed a school photo of a boy of about twelve with a head of tight blond ringlets, his face split into a grin, his teeth shiny with braces. 'When he still allowed me to walk with him to school,' she joked and Kate laughed with her.

'Did your son swim here? I was actually thinking about lessons for my son,' Kate pressed on, nudging the conversation back towards her object. She assumed there was little risk of Carlie picking up on her white lie. The café didn't face the pool area, and it was unlikely that Carlie would have seen Kate and Archie together today or picked him out as one of the multitudes of kids already enrolled in classes at the centre. Kate pushed on.

'One of the mums at playgroup was telling me there's an instructor here who's really good with the little ones. This is a few months back, mind you. I think she said her name is Gail, or Gabby maybe?'

'Yeah, Gabby Marshall; she taught the under-fives on and off. Although, she mainly taught the supported swim classes and the squads. But she's not here anymore. She left straight after her husband died. In the flood.' She paused to allow the significance of the information to sink in.

Pretending to realise who they were talking about, Kate exclaimed in mock amazement, 'Hang on! Do you mean the Gabby Marshall on TV? She's the instructor? Oh my God! That was such a tragedy.'

'Yeah. It was terrible,' Carlie agreed, not appearing the least bit perturbed. 'I knew her really well, actually – and her husband. I went to school with him.'

Kate looked suitably impressed by this information. If indeed Carlie had been in Gabby's confidence, she clearly had no compunction about revealing personal information about her. Now that Gabby had moved on to the 'celebrity' sphere, it appeared that all bets were off.

'There was a whole feature on her in *New Idea*, I remember. Last month, wasn't it?'

'*Woman's Day*,' Carlie clarified.

'She said she misses him every day.'

'Pfft!' Carlie snorted. 'I wouldn't be so sure about that.' Quickly checking to see if anyone was near enough to hear, she stage-whispered, 'She was having an affair.'

'No!' Kate did her best impression of a shocked housewife.

Carlie raised her eyebrows significantly and turned to the register to attend to a group of customers who had just arrived. Kate nursed her impatience as Carlie served two sweat-bathed women fresh out of a spin class – two muesli bars and a bottle of water – followed by a little boy trying to decide which flavour of Chupa Chup to purchase. Finally, Carlie was back at her side.

'So, how do you know she was having an affair?' Kate whispered conspiratorially.

Carlie grinned at her with a knowing look, stretching the moment for as long as she could. 'Because he works here.'

'No!' exclaimed Kate again, her hand to her mouth. She hoped she wasn't overdoing it, but from Carlie's pleased reaction, she figured not.

'Yep. He's a swimming instructor here, too. Name's Cameron Archer. Big body-builder type. If you're into that kind of thing. Not really my taste.' She made a moue of distaste.

Kate rather suspected otherwise, but let it go. 'And do you think Joel knew?'

Carlie paused, clearly trying to determine how far to stretch her knowledge. In the end, she settled for admitting that she didn't think so.

'But you think their marriage was on the rocks?'

'Oh, definitely. In fact, they were arguing even on the day of the flood. You know, the day Joel died?'

'Oh, really?' Kate's interest was piqued.

'Yep. Her car had broken down and she had to rely on Joel to drop her and pick her up from work each day. He was always running late and it was driving her spare. He was late that evening, too.' Carlie winked at her. 'He was probably at the pub.'

She laughed and continued, 'Well, Gabby was well and truly fuming by the time he got here. It was pouring outside and she was practically the only one left in here, still waiting for Joel. I was just doing the final clean-up of the café. That's how I saw them. You should have seen her face when he finally turned up. If looks could kill, I tell you.'

'Had you seen them arguing before?'

Carlie hesitated again. 'They kept it quiet. But you can tell when people aren't happy, you know?'

Kate made appropriate appreciative noises.

She kept Carlie talking for a few more minutes, but it was plain she had little more to give. Despite her talk, she obviously had no concrete proof of the affair. No actual sightings. It was all puff built on guesswork.

When she was sure there was nothing more to be gained by the conversation, Kate thanked Carlie for the tea, the majority of which remained untasted in the pot, and made to leave.

'You should speak to the office about swimming classes for your little one. They'll be able to help you out.'

'Yeah. I will. Thanks again.' She made her escape.

Leaving the café, Kate walked past the wall of photos next to the office showing each of the instructors currently employed by the centre. She scanned the multitude of smiling faces and located a blond-haired man with a broad smile above the name Cameron Archer. Even though the image was cropped at the face, Kate could tell he was well-toned and muscular. He had the square, jutting jaw and thick neck of a gym devotee. He smiled down at her with an air of easy confidence, a man who knew he looked good and didn't mind you noticing.

Gabby Marshall and Cameron Archer. The affair theory was gaining legs.

In Geoff's car heading home, Archie was asleep in his booster seat within minutes, lulled by lunch and a long morning of water play.

With one eye on the road, Geoff fiddled with the radio dial, unable to settle on a station. Kate swatted his hand as he tried to switch away from the news. 'Hang on,' she said, turning up the volume. A shot of adrenaline coursed through her body as she took in the words of the newscast.

'… *What happened to my Josephine is unacceptable. These boys are cowards without morals. The lowest of the low. They need to be caught before they do this to anyone else's son or daughter. I've had personal reports of incidents all around town. Young thugs terrorising innocent citizens and small businesses…*'

What incidents? What young thugs? Kate asked herself. Apart from the bakery and McDonald's holdups, there had been no other reported attacks involving masked assailants. There had been reports of thefts at one of the caravan parks near the river and the usual drunk and disorderlies from the weekend. But no incidents that could be remotely linked to the holdups. Roman Allen was sensationalising. Linking his daughter's attack with every petty offence in the area. Giving the impression of a town gripped in a crime wave perpetrated by young offenders, which the police were doing nothing to prevent. His next words confirmed her fears.

'... *They need to be stopped. They need to be found and put away. That is why today, I am pledging a reward of ten thousand dollars for any information that leads to the apprehension and arrest of these youths ...*'

The news reader's voice broke through. '*That was Councillor Allen speaking at a press conference held half an hour ago outside the Esserton Central Hospital, where his daughter, Josephine, sixteen, remains in a serious condition after she was attacked during a holdup of the Tweed Valley Way McDonald's restaurant in the early hours of Thursday morning. Police are yet to make an arrest and enquiries are ongoing.*'

Kate rummaged in her bag for her phone. Three missed calls from Josh. *Shit!*

THEN

Fuck! Fuck! Fuck!

Gabby sat slumped in the passenger seat of the ute as Joel navigated the traffic. They were stuck behind a long line of vehicles heading west. The normally dual-lane road had been blocked by an accident up ahead and they were crawling along in single file. The car's windscreen wipers worked furiously to clear the driving rain. Outside, the free-moving traffic on the opposite lanes was barely visible through the rain haze and sickly glow of vehicle headlights. The miserable weather reflected the mood inside.

Joel had been over an hour late picking her up after her shift. The centre was practically deserted due to the rain, the staff going through the motions until closing. A dead-end reception shift that had stretched out even longer than necessary. She had been itching for a fight by the time he had showed up, the wait giving her ample opportunity to nurse her grievances and build a head of steam.

The moment she was in the car, she had pounced.

'Why don't you ever answer your phone? I tried calling you, like, ten times.'

'What's the big deal? I've picked you up, haven't I? You said you were on till six-thirty.'

'No, that's next week. I told you this morning, I finish at five. You never listen. I've been waiting for ages.'

'Yeah, all right. It's only the one time. Keep your hat on.'

'That's not the point. You need to answer your phone. You can't keep it on silent all day. What if it had been an emergency?'

'What emergency? Why are you trying to make something out of nothing? I'm here now. Let's just get on with it.'

'Don't do that. Don't tell me to get over it. I hate it when you do that.'

And so it had begun. It was his easy dismissal that she couldn't bear. When he made out like she was over-reacting, swatting her concerns away like a whining child. Putting her back in her box. That was when her fury ballooned, uncontained and spiteful, picking on everything; old, new and buried. Dredging up old resentments and goading past sores, to score cheap points. But he would never admit any fault, never apologise. There had been no explanations. Where he had been or why he had been late. Not that she couldn't guess. He would have been with his footy mates the whole day playing Xbox and drinking beer. She could smell the alcohol and cigarette smoke on his breath and the tang of junk food on his clothes.

And just when their fighting had reached fever pitch, he had, as usual, abruptly lapsed into silence.

Inside, she felt like she wanted to rave and sob and scratch his face off, make him hurt like he hurt her. Provoke a reaction. Anything but this bitter silence. His silence completely overpowered her. She hated how he had so perfected this defence over the years that he was able to effortlessly control each of their fights.

She had no ammunition against it. Everything she had to give was ultimately defeated and swallowed up by his refusal to engage. Her tears, screams, arguments, rages, and even her own silences – none of them were a match for his all-absorbing, self-contained armour of muteness. The perfect hidey-hole he retreated to when he'd had enough of her. Where she couldn't follow, so nothing was ever resolved, nothing ever ended. Just a million starts and everything left hanging. Hot tears threatened to overwhelm her and she blinked them away.

They had finally made it to the accident site. A rear-ender between a Honda Civic and a transit van. Gabby could make out a couple of police cars and an ambulance parked on the side of the road, the officers in full rain gear directing traffic. The prang just serious enough to cause traffic chaos. As they passed the glow of the police lights, the traffic started to move again, separating once more into two lanes.

They were not long from Joel's parents' place now. She had a whole night to get through with her in-laws. She could feel a headache coming on and an ache in her jaw from clenching her teeth.

She glanced sideways at Joel. He was staring straight ahead, absorbed with the task of driving. To her, it looked like he had completely forgotten about their fight. He was over it and had moved on, his mind now on something else. Did he care at all? Was it really all in her head?

Anger settled in her chest like a coiled fist. She rested her head against the car window, trying to find relief in the cool glass for her throbbing temples. Staring unseeing at the streaming droplets of rain, she willed herself to get through the night.

16

An intense pain rent through her lower abdomen and Kate was instantly awake. She fumbled for her phone: 10.42 pm. The pain was immediately familiar and terrifying. A slow, primordial wave building to a crescendo. It was unmistakable. She was in labour. Fear gripped her. The baby was not quite thirty-six weeks. Was it too soon?

'Geoff.' She shook her husband's sleeping form. 'Geoff. Wake up. I think the baby is coming.'

'What? Right now? Okay. All right. Are you okay?' He was up, bleary-eyed and flustered.

'We need to get to the hospital. Give Nidah a call.'

Nidah Khan was their kindly neighbour: a retired school teacher and widow, grandmother to four boisterous grandsons whom she babysat regularly, and a favourite emergency sitter for Archie. They had already spoken to Nidah about exactly this situation weeks ago, knowing that Gray, living out of town, wouldn't be available to mind Archie at short notice.

While her husband hastily pulled some clothes on, Kate tapped her phone for the number of the maternity ward. Anxiety flooded her veins. Had she brought this on herself? She had been warned repeatedly by her ob-gyn about overdoing things. The spotting a few weeks ago had been a warning. She hadn't mentioned it to Geoff; she'd been too afraid that he would insist she leave work, start her maternity leave early. Women in other countries worked till the day they gave birth, didn't they? Taking early leave would only prove her detractors right, confirm the need for different rules. She had wanted to keep going.

Yet now, as her hands clutched the bedhead and she breathed through another wave of pain, the weight of her decision crashed over her. Her finely crafted reasonings and justifications falling to ash around her. Her throat felt dry as raw panic clawed at her throat. She held her belly, murmuring silent entreaties at her unborn child. *Please be okay. Please be okay.*

The connection clicked through. Yes, she was experiencing labour pain. No, her waters had not broken. Yes, the contractions were intense. As she spoke, another sharp wave made her double over in pain. She gave her obstetrician's name and hung up.

Geoff had gone to fetch Nidah. Kate looked around the room, suddenly lost. She wasn't ready for this yet. She had so much left to get done. The entire mess with the Allens had to be resolved. She hadn't completed her transition with Josh. She hadn't handed the Marshall file back to Skinner. She hadn't even packed a hospital bag, she realised in dismay. Gingerly, she got up and started to get dressed.

* * *

Two-and-a-half hours later, Kate lay in a maternity suite, her belly hooked up to a foetal heart monitor. The steady drum of the monitor display and an ever-increasing printout of a regular heartbeat pattern told her that her baby was fine.

They had reached the hospital within minutes, the night-shrouded streets empty of traffic. Kate's mind had been a whirl, distracted by pain and yet succumbing to the realisation and mounting anticipation that this was actually happening. She would be having her baby tonight.

Less than an hour later, the intermittent waves of pain that had raged so intensely had started to wane, receding until they had ceased altogether. After examining her and conferring at length with Kate's obstetrician over the phone, the on-duty registrar had pronounced severe Braxton Hicks contractions, phantom labour pains. There was nothing to worry about. Kate's weekly appointment with her obstetrician had been rescheduled for the following day for peace of mind. As a precaution, they would keep her in to monitor the baby's heart rate, after which she was free to leave.

Kate lay alone in the suite with just her baby's heartbeat for company. Geoff had stepped outside to find a vending machine. Lying there, she felt strangely deflated; overwhelming relief that nothing was seriously wrong mixed with a sense of foolishness. She had the vague feeling that the doctor and midwives were slightly impatient with her for not being able to distinguish between Braxton Hicks and the real thing, for wasting their time in the midst of a full maternity ward. This was her second pregnancy, after all.

Wanting to escape her own woes, her mind flickered to Josephine lying two levels up. Was she sleeping peacefully, Kate wondered, or suffering from nightmares? Her unconscious mind churning up what her conscious mind refused to face.

She knew Josh had visited Josephine in the afternoon, within an hour of Roman Allen's impromptu press conference. He had been planning on visiting anyway, but the timing after Allen's stunt had made it seem like the police were playing catch-up. Josh had walked into a mass of reporters and she knew he was anything but happy. Kate had born the brunt of his frustration when they had finally caught up on the phone. Skinner had scheduled a media conference for first thing in the morning and she knew she would be walking into a storm of press enquiries when she got back to the station.

She felt exhausted just thinking about it. During that brief period less than an hour ago when childbirth had seemed a certainty, she had mentally cast aside her work as someone else's problem and now she had to find the energy to pick up the threads again. She closed her eyes, concentrating on the sound of the heart monitor.

She was suddenly impatient to get back home. She wondered where Geoff had got to. She shifted her position, careful of the wires, and reached for the remote, turning on the mounted television, needing a distraction. She flicked through the late-night offerings: evangelical prayer services, home shopping, subtitled movies and back-to-back repeats of daytime TV. Her attention was caught by an advert for an upcoming episode of a network current affairs program, one of those sneak-peek extended ads: a spotlight on the flood recovery. The centrepiece was an interview with Gabby Marshall three months on.

Kate grimaced. She couldn't seem to escape the woman. She levelled the remote once more at the TV, intending to change channels.

'Oooh. I love her, don't you?'

One of the midwives had entered the room without Kate noticing. It was the fresh-faced, short-haired nurse who had admitted her into the ward earlier in the night. Smiling, she moved closer to the bed, her eyes fixed on the wall-mounted TV.

Resignedly, Kate turned up the volume and followed the nurse's gaze.

The TV was showing high aerial shots of South-east Queensland and New South Wales at the height of the flood. Mini islands of settlement marooned in brown-grey soup. Floating hulks of vehicles and farm machinery. Families stuck on corrugated iron roofs, waving to rescue helicopters. SES boats transporting people and pets across liquid streetscapes. Paddocks of huddled stranded stock; horses, cattle and sheep. No footage of the bloated carcasses of the animals that hadn't made it.

The scenery changed to a view of Gabby Marshall, sombre and beautiful, austere in a shapely, full-length black dress, standing reflectively beside her husband's tombstone and then walking alongside her interviewer. It was clearly going to be a fluff piece. The interviewer was not one of the usual pack of hard-nosed journalists that hosted the flagship news program, but a guest presenter, the co-host of a morning show brought in to do a human-interest story.

Music swelled in the background. There was a quick recap of Gabby's life, a suitably grave voiceover set to a series of faded photographs: the sun-kissed only child on the southern beaches of Sydney, her teenage sporting achievements competing in several Iron Woman Championships, and the loss of her parents in a light-plane accident in her early twenties. Then the chance meeting with Joel Marshall, an Esserton local on an end of year footy trip to Sydney. The whirlwind romance leading to her move up north to be with her man. The starry-eyed couple on their wedding day. And finally, the tragedy that had ripped them apart.

Kate cringed at the overdone sentimentality. The Marshalls' story was being blown into a Hollywood-esque tale: the loving couple being washed away in floodwaters, Gabby having to watch helplessly as her husband succumbed to the raging torrent, and her own miraculous rescue.

Kate noticed that the young midwife was transfixed by the piece. This was, Kate realised, part and parcel of the fairytale fed to women: love at first sight and undying love even in the face of tragedy. She must have believed that once, she reflected, before her job had rubbed reality into her face one too many times.

Kate's eyes returned to the screen in time to take in a last shot of the interviewer's face, a study in sincere empathy expressing deep admiration for Gabby's bravery and grit. The promo was finally at an end, one last banner declaring the date and time of the program. There had been no mention of Joel's family, Kate noticed. She wondered if Annette had seen the promo, and if so, what she made of her daughter-in-law's portrayal.

A small sigh escaped the nurse's lips. 'She's so beautiful, isn't she?'

Kate made a vague sound of agreement. Watching the nurse efficiently go about her business, taking down notes from the monitor readout and fiddling with the wires, Kate couldn't help but think of Annette. The mother who was also suffering, but who wasn't sexy or interesting enough to warrant her own TV special. She felt a pang of sympathy for the lost and grief-damaged woman sitting alone at home.

The door opened and Geoff walked in, clutching a can of lemonade. The nurse glanced up at his entrance. 'Perfect timing,' she said, turning back to her notes. 'I was just about to tell your lovely wife here that she's all good to go. Your little one is just fine. All the readouts look normal. I'm just going to get the discharge papers and then you're fine to go home.'

She turned and spoke directly to Kate's belly. 'Try to stay in there for a while longer, little one, and we'll see you in a few weeks' time.' She patted Kate's hand, and with a nod to Geoff, exited the room.

17

Monday

It was mid-afternoon by the time Kate arrived at the station.

The morning had been a whirlwind. She and Geoff had both slept in after their disrupted night, hardly noticing when Archie crawled into bed with them in the early hours. When she finally woke up, it had been a scramble to get ready and get to her rescheduled ob-gyn appointment on time. She had driven off, leaving Geoff on the couch, yawning and sluggish, and Archie hyper and bouncing off the walls.

Arriving at her obstetrician's offices in Tweed Heads, she had been unable to find parking anywhere near his rooms. After circling the block, she had been forced to duck into the vehicle bay of the Tweed Police Station to find a park and make her appointment on time. With her night-time scare, it had been a longer-than-normal check-up; the hours she put into work and her proposed start date for maternity leave, all up for lengthy discussion. Afterwards, works on the Pacific Highway had stretched the usually forty-minute journey back to Esserton to over an hour, making her miss the press conference.

Josh and Skinner had handled it without her, after she had made a hurried phone call explaining her absence, much to Skinner's annoyance. She had made mention her revised appointment but had not divulged anything of the night's events. As far as she was concerned, what had happened was nobody's business but hers. She didn't want anyone at the station treating her differently, like she was suddenly fragile, expected to break and be rushed to hospital at any second.

It didn't surprise her that Skinner was the first person she saw when she walked into the office, collecting paperwork at the photocopier. He caught her eye and she knew there was no way of avoiding a meeting. Inside his office, she remained standing as he shuffled through notes at his desk, taking his time.

'How was the press conference, sir? I'm sorry I wasn't able to make it in time.'

'It could have gone better. Would have helped if we had any concrete leads.'

Kate accepted the rebuke without comment. There was no point arguing. Skinner was under pressure and he was taking it out on her. That's how it went.

'Where are we with this security image? Have we got any hits yet?'

'Nothing yet, sir, but we're working on it. Josh and Constable Harris are visiting the local high schools today to target the teachers and principals. We think there's a good chance that one of the staff could recognise it and match it to one of their students.'

'Hmm.' Skinner sounded unconvinced. 'It's going to get more complicated with this reward business. You're going to get more time-wasters on the phone. I've asked Josh to put more resources on the info line.'

'Sir.' Josh had updated her by text that morning that two more constables were now helping Grant and Roby to weed through the incoming calls.

'And where are you with the Marshall issue? Have you got anything yet?'

Kate had been waiting for the inevitable question and was prepared. She opened her backpack and pulled out a typed report that she placed on his desk. 'I've written it up. The investigation was solid.' She nodded towards her report. 'It's all in there.'

'Excellent,' said Skinner, looking slightly mollified. He reached for the file and flicked it open. 'I'll send it up the line today. Preston's office should be happy. This'll hopefully shut the old bat up. Good work, Miles.'

Back at her desk, she skimmed through the endless press enquiries littering her inbox, before turning her attention to the fresh reports awaiting her review. A summary of the calls that had come in over the weekend. Nothing particularly promising, though a couple of leads involving known teen offenders had been marked for further follow-up. She knew that Josh and Vickie would be at the high schools all day. That left Darnley.

Kate stood up and stretched. Four desks down, she could see Greg's neatly shaved head firmly facing the computer. She headed for his workspace.

'Greg, talk to me. What's going on with this traffic footage?'

Darnley swung his chair around at the sound of her voice. 'Sarge. I'm just about done. I was just double-checking some of the footage Vickie was reviewing.'

Code for *I don't trust anyone but myself to do the job right.* She made no comment but pulled up a chair and waited.

'So basically, we focused on the Tweed Valley Way footage from the Rose Street and Findlay Street intersections in the half an hour leading up to and after the Macca's holdup. We went through the vehicles to see if we could find any matches to the footage from the bakery incident.'

Kate nodded. The McDonald's and neighbouring Hungry Jack's were both located on the western side of Tweed Valley Way, with the closest cross-streets being Rose Street to the south and Findlay Street to the north. She pictured the vehicle approaches to the site from her drive there on Thursday. Northbound vehicles, she knew, could access both restaurants from Tweed Valley Way via a left-in shared access, while southbound vehicles used a dedicated right-hand turning lane. Both the restaurants only provided for left-out access northbound, with a U-turn bay a short distance away catering for vehicles turning back south along Tweed Valley Way.

'As you know, Sarge, there isn't much to work with from the bakery site,' Darnley continued. 'There's very little traffic footage available from that part of town. It's all local roads. And we only recovered two sets of CCTV from surrounding businesses at the time. So, there's not much to compare against.' Darnley met Kate's gaze. 'Basically, there are no matches, Sarge.'

Kate nodded. It had been a long shot. 'What about the Tweed Valley Way footage itself? Any likely candidates?'

'Well, there's no shortage of traffic footage.'

Kate knew what he was referring to. A recent spate of accidents and talk of upgrades to Tweed Valley Way meant that Transport had installed a raft of new traffic-survey cameras along that stretch of the road in the last year. They had got lucky with the available footage. Yet, Kate didn't miss the hesitation in Darnley's voice.

'But?'

'The thing is,' Darnley noted slowly, 'most of the vehicles are pass-bys, showing up from one intersection to the next within minutes, meaning that they are travelling straight through without stopping. We've only focused on the vehicles that show a time gap between the two intersections, meaning they stopped in between, we assume, at one of the restaurants. It's an empty stretch along that way. The only premises are industrial businesses – closed at that time of the night – and the two fast-food outlets.'

Kate nodded, absorbed as Darnley continued. 'So far, we've got a couple of vans, a ute and a semi in the timeframe, all of which I've crosschecked against drive-through records and accounted for in the intersection pass-bys. The thing is, there don't seem to be any vehicles that stop in the ten minutes directly before the holdup.'

'You're not suggesting they walked there?'

Darnley's face crinkled into a smile. 'No, Sarge. It would be a bit of a hike from town.'

Kate shrugged her shoulders, stumped. 'So what, then?'

'There's one more thing I wanted to check. Actually, I was just looking into it before you came.'

He quickly clicked out of the traffic footage and brought up a view of Google Maps. He zoomed in on the McDonald's restaurant and the Hungry Jack's next door, pointing the curser at the property that the fast-food restaurants backed onto.

'It's a warehousing business,' Darnley clarified. 'Except, see this.' He switched the field into 'Street View' and manoeuvred the toggle to travel south along Tweed Valley Way, stopping at what appeared to be a private, sealed road a few hundred metres south of the restaurant. 'It's a private-access road that leads from Tweed Valley Way into the property.' Darnley glanced at Kate.

'Can we see in?'

Darnley moved the curser once more. 'Not fully, because Google Maps doesn't cover private roads, but you get an idea of the view from Tweed Valley Way.'

Kate stared at the screen. It showed an angled view of the private-access road looking north-west from Tweed Valley Way and she could see what Darnley was trying to show her. 'If you're standing on that road, you would have a full view of the Macca's carpark.'

'Exactly.' She could hear the anticipation in his voice.

'What are you thinking? The boys hid down this road?'

'It's possible, Sarge, don't you think? They'd know that the traffic footage is the first thing we'd check to see what cars would show up before and after the holdup. Maybe they drove here nice and early and waited, scoping out the McDonald's carpark to make sure there was nobody else at the restaurant before heading in. And maybe, afterwards, they stayed put in the car for a while before driving off. So, their vehicle wouldn't be connected with the holdup.'

It made sense and Kate felt a prickle of admiration for the resourcefulness of the teens. 'Smart.' She nodded.

Darnley turned back to his computer screen and switched over again to the Tweed Valley Way traffic footage. 'I was just going to extend the time window by another thirty minutes either side of the holdup to see if it made a difference.'

Kate drew her chair closer and they both leaned in to view the extra thirty minutes of footage. The static image of the road flickered into life. They watched as a smattering of vehicles drove in and out of view, the traffic volume slowly increasing with the dawning light. It was slow, repetitive work. Making sure they clocked each vehicle as it passed through both intersections. She could feel tension building in her neck and shoulders as she leaned in.

'There!' Kate pointed, almost shouting in her excitement. The time stamp read 5.22 am, forty-four minutes after the holdup. A maroon Toyota Corolla hatchback could be seen heading south along Tweed Valley Way through the Rose Street intersection. 'That's it. I have that Toyota heading north at Rose Street at 3.52 am and it doesn't appear again at the Findlay Street intersection. That's an hour and a half time gap. It's got to be them.'

Darnley shook his head in disbelief at the time stamp. 'Jesus! Vickie and I were at the scene by then. The little shits were watching us all that time.'

'Hope I'm not interrupting anything.' Kate and Darnley looked up to find Skinner observing them without a trace of humour. 'Kate, can I see you, please. In my office.' He glared at her meaningfully, and without waiting for an answer, turned on his heel, expecting her to follow.

Kate ignored the interruption. She patted Darnley on the back. 'Excellent work, Greg. Can we get a licence plate from that, do you think?'

Darnley studied the image. 'I can try, Sarge. Maybe a partial.'

'Do what you can. I'll be back soon.'

She rose to follow Skinner, but within seconds had wheeled around. 'Also, can we check with the warehouse business – see if they have any security footage of that access road from their premises? Maybe we can get some proof that the car was parked there the whole time. Even get a view of the boys, if we're lucky.'

'Will do, Sarge. And I'll try to crosscheck the car with the bakery footage, too,' added Darnley, the excitement in his voice mirroring Kate's. 'See if we can get a match this time.'

'Yes. Perfect. Let me know as soon as anything comes up.' She turned and lumbered to catch up with Skinner, who had already disappeared into his office.

18

'Have you got any doubts?'

'Sorry?'

'Don't fuck with me, Miles. It's a simple question. Have you got any doubts?'

Kate didn't answer straightaway, gathering her thoughts.

'The investigation followed *standard* police procedure and the conclusions reached *appear sound* based on the investigation carried out ...' Skinner was reading from her report on the Marshall case, heavily emphasising certain words, his voice dripping with sarcasm.

'Well, doesn't it say what you want?' She regretted the words almost as soon as they were out of her mouth.

Skinner's neck turned red, but his voice remained controlled when he replied. 'Being a smartarse isn't a good look for you, Miles.' He paused. 'But try it on again and let's see where it gets you.'

'Sir.' Kate bit down hard on the inside of her cheek. She chastised herself for losing control. He would make her pay for that moment of weakness.

Skinner stared at her and tossed the report back. A few of the papers came loose and scattered on the floor.

Kate remained standing, not moving a muscle.

'I know you. I know your reports. I know when you're trying to dance around an issue. Explain.'

She began, choosing her words carefully. 'Murchison's investigation followed all the right protocols. There's no case to answer on procedural grounds.'

'Fuck the procedure. Did he cover all bases? Do you think he missed anything?'

'I think it was a forgone conclusion from the start, sir. I don't think it occurred to Murchison to consider any other avenues.'

'In my day, that was called good policing, not wasting public money on chasing after ghosts without any evidence,' Skinner retorted.

She sighed. 'It was in the middle of the flood, sir. It's understandable that everything was assumed to be flood related. It's nobody's fault. But I think Annette Marshall is right. We didn't dig very far with Gabby. I've come across some details about her personal life and the life insurance she inherited from Joel, which I think are worth looking into.'

Skinner rubbed his hands down his face and exhaled. 'Have you got anything more concrete?' He glanced at her silent expression and grimaced. 'I'll take that as a no. So it's a gut thing, then? The famous bloody Grayling gut. Like father, like daughter. How long do you think you'll need to work out if it's actually something and not just bloody indigestion?'

'Give me until the end of the week. If I don't find anything new, you can send it up the line. And … I'd like your permission to speak to Gabby Marshall.' She waited and he flicked his hand impatiently in agreement. Her spirits rose.

'What about Superintendent Wright?' she pressed.

'I'll deal with him.'

She nodded and bent down to pick up the scattered paperwork with a grunt. She handed the file back to him. 'Thank you, sir. I appreciate it.'

'Take it with you. Bring it back on Friday once it's been rewritten.'

'Sir.'

Outside his office, with the door closed behind her, she exhaled sharply. The whole interview had disconcerted her. Her view of Skinner had been shaken. She had been so sure that he would just accept the report, blithely swallowing the bureaucratic, meaningless findings, happy to serve up to his masters exactly what they wanted to hear. Yet he had picked out the doubts behind her carefully chosen words and was willing to stick his neck out to uncover more. Maybe he actually gave a shit about finding the truth, or more likely, he wanted to cover his arse if it all went tits-up. Either way, she had underestimated him and what he was capable of. He had called her out. It was a mistake she couldn't afford to make again.

* * *

Josh and Vickie had returned by the time Kate got back to her desk. They were crowded around Darnley's computer terminal and she assumed he had updated them on what they had discovered. She tossed the Marshall file on her desk and joined them.

On seeing Kate, Josh quickly filled her in on the results of the school interviews. 'Basically, no luck,' he summarised. 'The form teacher at St Therese's had no idea about Abigail's personal life, current or former, and none of the staff at the schools recognised the security image. I'm starting to think these boys don't bloody go to school.'

Kate was sympathetic, but distracted by their more recent find. She turned to Darnley. 'Anything further at your end, Greg?'

'I've rerun the footage, Sarge and I don't think there's any doubt. There are no other vehicles with a time gap that aren't otherwise accounted for. All the other vehicles that show an interval between the intersections are either explained by cash-register records at the restaurants or come and go well outside the holdup period.'

'So, we've got them,' Josh broke in. 'They were parked in the warehouse road the whole time.'

'There's just one other possibility. There's a side road – Turner Road – north of the McDonald's and just before you hit Findley Street. They could have turned in there. It's a rural road with no cameras that eventually ends up at Smith's Creek. If the car did head in there, it was more than an hour-long round trip wherever they went because we have them coming back south on Tweed Valley Way passing Rose Street at 5.22 am.'

Kate nodded, frowning. 'If the Toyota is a blameless joyride, though, the only other explanation is an unknown vehicle originating from Turner Road. If they parked somewhere along the stretch of Tweed Valley Way, between the intersections, and accessed the restaurant on foot, then we have no record of the vehicle at all.'

There was a silence as the team contemplated the possibility.

'My bet's still on the warehouse road, but we need to shore it up. Have we followed them up yet for any CCTV?'

'I've got Roby on to that, Sarge.'

'Okay. What about the licence plate? Have you had any luck with that, Greg?'

On his computer screen, Darnley brought up a zoomed-in still of the vehicle licence plate captured from the traffic-camera footage. 'This is the best I could do, Sarge.'

With the pixilation, the image was grainy and ill defined. Kate could just make out the outline of a few blurred letters and numbers. 'It looks like a NSW plate,' Darnley noted, pointing to the faint outline of a smaller 'S.W.' stamp along the side of the plate. 'I reckon that's an X and a T maybe,' he said, pointing to the nearest characters. 'That's an eight or possibly a three. I couldn't make out the rest with the resolution and the glare from the headlights.'

He turned back to Kate and resumed. 'I've run a search for Toyota hatchbacks, maroon with a licence plate ending with 8-X-T and 3-X-T. There are over two thousand registered across New South Wales, but narrowing it to the Esserton area only got one hit with the 3-X-T tag. The next closest is a plate ending in 8-X-T in Cabarita Beach.'

Kate leaned in. 'And the Esserton plate?'

'Registered to a Mrs Margaret Henshaw, seventy-two. An address in East Esserton.'

'A delinquent grandson maybe, or a boarder?' Josh mused aloud.

'Yes, we definitely need to visit Mrs Henshaw. But not yet,' Kate clarified, seeing Josh immediately stir. 'I don't want her warning off her favourite grandson and his mates, if it's them. Let's rule out any security footage from the warehouse first. If we get some clear images placing the car at the warehouse road, then we're on much stronger ground. Right now, Turner Road still gives them an out and any good lawyer will be throwing that in our face.'

She turned to Harris. 'In the meantime, Vickie, can you crosscheck the bakery footage and see if you can find a match for the Toyota? I'd like to have something firm linking them to that incident, too, if we can.'

'Will do.' Vickie made to head back to her desk, but was forestalled by Josh.

'Actually, Kate, Constable Harris also had a couple of thoughts on the wrist marking, which I think you should hear.'

Kate glanced at Vickie. She didn't miss the flicker of irritation that passed across the constable's face at Josh speaking for her.

Vickie turned to Kate and addressed her without reference to Josh. 'Yes. Well, I've been thinking about why nobody seems to recognise the marking, Sarge. I was watching the students from Esserton High and Esserton West today at recess and lunchtime. Apart from watches, a lot of them were wearing bracelets on their wrists. Even the boys were wearing those thick, surf-brand leather bracelets or threaded bands. It's the perfect way to hide something on your wrist.'

Kate listened, waiting for her to get to the point.

Vickie continued, stumbling slightly in her rush to get her theory out. 'I was thinking about the marks that people, especially teens, don't want anyone finding out about. I'm just wondering if he self-harms?'

Pausing a second to let this sink in, Vickie went on. 'If he's cutting himself, he'll be going to any lengths to hide it. If he normally wears some sort of wrist gear, it would be the perfect place to cut himself, in a place that's already covered. But when we show people the security footage, they're thinking of someone who has a tattoo or maybe an old scar from an accident or something, not self-harming. There's a good chance that none of his friends and family even know it's going on, especially if it's only begun recently.'

Kate nodded slowly, her mind going back to their interview with Abigail Masters. How viewing the security footage of Captain America's wrist had seemed to change her mind about who she thought the assailant was.

She smiled and nodded at Vickie. 'I think you've definitely got something there. It's worth checking out tomorrow. Maybe you can go back to the schools and target the school counsellors? See if they can point out some likely candidates.'

Vickie beamed.

'But let's focus on the traffic footage today. It's the priority.'

She waited for the team to disperse before turning towards her desk. She felt energised and full of purpose. She could feel the familiar anticipation of a case nearing its close. With any luck, the warehouse-road lead would pan out and she would have this one done and dusted before she went on leave, so Josh would have a clear caseload.

She sat down heavily, her eyes drawn to the Marshall folder lying abandoned on her desk, the loose papers still out of order from when she had retrieved them from Skinner's floor.

She sighed as she pulled the papers towards her. All she needed now was to find her way clear of Gabby Marshall.

19

Kate drove into the back lot of the greengrocer. She was just in time. The store was still open, but only just. She parked and hurried in as best she could, grabbing a two-litre bottle of milk and the jar of pasta sauce that Geoff had texted her to pick up on the way home.

She was the last customer. The trays of fruit and veg were almost packed away, ready for cold storage, and the remaining cashier on duty was pointedly counting out coins at her till as Kate placed her items on the counter. Kate waved her credit card and was out of there quickly. The 'closed' sign went up as she stepped out into the darkened carpark.

Walking through the empty lot in the cool, enveloping dusk, she noticed a dark-blue Ford Falcon ute parked unevenly, two spaces up from her Commodore. A tiny shot of electricity passed through her spine as a number of unconnected memories all at once fused together in her mind. The dark-coloured falcon ute she had noticed in passing over the weekend, keeping its distance behind her vehicle: driving to her father's with Josh, and then on their way back from Abigail's. The ute that had driven past her on Friday before she crossed the street to the Marshalls' residence.

A man was leaning against the ute cab, watching her make her way to the car. Short, cropped hair. Sweat-marked shirt over jeans. She looked around. They were alone in the carpark, the shutters closed behind her at the greengrocers. Her senses heightened, she felt the reassuring press of her Glock under her jacket. Adrenaline flooded her and she took a steadying breath.

'Constable Murchison. You're too late for the greengrocers. They just shut. I only just made it myself.' She had reached the car. Placing her grocery bag down, she stood her ground, making no move to get inside the vehicle.

Murchison slowly straightened up, making the most of his height advantage. He emanated a feral stench: drink and sweat and cheap aftershave. He spat on the ground, a speck of spittle landing on Kate's boot.

'What were you doing at Tweed Station today? Making a report against me? You said I didn't have anything to worry about. And then I hear you're off rooting around at Barlow's? What did he say? What have you got against me?' He stepped towards her.

'Constable. You need to calm down and you need to step back. I don't have anything against you and I wasn't at the station today. I only used the carpark because I couldn't find a parking spot and I had an appointment with my obstetrician—'

'Do you think I'm stupid? What? Because I haven't got a fancy degree, I can't put two and two together? Because I'm not the chief's daughter, I'm not as good as you?' His eyes raked her skin. 'Don't you think you're better than me.' He was stepping closer now, his eyes livid and his hands trembling. 'I was working cases before you were out of school. Some of us worked to get where we are. We didn't just walk into promotions because of who we're related to.' His face moulded into a sneer. 'And don't think no one knows about what he got up to in that *cottage on the hill*.' He spat out the last words, his face twisted in disgust.

'Constable, enough!' she broke in, her voice sparking with anger. 'That's enough.' She struggled to contain her fury, ignoring the snipes aimed at her and swallowing the venom directed at her father with effort.

She focused on his accusations about the case. 'Constable, you're currently putting two and two together and coming up with fifty. I was not at Tweed Station today beyond using the carpark. Check with the duty sergeant. Ask Superintendent Wright, if you must. I was not there.'

Murchison glared at her and muttered under his breath, 'Lying bitch.'

'Excuse me? Do you want to repeat that, Constable?'

He glared at her, but said nothing.

'Constable, you are on very thin ice. I don't give a shit what you think of me, but I outrank you, and from now on you will address me as Detective or Sergeant. If you wish to speak to me, you will do so in a civil manner or not at all. Do I make myself clear? Constable? Do I make myself clear?'

'Yes – Detective.' His face was sullen and set.

'Now, I've told you everything there is to say about this investigation. I have been asked to review the file and that is what I intend to do. Who I speak to and what I do as part of

that review is up to me and the chief inspector. If I need to talk
to you, I will send for you. Until then, Constable Murchison,
I do not expect to hear from you or to see you – and I expect you
to stop following me.'

His face blanched at that. He had thought she didn't know,
that he had been good enough to have gone unnoticed.

'Do you understand?'

'Yes.'

'Yes, what?'

'Yes, Detective.'

'Good. Now fuck off home, Constable, before I call you in for
drink driving.'

20

Kate drove with one eye on the rear-view mirror, on alert for any suspicious vehicles that could indicate Murchison.

She was still in two minds on whether or not she would report him. Part of her wanted to see him humiliated as he had her, yet the other part, the clear-headed, strategic part of her, wasn't sure it was worth the trouble. Murchison was close to retirement and would be out of the force in a few years, anyway. He had spent over thirty-five years in the force, only to rise to the rank of leading senior constable. It must rankle. Did she really want to make a fuss when he was only a handful of years from his pension? She knew he was not alone in the opinions he had voiced, though no one else had been stupid enough to say them to her face. She was used to it. No matter what her achievements, her detractors would always say she had got there because of her father and her skin colour. A diversity hire. It was a cross she had always borne and would have to bear for the rest of her career. Punishing Murchison would make no difference on that account.

Pulling up at her destination, in front of a high metal grate fence, she forced the constable from her mind. Extricating herself from the car seat – an increasingly difficult task – she took in the premises set back behind the fence line. An industrial block made up of huge warehouse buildings, blank imposing shells, set within an expanse of concrete pavement. One of the buildings abutted the front security fence, its cement wall panels forming part of the boundary line. The place looked brand new but shut up. There were no signs of any activity, vehicles or people. A sign on the closed and padlocked gate proclaimed *Collias and Sons Warehouse and Distribution*. A newly bought business that was yet to commence operations?

She noted down the number in her phone. She knew Roby had been trying to contact the company since yesterday afternoon, without luck. Her eyes scanned the site for security cameras, observing several discreetly positioned domes on the building façades. She noted with satisfaction one attached to the roof line of the building that formed part of the front boundary. Yet was it operational if the site was unoccupied?

Turning, she headed right along the fence line, stepping across weed-choked gravel and past scraggly scrub that formed a border of sorts with the neighbouring property. Within a few metres, the land gave way, sliding down into a shallow ditch filled with refuse: plastic bags and fast-food containers. Beyond, she could see the Macca's carpark and further on the neighbouring Hungry Jack's. It was an easy scramble down, she observed. At her feet lay a couple of longnecks and a discarded plastic juice bottle fashioned into a bong with a piece of hose pipe. Trekking back to the car, she returned with evidence bags, photographing and bagging the lot.

Her mobile buzzed as she fell back into her car seat. The irate voice of Roman Allen greeted her.

'I want to know what's happening with the investigation. I can't get a hold of Detective Ellis. He's not answering his mobile.'

Summoning up her patience, she spoke as politely as she could. 'Mr Allen, I'm sorry you haven't been able to get on to Josh. I understand you saw him on Sunday, at the hospital? Is there anything I can do to help?'

'Yes, but what's happened since Sunday? It didn't sound like you've had any leads at all.'

'Things have moved on, Mr Allen. We are following up some information that came to light yesterday afternoon. At the moment, it looks very promising and we're hoping to have a result soon.'

'So, you know who the bastards are? You've identified them.'

'I can't go into that, Mr Allen. All I can tell you is that we'll keep you informed once we make an arrest.'

'They should be shot for what they did to my Josephine.'

A memory of a Ferris wheel, carnival music and popcorn rose in her mind. The sickening crunch of boot leather on soft flesh. Kate shook her head, chasing away the scene.

'No one deserves that kind of violence, Mr Allen. Not Josephine. Not anyone.'

There was a silence on the line. She could feel her heart pounding in her chest. Had she gone too far?

'Rest assured we'll be doing everything we can to find the boys, Mr Allen. That I can promise you.'

'Damn right you will be.' The line went dead and Kate put away her phone, unease spreading. She had said too much. Knowing Roman Allen, there would be consequences.

* * *

Returning to the station, it took Kate a moment to catch the atmosphere in the room, like the aftermath of a dogfight. *What now?* Roby, quiet and self-contained, sat glued to his computer screen, his headphones on, studiously avoiding eye contact. Darnley was buried in files at his desk. Only Constable Grant – his face gleeful and flushed with excitement – met her gaze as she walked past. His stocky, gym-grafted body had the look of a highly charged Jack Russell, clearly bursting to spill whatever had just gone down. She only had to ask.

There was no sign of either Josh or Vickie.

Ignoring Grant, Kate walked to the evidence locker to log in the items she had recovered from the land adjoining the McDonald's restaurant. The items probably had nothing to do with the youths they were after, but it was a possibility. Returning to her desk, she waited until Grant had made himself scarce before approaching Darnley.

'What's happened, Greg? Where's Josh?'

'The detective and Harris had a bit of a bust-up, Sarge,' he replied, clearly embarrassed to have to go into it. 'They both walked out about five minutes before you got in. Detective Ellis looked pretty upset.' He nodded towards the fire-escape door.

'Did he hear?' she asked, motioning to Skinner's office.

'No, Sarge. He hasn't got in yet.'

Kate nodded. She was glad of that, at least. Whatever this was between Josh and Vickie, it was easier for all concerned if Skinner didn't get involved.

She chewed her lip, undecided whether to check on her colleagues or let things lie. She had no desire to meddle in either Josh or Vickie's personal lives, and yet if it was starting to spill into their work life, she had to do something. She grimaced. This was not what she needed this morning.

Her mobile rang again, saving her from having to make a decision. She checked the caller ID to make sure it wasn't Roman Allen again and answered. 'Hello. Detective Miles speaking.'

'Hello, Detective,' a chirpy voice bounced through the phone. 'This is Melanie Ashton. You left me a message over the weekend. Sorry, I was away at my cousin's out Stanthorpe way and they've got terrible reception out there. Only got back home yesterday.'

Kate's mind raced, trying to recall a Melanie Ashton. Whom had she rung over the weekend?

'You said you wanted to speak about Joel Marshall. Sorry,' the voice hurriedly continued. 'Chen was my maiden name. I'm married now. Hence, Melanie Ashton.' There was nervous laughter followed by an awkward silence.

She remembered. Melanie Chen. The only name that Neil had been able to provide her with when she had asked after any close friends of either Gabby or Joel that she could approach.

'Yes. Of course. Just give me a sec.' Kate pushed open the fire-exit door and escaped into the stairwell, sitting down heavily on the top step. She tried to recall what Neil had informed her about Melanie.

Melanie Chen, now Ashton, according to Neil, had been close to both Gabby and Joel, part of the loose pack of football buddies and WAGs that had made up Joel's social circle. Neil's impression had been that Gabby had never really taken to Joel's footy mates and Melanie had been her one and possibly only real friend in that group, before Melanie had moved to Queensland just on a year ago for work. Prior to her departure interstate, Melanie had been going out with one of Joel's football teammates and they had all spent a lot of time together. If anyone could shed light on the true state of his son's marriage, Neil had felt it would be Melanie.

Kate returned to the phone call. 'Melanie. Thanks for ringing me back.' She paused, trying to determine the best way to approach the conversation. The truth or some version of it, she felt, was her only option.

'Melanie, I'm following up on the coroner's findings into Joel Marshall's death on behalf of his family. Your name was given to me by Neil Marshall as being a close friend of both Gabby and Joel. I was wondering if you would be willing to talk to me about your impressions of the couple? Anything that struck you about their marriage or their relationship. Did they seem happy to you?'

There was a long silence on the phone as Kate waited. The reasons she had provided for asking Melanie questions had sounded vague, even to her own ears. She was fully prepared to be met with a curt refusal and the call being ended.

'Is this something to do with Joel's mum?'

The question took Kate by surprise. 'Why do you ask that, Melanie?'

'Because everybody knows she hated Gabby. Well, not hate maybe, but you know, she really, really didn't like her. Did you say this review or whatever was initiated by Joel's family?'

'That's right,' Kate replied.

'Well, then it must be coming from Annette. It wouldn't be from Neil. Gabby always got on great with Joel's dad. So, what's she been saying? That Gabby had something to do with Joel's death?' Melanie snorted down the phone. 'Trust Annette to try to turn even an act of God into Gabby's fault.'

Kate waited, not responding, knowing that Melanie had more to say. She was just gathering steam.

'I don't know what it was about the two of them.' Melanie's voice was back after a beat. 'They just rubbed each other the wrong way from day dot. Annette was super-attached to Joel, I guess 'cause he was an only child. It was like she couldn't bear it that he had chosen another woman or something. I don't know. Gabby and I used to laugh about it. But it was a bit sad, really. And now that Joel's gone, Annette's lost everything.'

'So, you could say there was nothing Gabby could do to please Annette?'

'Exactly. I'll just give you one example. The funeral: Annette just completely lost it and started bawling and screaming at Gabby because she wasn't crying. I mean, can you believe that? Like there's only one way of hurting? God! She was out of control. I just felt for Joel's dad. He was so embarrassed. The poor man.'

'Annette thinks that Joel and Gabby's marriage wasn't working out. That maybe Gabby wasn't being faithful.'

'Well, that's none of her business, is it? I mean, that's between Gabby and Joel—' Melanie stopped mid-sentence, as if realising she had said too much. Kate's mind flew to her conversation over the weekend with the café attendant at the aquatic centre. Maybe Annette's instincts had been right all along.

'Were you aware of any problems in the marriage?' Kate probed. 'Did you ever suspect Gabby or Joel of being unfaithful?'

There was a pause. Melanie was clearly deciding how much she should reveal.

'I don't know anything for sure,' she replied finally. 'Gabby just liked to flirt, you know? She's beautiful and all the men in the footy club were after her, even the married ones. Especially the married ones. Even my Adam.'

The last sentence was delivered matter-of-factly, but Kate wondered if there had been more to Melanie's decision to leave Esserton than just work.

'Gabby hated going to the footy and attending all the functions at the club. But Joel was the team captain and their highest scorer on record or whatever, so she was kind of expected to be there each week. She just flirted with the men to pass the time. It gave her something to do and she liked having power over them, getting free drinks and knowing that all the wives hated her. She never did anything, I don't think. It was all just a bit of fun.'

Kate thought about Melanie's words, pondering the true extent of the jealousies and animosities that had existed within the local footy fraternity.

Melanie continued, her voice more pensive. 'There was a time when I thought she had got more serious with someone, maybe someone from outside the club. But I can't be sure. She never said anything, and then of course I moved away.'

'Did you suspect any particular person of seeing Gabby?'

'I'm not sure, Detective. I really can't say.' Kate could hear the reluctance in her voice. Melanie had nothing further to reveal. It didn't matter. Kate had received all the confirmation she needed. She thanked Melanie for her time and ended the call.

Kate sat at the top of the stairwell, absorbing what she had just learned. She really needed to speak to Gabby. She had attempted to make contact yesterday after her meeting with Skinner, but Gabby was proving difficult to reach.

The sound of low voices rising from somewhere below her pulled Kate out of her reverie.

Through the railings, she peered down at the steps leading to the basement level below. The fire-exit door had opened and Josh had entered the stairwell with Vickie. At the base of the stairs, Vickie whispered something into Josh's ear and pulled him into a kiss, their bodies pressed hard against the wall.

Kate looked away. Well, they seemed to have worked out their differences, at least.

21

The sun directly in her eyes, Kate negotiated the after-work traffic of central Esserton, such as it was. It was a quarter to five in the afternoon and she was on her way to meet Gabby Marshall. It had not been an easy appointment to schedule. Kate had tried her mobile throughout the day and Gabby had finally answered late in the afternoon, agreeing to a meeting at five. It was Kate's last errand of the day before she had to pick up Archie from her father's house. Gray had agreed to mind Archie while Geoff attended a rare work appointment with clients in Grafton.

Kate squinted through the brightness, taking it slow as she crested a rise, feeling the full brunt of the sun's glare. Her mind swept through the day's events as she navigated the familiar roads by rote.

After her run-in with Roman Allen, she had expected a complaint to Skinner all day, some sort of reaction – a retaliatory press story maybe – but nothing had materialised. Josh and Vickie also seemed back to normal, much to her relief. Kate had debated having a quiet word with Josh, but had desisted in the end. She was his partner, after all, not his mother. She had opted instead to send them out together to follow up on Vickie's hunch regarding self-harming students. If they had any residual issues to work out, they could do so away from the office.

Though they had spent the day with the school counsellors of Esserton High and Esserton West, nothing useful had emerged. Of the possible candidates the counsellors had identified – three kids in total, two of them girls – none fitted the bill. However, both counsellors had admitted there was a good chance they weren't even aware of the affected teenager, given the long waiting list to see a counsellor at both high schools.

Kate knew Harris was disappointed. She had seen it in her face on their return. Vickie, she knew, wanted desperately to match Darnley with a concrete breakthrough. It hadn't helped that she also had no luck cross-referencing the Toyota from the Tweed Valley Way footage with any CCTV from the bakery holdup. It was disappointing, but not unexpected. There had always been a possibility that the boys had travelled by foot to that first mark. Kate sympathised but hadn't wasted time on platitudes. Vickie would just have to dust herself off and get on with it.

Waiting for the lights to change, her mind settled once more on the warehouse access road. Her gut told her that they were on the right track there. She toyed with the Turner Road loophole, but in the end shrugged it away. The warehouse security was the key, she was certain.

Roby had informed her that he had finally managed to chase down the owners. As she had suspected, the warehousing business had only just been purchased, with the business due to commence operations in a few weeks, once the owner, Mr Collias, returned from an overseas holiday. He was currently away with his family visiting relatives in a tiny village in Greece. With the time difference and non-existent phone reception, they had only managed to get Mr Collias on his mobile late that afternoon local time, early morning in Greece. After the situation had been explained, Mr Collias had been only too happy to help. He had confirmed that security cameras were indeed in place, a new system having been installed by a security firm, GuardSafe. He couldn't confirm, however, if the cameras were currently in operation, referring them on to the security company.

The firm, GuardSafe, had been contacted late in the day. After being relayed from one supervisor to another, they had finally managed to confirm that the security system at Collias and Sons had been functional over the relevant period, with the firm in the process of running back-to-base testing ahead of the site commencing operations. Roby had received assurances that the relevant footage would be tracked down and sent over to the police station first thing in the morning. It was now a waiting game to see what it would produce.

Nearing the turnoff to her destination, Kate deliberately put the holdup case out of her mind. Checking her scribbled note to make sure she had the correct address, she turned into the carpark of a Homemaker Centre.

She found a parking spot and glanced around, taking in her surrounds. Gabby had chosen an interesting spot to meet. An out-of-the-way homewares shopping strip on the outskirts of town. Across the almost empty concrete car lot, a line of shopfront windows glinted in the late-afternoon sun. Kate spied the usual suspects: furniture, electrical, lighting, carpet and flooring. She was meant to be meeting Gabby at a café. She finally spotted it at the far end of the strip, its presence proclaimed by nothing more than a purple banner stuck out the front. She wondered what time it was due to shut. Kate heaved her body out of the car and made for the eatery.

The café was a surprise. An authentic French bakery squeezed into the middle of a commercial retail block. Kate assumed the rents must be cheaper out here. The front counter groaned with a bewildering assortment of pastries and sweet treats, all of which she resisted with difficulty. She didn't want any distractions when Gabby arrived. With only a few tables tucked inside, she noted it was a good spot for a private meeting, away from prying eyes.

Kate was right on time, but there was no sign of Gabby. Purchasing a bottle of water, she found a table outside. Twenty-five minutes later, Gabby was obviously a no-show and she was at the point of leaving. The café and stores were closing up for the day. She made to rise, watching a couple of straggling customers lugging something bulky in a trolley to one of the lone remaining vehicles in the carpark.

She stopped at the sight of Gabby Marshall standing near the café door staring directly at her. Gabby approached the table and sat down abruptly, making no move to speak. For a second, Kate wondered if Gabby had been somewhere in the carpark all this time, watching her and contemplating whether to keep her appointment.

Kate observed her guest in silence. She wore an overcoat

against the cooling evening and large dark sunglasses. Gabby's long, dark hair – which Kate had only ever seen worn down on her shoulders in every TV appearance and photo she had viewed – was pulled up into a tight bun. On casual observation, no one would pick her for the Gabby on TV, and Kate assumed that was her intention. Despite her altered appearance, Kate noticed that she was still perfectly made up, her clothes chic and well fitting, her legs shapely in perfectly moulded jeans, her feet encased in fashionable leather boots.

'Well, what's this about, Detective? I don't have much time.'

There was no hint of apology for her lateness.

'Thanks for agreeing to meet with me, Mrs Marshall. As I mentioned to you over the phone, your parents-in-law, Neil and Annette, have requested a review of the circumstances surrounding your husband's death—'

'Pfft!' Gabby snorted out loud. 'It wouldn't be Neil. Don't bring Neil into it. This will be all Annette's doing. So, what's she been saying? Let me guess? That I killed Joel? That I somehow hit him on the head and chucked him in the water? I'm right, aren't I? It'll be something stupid along those lines.'

Kate paused, taking in Gabby's expression and posture. She was on the offensive. Ready for a fight.

'Mrs Marshall, I want to clarify there is nothing in the way of new information. I believe Annette just wants reassurance that we have considered all possibilities—'

Gabby snorted again. 'Yeah. I bet.'

'Mrs Marshall … May I call you Gabby?' At a nod from her, Kate continued. 'Look, Gabby, I am here in good faith. You're right.

Your mother-in-law doesn't have the nicest things to say about you, and I'd like the opportunity to hear your side of things.'

Gabby suddenly erupted into throaty laughter. 'Do you hear yourself? Jesus, what a joke! You just said you have no new information. So, what is it exactly that I need to answer? What? You think I need to disprove all her conspiracy theories? You know very well this is all bullshit, Detective. So far, nothing you've told me justifies this discussion.'

Kate could feel the conversation slipping away. The stark accuracy of everything Gabby was saying was steadily unpicking the straw house of doubts that she had so painstakingly constructed.

'Gabby. Please calm down. No one is accusing you of anything. I just wanted to clarify a couple of things. Just some details about the night. Some background.'

She was up and off her chair now. Almost spitting down her words. 'You want details, Detective? Read the coroner's file. It has all the details you need. My husband died in a flood. I am not going to apologise to Annette for the rest of my life because her son died and I survived. That's what happened and we all have to learn to accept it and move on.'

She paused to take a breath before resuming more calmly. 'Annette's grieving, Detective, and she doesn't know what she's saying. The police shouldn't be giving her air time and making it worse. You should know better.'

And with that, she turned and walked off, leaving Kate with the sour weight of her words ringing in her ears.

THEN

Gabby stepped out into the warmth of the night. The footy club Christmas party was in full swing inside and she needed to escape its over-air-conditioned confines and alcohol-soaked rowdiness disguised as hilarity. Everyone had moved indoors for the awards presentation. The speeches were about to begin and it was a good time to escape.

A hint of a breeze filtered in from the banks of the Tweed River, fluttering across her goose-pimpled skin that was still cool from the air-con turned to maximum inside. She moved to the darkest corner of the balcony, away from prying eyes. The jutting angle of the building protected her from the blazing glass walls that provided party-goers with vistas out to the water. Occasionally, she could hear snatches of laughter and loud clapping, and the drum roll of the band. She tuned out, staring across to the river, an uninterrupted view framed by the occasional palm tree and eucalypt.

She breathed in the still humidity of the evening, feeling just on the right side of tipsy. Tingly and full of anticipation.

She felt rather than saw him step out after her into the balcony. She had spotted him inside, had felt his eyes zooming in on her in her strappy dress and heels. Felt his need like a beacon across the room. She had mentioned the event to him, but had not expected him to show. Not that he would be particularly noticed. Half the town had turned up.

There was no need for words. She neither turned nor acknowledged his presence. His hands found her body, slipping inside her dress to where they needed to go. His lips grazed her neck, his breath hot and urgent in her ear. She moved with him, practised and in synch, their proximity to everyone inside and the possibility of getting caught adding to the rush of the moment and fuelling her desire. Loud cheering and clapping from inside drowned out her moment of release.

He bit her ear lightly as she slipped away.

Back inside, Gabby joined her in-laws in the crowd for the final presentation, Player of the Year. She sidled up next to Neil, clinking her glass of wine to his raised bottle of Peroni. She felt Annette's eyes run down her body, bracing herself for the inevitable question.

'Where have you been? The speeches are almost over.'

'I ducked out for some air and then went to the loo.' Stick to the truth as far as possible. It was always the best policy.

Annette didn't reply.

Gabby searched the crowd for Joel and spotted him standing to the side of the stage with his four fellow nominees, no doubt on tenterhooks until the winner's name was read out. She felt the familiar rush of annoyance mixed with affection for his need for this recognition every year and his genuine amazement at winning the prize each time, when everyone knew there was no real competition. She hated that he set his sights so low (at the level of a local football club, for Christ's sake) and then was so pathetically grateful for each tiny victory.

There was a drum roll and Joel's name was read out. Wild cheers erupted and Gabby joined in the clapping as Joel ran up the steps, a look of pure happiness on his face. Beside her, Annette appeared to be fighting back tears. Joel raised the trophy in triumph above his head and Gabby drained the last of the wine in her glass.

22

Kate made her way slowly and carefully up the rutted dirt track to her father's house. She had done her best to put her disastrous interview with Gabby out of her mind, although the memory of it still stung. Was Gabby right? Was she really chasing shadows? Making promises to Annette that she couldn't keep? Convincing Skinner that there was something to pursue when there wasn't? She shook away the unhelpful thoughts as best she could, concentrating on her driving.

Despite her best efforts, she was late picking up Archie and the afternoon had well and truly bled into dusk. As she pulled up, the headlights of her car caught an arbour draped in carefully tended wisteria climbers waiting for spring time to flush into lilac bloom. She wondered again how her dad could stand all that gardening to keep up the looks of this very English garden.

She turned into Gray's gravel parking area and was surprised to see a car next to her father's ute. She stopped further up to allow space for the unknown vehicle to reverse out. Exiting, she stretched deeply to try to remove the kinks from her neck and shoulders, and slowly made her way to the house.

The door was opened by a woman wearing grey cleaning overalls, her dark-blonde hair held firm in a ponytail. She seemed familiar. Kate had seen her somewhere quite recently.

The woman smiled and let her in. 'You must be Kate. Your dad mentioned you'd be here soon.' The faintest lilt of a European accent. She held the screen door open for Kate to enter. 'He's out on the deck with the boys.'

Boys? Plural? Kate's curiosity was piqued. She followed the woman's lead through the back of the house. Bunty the tabby was in his usual spot on the sitting-room sofa. On seeing Kate, he deigned to lift his head in greeting. As they passed, he jumped down and ran ahead of them. The woman momentarily pressed herself against the wall to let him pass. *Not a cat person*, thought Kate.

They made for the outdoor deck, where Bunty went straight for the padded wicker chair in the corner. Kate found Gray sitting on the timber steps in the fading light, his attention on the back shed, a sort of converted workshop and half-hearted gym. Through its open door, Kate could make out Archie seated at her father's ancient desktop computer, beside an older, school-aged boy, dressed in a plain red T-shirt, who she didn't know. Lengths of dark hair reached down from under the boy's baseball cap to his shoulders. They seemed to be engrossed in some sort of computer game.

Though the boys' backs were turned, Kate felt a stirring of recognition. It came to her: the woman and the boy from the swimming pool, the one whose swimming lesson had been cut short. Kate looked back at the woman, curious. She was staring across at the boys with an oddly intense expression on her face. She noticed Kate studying her and broke her gaze.

'Kit!' Gray had got up to greet her and grazed her cheek with a quick peck.

'Dad.' Kate returned his embrace. 'Sorry I'm late. It's been non-stop today.'

'Not a worry. The chickens have kept them occupied and then they got on the computer. I haven't had to do a thing.'

The woman came forward, an uncertain smile playing on her face. 'Yes. I hope you don't mind. It's only Minecraft. Noa loves it and he usually doesn't like anyone watching, but he seems to have really taken to Archie ... It's a really safe game. Just building different worlds and things ...' The woman's expression had become anxious, waiting for Kate's reaction.

Kate hesitated. She knew little of the game and her immediate reaction was an urge to intervene and limit her son's screen time. But the woman's tense expression, clearly expecting some kind of censure, gave her pause. She wavered. The boys looked so settled. It seemed churlish to create a fuss.

'It's fine,' she said with a smile. 'Is Noa your son?'

'Yes and I'm Ester,' the woman introduced herself with a small wave, relief tinging her voice. 'I'm with the cleaning company.' She glanced at Gray. 'Your dad's request was a bit short notice, so I had to bring Noa along, too.' She met Kate's eyes, a hint of laughter in her gaze.

'It's the bloody booking website.' Gray joined them, oblivious to what had passed between the women. 'The emails end up in the spam folder. I didn't realise the cabins had been booked until the woman called at three o'clock to check if she could bring her dogs.'

Kate shook her head at her father. This wasn't the first time the cabin bookings had gone astray.

'Anyway, thank God they were able to send Ester. Otherwise, I would have been stuck cleaning all tonight.'

'God forbid!' retorted Kate.

Ester chuckled.

'Don't you start,' said Gray. 'Remember who's been minding your child all day.'

'And I'm sure you've done an excellent job, Dad,' Kate replied, taking him by the arm. 'Has he been any trouble?'

'None at all. We've had a great time, haven't we, mate?' he called out to Archie.

Archie reacted to the sound of his grandfather's voice. Seeing his mother, he jumped from his seat and ran in for a hug. 'Mummmyyy!!'

After a suitably brief demonstration of affection, Archie drew back and urgently accosted his mother. 'We're not going yet, are we? Noa's building a house. It's made out of *crim-son* wood and can't be burned. Now we're building a moat that's sixteen blocks long so it's safe from the *ender-men*.'

Kate smiled, bemused at the mysterious words tripping from her son's mouth; his careful pronunciation of the unfamiliar names. 'Wow! Wood that can't burn. That sounds amazing. No, we don't have to go yet.'

'Yay!' His objective achieved, and not hanging around for his mother to change her mind, Archie raced back to join his companion, who had barely looked up at the interruption.

'All right, I guess we're staying until the moat's finished.'

Ester chuckled. Her face was transformed by laughter, Kate noticed. The tight worry lines smoothed away, showing a glimpse of a younger, more carefree version.

'It won't be too much longer, I promise,' noted Ester. 'I just have to do the beds and then I'm done. I only came up to the house to pick up the linen.' She glanced back at her son. 'Noa won't want to go home, either.'

'It's all good. Take your time. They're fine. We don't have to leave straightaway.'

Gray turned to Ester. 'There should be sheets in the hall closet, but check the laundry cupboard, as well. The doona covers may be in there. C'mon, I'll give you a hand.'

Kate waited until her father and Ester had disappeared inside the house before turning towards the shed, her curiosity getting the better of her. Standing at the open door, she observed the computer screen from behind the boys, taking in the block-like characters and landscape. The boys appeared to be deep in conversation. The older boy was describing in minute detail the various attributes of the figures and materials populating the game, his hands moving with confidence across the keyboard and his gaze not leaving the computer, while Archie listened, completely entranced. Even to Kate's untrained eyes, Noa's on-screen construction looked impressive, involving several intricate levels and multiple building materials. Archie asked something and Noa nodded, rapidly switching screens to open up a YouTube video showing a Lego construction of a lumbering machine that looked like a metallic species of dinosaur making its way across a mock snowscape. She had seen Archie view similar Lego construction videos with Geoff. Archie shuffled closer as Noa pointed something out on screen.

Watching them Kate had a glimpse of what a future with two boys in the family could look like. Would Archie be as patient, an older brother as this young boy seemed to be? She hoped so. She cupped her belly, where her skin was drawn tight across the solid shape of her baby – an as yet unknown entity waiting to be born.

Archie caught her eye and she winked back. 'You're all good in here, boys?' she asked entering the shed proper. 'I'm Kate by the way, Noa. Archie's mum.'

'Hi,' the boy answered, glancing her way briefly before returning to the screen.

'Mum, do you know how an AT-AT walks?'

'Er not sure, buddy. What's an at-at?'

'It stands for All Terrain Armoured Transport,' Noa answered calmly. 'They are four-legged transport and combat vehicles used by Imperial ground forces in the Star Wars universe. They move by placing each leg forward on one side first and then the legs on the other side. Front to back.'

'Oh right.' It dawned on Kate that the boys were talking about the walking Lego machine playing on the clip.

'Mum, can Noa come over for a play date? We can watch Star Wars together.'

'Oh, buddy, not sure if you're old enough for the movies yet. And we'll have to check with Noa's mum first if he can come over.'

'Muuumm.' Archie rolled his eyes at her. A momentary glimpse into the future with a teenaged version of her son. 'Not the proper movies. Lego Star Wars videos.'

'They are only short YouTube clips, Kate,' Noa interjected, patiently. Kate had the strong impression that she was failing some kind of Star Wars test. 'But if you prefer, we don't need to watch anything. If Archie has Lego, I can show him how to build some of the craft. I have the sets and the instructions too, which I can bring over.'

'Can he, Mum? Please?' Archie was insistent.

Kate hesitated. Archie tended to do this. He latched onto kids that he met – at the park, at playgroup, at birthday parties – and begged for play dates that he later lost interest in. Noa seemed like a nice kid and she didn't want to disappoint him. If Archie remained enthusiastic in a few days, she would call Ester and organise something.

'That sounds good, Noa. I'll check with your mum and we'll try and set something up.'

The boys seem satisfied and she left them to it.

Her attention drifted. In the dwindling light, she took in the fruits of her father's efforts in the garden. The backyard wasn't as sculpted as the front of the cottage, but the theme of an English garden with structured hedges and planted garden beds still persisted. Her gaze wandered, not focusing on anything in particular. It was peaceful with just the soft clucking of her father's chooks shut away for the night in their wire enclosure and the snatches of sound from the computer.

She heard shouts of laughter from the shed and looked over. The boys appeared to have swapped from Lego clips to videos featuring Minecraft animation. The screen showed a group of blocky characters dancing to music and banging into each other, while the boys laughed uncontrollably.

Kate smiled to herself, the action in the videos making little sense to her. She noted that Archie was wriggling on his seat as he watched.

'Archie. Do you need to use the toilet, matey?' she called out.

'No thank you.' Always so polite when he didn't want to do something.

His legs were now firmly crossed, his small body a squirming bundle of movement, even as his eyes remained determinedly trained onto the figures on screen.

Kate stepped to the shed door. 'Come on, Archie. You need to go, otherwise you're going to have an accident.' She held out her arms to him and he stood up reluctantly to run to her.

'We're just going inside for a minute, Noa. Just taking Archie to the toilet and we'll be right back.'

'C'mon, Mummy.' Archie plucked at her hand, suddenly all urgency. They ran inside to the toilet, where Archie almost made it, but he had left it too late and the final hurdle of wriggling out of his pants proved too much.

Kate had dealt with the spill in the bathroom and was in the spare room rummaging in Archie's daypack to find him a change of clothes when Gray stuck his head through the door. By the expression on his face, Kate could tell something was wrong.

'Do you know where Noa is?'

'He's outside in the shed, isn't he? He was on the computer when we left. I had to take Archie to the toilet.'

'When was that? He's not there now.'

'It was only about ten minutes ago.' She motioned to the clothes in her hands. 'Archie had an accident, otherwise we would have been out sooner.'

'He can't be left alone, Kit. He doesn't like it.'

Kate's eyes widened, a feeling of unease spreading through her. 'I'm sorry. I didn't know.'

Gray held out his hands. 'I know. It's not your fault. I should have said something. He's probably trying to find Ester.'

Kate hurriedly got Archie dressed as they spoke. 'Well, he can't have gone far. Is Ester out looking?'

Gray nodded. 'I came in to find the torches.'

'Okay, I'll meet you out the back.' Neither had given voice to their fears. Gray's property backed onto endless sheep paddocks fringed by dense stands of bushland. If Noa had managed to negotiate the fence and wander away in the dark, he could be anywhere.

She turned to Archie, who had not missed the change in the adults' voices. 'Matey, it sounds like Noa might have gone for a walk. Mummy and Grandpa are going to go out and search for him, okay? He'll be fine. He just doesn't know Grandpa's place very well. Do you want to come and help? You can walk with Mummy.'

'Carry, carry.' Archie's voice had crumpled and he held out his arms for comfort. Kate didn't have time to argue. She hefted her son onto her side and made her way towards the back, where Gray was waiting for her by the deck.

Seeing her carrying Archie, he offered to take him off her, but Archie protested, clutching even more tightly to her neck, and Kate resigned herself to his weight.

'He's definitely not in the house?'

Gray shook his head. 'We checked.' He started down the grass in quick, long strides with Kate at his side. They crossed the hip-height inner fence armoured with chicken wire Gray had set up to divide the backyard in two and keep his chickens from the extensive vegie garden he had established. As they crossed the simple latch gate, Gray answered her unspoken question. 'The boys have been going in and out all afternoon.'

They crossed the remainder of the garden, navigating the multiple raised beds of planted veg protected by bird netting, and found Ester calling out Noa's name at the back boundary of the property. She stopped as they approached.

'I'm so sorry, Ester—' began Kate.

Ester cut through her. 'It's okay, really. He does this at home too.' Despite her words, Kate could see Ester's face was pinched with worry, her accent more pronounced.

Kate examined the back fence with increasing apprehension. It was a typical metal, wire and timber affair, easy to climb over. Even Archie with a bit of effort could navigate it, except that he had never shown the slightest interest in wandering off by himself.

Gray unwound the chain securing the gate and swung it open, allowing them to follow. Evening had well and truly set and the paddock lay dark and shadowy. Clumps of trees made shapeless silhouettes on the horizon. A sharp breeze had whipped up and Archie's cheeks felt cold on Kate's face. She could feel him snuggling in closer. Her thoughts flew to Noa with only a thin T-shirt for warmth.

'Let's try along the fence line first. He can't have gone far.'

They split up, Gray walking north-west, with Ester, and Kate going in the opposite direction downhill. She tramped down the uneven ground, trying to dodge sheep pats, a white-hot ache starting to spread down her right side from carrying Archie. She held the torch awkwardly in two fingers as she tried to support Archie's body with both arms, the light making jagged stabs in the night as it moved unevenly with her stride. She called out Noa's name, sweeping her torch as best she could, but apart from startling a group of resting sheep, there was no sign of him. Sweating, despite the nip in the air, she rested for a moment against the fence line, shifting Archie slightly to redistribute his weight and find temporary relief for her straining muscles. They would have to ring the station and call in a search team if they didn't find him soon.

She felt Archie relax against her. Despite the chill and her calling out for Noa every few minutes, he had nodded off. She paused a second longer, savouring the feel of his warm breath on her neck. But thoughts of the lost boy made her straighten up again and keep going.

It was then that she heard it. The sound of running footsteps and her name being called. It was Gray. He was running towards her, waving his arms. His voice carried down the slope. 'We found him, Kate. He's fine. We found him.'

23

Utterly spent, Kate collapsed onto the couch, a mug of hot Milo in her hand. Archie had woken up briefly to request the drink before crashing again without tasting a drop. He now lay curled beside her on the couch, Bunty a small furry ball beside him.

Kate rubbed her aching shoulders. Her father had ended up carrying Archie back to the house, still asleep. She had not been able to manage it. In the end, Noa had been located very close to the back gate. He had squeezed himself inside a hollowed-out tree trunk among a dense stand of tea tree. Although Gray had already passed that way, Noa hadn't responded to his calls, the urgency in Gray's voice not making an impression on him. Ester had spotted him when she had accompanied Gray on their second pass, catching a glimpse of Noa's red shirt among the scrub in the torchlight.

They had finally left, Ester leading a compliant Noa pressed to her side. Kate hoped he was okay, the bite of guilt at having left him alone in the shed still playing on her mind. Despite her own remorse, it was Ester who couldn't stop apologising. There had been a nervous mention of her work contract, which disallowed family members from accompanying her on cleaning jobs for insurance reasons. Kate's heart went out to Ester, as Gray had hurried to reassure her. They would not be contacting her work. Such a course of action had not occurred to either of them. Gray had left to see them out and lock up the cabins.

Kate glanced at the time on her mobile. Geoff had phoned. He was still on the highway driving back from Grafton and was about thirty minutes from home. If she left soon, she could get home in time to meet him.

She sipped the hot drink, but it was too sweet, made to Archie's tastes. She placed the mug on the coffee table, accidentally flicking a piece of paper onto the floor. Grunting, Kate reached for it, glancing without interest at its contents. It was the invoice Ester had left, the logo 'Premier Cleaning' in bold pink font on the top left-hand corner with an image of a dustpan and brush.

Her gaze was drawn to the name at the bottom of the page: Estelle Pavić. *Pavić.* A buzzing in her ears. Kate's mind was alive, suddenly burning with questions. Ester was the Estelle Pavić from the witness statement in the Marshall file. She had been present on the night of Gabby Marshall's rescue. But what did that mean?

Kate's thoughts flew to her father. Had he known who Ester was? Had he deliberately organised this meeting intending it as … What? An opportunity for her to talk to one of the witnesses informally, to assuage Kate's concerns over the case? All before it had gone to hell with Noa's disappearance.

Would her father do that – deliberately insert himself into one of her cases? He had meddled in her life before, trying to fix things when she hadn't needed his interference. She had asked his advice on the Marshall case, sure, but this was a step too far. Did he think she couldn't handle things without his machinations, without his packaging everything up for her in a nice tidy bow?

Anger and frustration sparked through her. She looked around the room for something to distract her, her eyes flicking past the framed photographs scattered around the room. She had seen the photos dozens of times before. They were of herself and her brother at various stages of their lives. Family holidays at the beach with their mum. In uniform on their respective first days of school. Kate on her first day as a police officer and a wedding photo of Geoff and her. Numerous photos of Archie were the latest additions. Her eyes rested on a photo of Gray in a fishing boat with Martin Jackson, the former New South Wales Attorney-General and a friend of her father's since childhood. The men were laughing at the camera, holding up a giant barramundi. The photo had been taken during a trip to Cairns, three months before the attorney-general had dropped dead in his office from an undiagnosed heart condition.

She heard noises in the kitchen signalling her father's return and tried to swallow her misgivings. She didn't want to start something with him tonight.

Gray entered the room, beer in hand, and sat down in the chair opposite with a deep sigh. He took a swig of his beer and glanced at her. 'Do you want to stay for dinner? I could knock up an omelette or some sausages for the little man.'

She made herself answer him calmly. 'No. Let him sleep. He's tired out. Geoff's almost home, anyway. We'll need to head off.'

He nodded and lay his head back on the chair, closing his eyes. 'What an end to the day, eh?'

Kate hesitated, and then blurted out before she could stop herself, 'Did you know about Ester when you called her? You didn't get her here for me, did you?'

'Sorry, what? What do you mean?'

Frustrated that he was pretending, that he was making her explain, she said more forcefully than she had intended, 'Do you know who Ester is? She was there on the night of Gabby Marshall's rescue. Gabby Marshall washed up on the creek bank at the back of the Pavićs' house.'

Gray stared at her. 'Kit, I have no idea what you're on about. I called the cleaning company and she's who they sent. I've never set eyes on the woman before.'

She could see the truth in his eyes. She turned away, embarrassed by her mistake. Of course it had been a coincidence. How could she have considered otherwise? Why would her father go to the trouble of orchestrating such an elaborate and ultimately pointless arrangement? Her preoccupation with the Marshall case was spilling into everything. Her earlier failure with Gabby Marshall was making her question too many things. She was losing perspective.

Gray had paused and was watching her. 'Are you still on about that file Skinner gave you? Didn't you make up your mind that there was nothing in it.'

Her answer was quick, unthinking. All she wanted now was to get off the subject. 'I did. I thought I did, but Skinner agreed that I could dig into it a bit more.'

'Oh, he did, did he?'

'He was actually very good about it, better than he could have been.'

Gray watched her silently, not saying anything. Kate was up from her chair, avoiding his eyes. She walked to the bank of photographs on the mantel, her gaze rolling across the score of frozen smiling faces, zeroing in on the image of Gray and Martin Jackson.

'Why do you keep photos of Mum here? What's the point?' It was out before she could think. Her exhaustion from the day, the sudden anger and confusion directed at her father had all muddled her. Her normally carefully maintained reserve had been shattered. She wanted the searchlight of attention to be directed at someone else's vulnerabilities.

Her words were met with silence.

And then a single word bathed with heat and warning. 'Kit—'

But she refused to heed it and went on before her nerve failed her, 'Do you miss him?'

She didn't dare turn around. She had never before directly broached the subject with her father, and she didn't know why she was pushing it now. All the questions she had painstakingly skirted around for so long and her meticulously compartmentalised emotions had been breached today. She had thrown caution to the wind and she had to see it through. She had to learn everything or she would never again find the courage. She remained with her back turned, pretending to concentrate on the photographs.

'Kit, your mum and I ... we made it work.' His words were cautious and tinged with sadness. Not answering her directly but navigating the unexploded ordinance of their family's past. 'She made space for Martin and I loved her for it.'

Kate screwed her eyes shut, a sensation of shivery light headedness at his words. A slight shifting of a weight wedged deep within. She opened her eyes and faced him. 'And Lindsay?'

Gray sighed and rubbed his face. 'Lindsay knew. Martin never really talked about it, but I believe they had an agreement.' He looked away from her. 'Martin was plenty enough for me but … well, it was different for him.' He laughed, a sound filled with pain.

Just as quickly as it had arrived, Kate felt her emotion drain away. She said softly, 'I'm sorry, Dad. I shouldn't have brought it up. I don't know why I did. We don't need to go into it.'

'You asked because It was on your mind. All these years, you've had questions that you've never voiced. Probably like your mum all through our marriage.'

Kate felt a stab of hurt for her dead mother.

'I'm glad you brought it up. I should have talked to you about it earlier – and to your brother. Cleared the air.'

They fell silent, both their thoughts on Luke, holed away in Sydney, avoiding his father.

Gray took a deep swig of his beer and continued. Now that he had started, he couldn't seem to stop himself. 'Lindsay got her revenge. Don't you worry.'

'She told the commissioner and made you step down.'

'That. Yes. A bit of judicious political manoeuvring. But that was nothing. I always expected something like that to happen. There are always repercussions when you're as high-profile as Martin was. After your mum died, we were living on borrowed time.'

Kate recalled Murchison's barb that everyone had known about her father's personal life.

Gray drained the last of the bottle and smiled at her sadly. 'Lindsay's revenge was a bit more personal. She insisted on a private memorial. Family only. To make sure I never got to attend the funeral to say goodbye.

'He was my best friend, you know. Before any of this. I had known him a good ten years before Lindsay, before your mum. But it didn't count. Only those last few years mattered in her eyes.'

Kate gazed at her father, somehow small and diminished in his chair, and she didn't know what to say. Archie stirred and murmured something in his sleep. Bunty leaped lightly off the couch, disturbed. Kate moved to sit beside Archie, straightening his blanket and stroking his hair, glad of something to do. 'Does Skinner know?' She knew she should let it rest, but she had to ask.

Gray looked up. 'I don't know. I'm sure he's guessed.' His voice was resigned. Uninterested.

Kate had figured as much. Her mind combed over Skinner's periodic snipes at her father. The little reminders he sent her way, never letting her forget that he had won and Gray had lost.

'To answer your original question, yes, I miss him. Every single day. Why do you think I keep up this house and that bloody stupid garden? It's the property I bought for us. To spend the few hours we could steal, when he could get away from Sydney. This is the house he wanted. This view and this garden. So I take care of it.' His voice was barely a whisper.

Kate hesitated, wanting to provide comfort but not knowing how. They had never been an overly demonstrative family. Her father had always been larger than life, stoic and in control. Seeing him now, so exposed, was disorientating and unnerving.

Kate reached for her father, an unspoken bridge across the space between them. His palm felt rough and warm. She couldn't remember the last time she had held her father's hand. Probably when she was still a little girl, when he had been able to completely encircle her small digits in his. Now, she realised his fingers were the same length as hers – average and ordinary. His skin had stretched and was marked with sunspots and wrinkles. He had aged into an old man without her noticing.

He squeezed her hand, a lifetime of emotion and apology in the gesture, and she didn't let go.

24

Kate turned heavily on her side. She was exhausted, but wide awake. The events of the day, and her father's revelations, chased around in her head on an incessant loop. She glanced at her alarm clock: 11.53 pm. She sighed and heaved herself up, sitting on the edge of the bed for a moment, feeling lightheaded. She rose and exited the room as quietly as she could.

She paused outside the adjoining room, set up as the new baby's nursery, then stepped inside. In the glow of the corridor night light, her eyes took in the fully furnished space – all of Archie's old baby things, the cot and change table and old toys – carefully washed and scrubbed, mostly by Geoff, and awaiting the new arrival. She turned to the chest of drawers, gazing inside at the tiny onesies, swaddles and booties, all neatly folded.

She chose one of the baby blankets, pressing the soft cloth to her face, breathing in the new fabric smell. As she folded and replaced the material, she noticed a faded knitted quilt tucked into the linen. A comforter from her own childhood, handmade by her mother, which had been one of Archie's favourites only a few short months ago. Pulling it out and taking it with her, she navigated the silent house into the lounge room.

Turning on the telly, and flicking aimlessly through the late-night offerings, she finally settled on the home-shopping channel. Turning the volume down to almost nothing, she curled up on the couch and pulled the blanket close, for comfort more than warmth.

She gazed at the screen. A man with a made-for-TV smile was handling a steam mop and demonstrating its many virtues to a woman with an equally inane grin. Kate watched without really seeing. She knew she needed to get some sleep. She had a full day ahead and she needed to rest. Her body ached, tightness threading her back and neck. Her hands automatically reached for her belly, rubbing where she could feel the hard bump of her unborn child, as if that would make up for the little care she was taking with her second pregnancy.

Her mind returned to her father. She felt a pit in her chest as she recalled his face when he had hugged her goodnight. His loneliness had affected her more than she had expected, and more than she had wanted. She didn't want to feel responsible for him.

On impulse, she grabbed her mobile, which she had brought out of the bedroom by habit, scrolled through her contacts and dialled a number. It rang four times and went to voicemail. It had been stupid to expect him to answer. Even her ever-partying brother must sleep some nights. The phone buzzed in her hand and she glanced at the screen. Luke.

'What's wrong? Why are you ringing so late?' Her brother's voice sounded muffled, like he had just woken up, but the note of alarm was clear.

'Sorry. Didn't mean to worry you. I couldn't sleep and I figured you'd still be up. Don't tell me I woke you?'

'I wasn't sleeping.'

'Ah, sorry, didn't mean to disturb. How is ... Ellie, isn't it?'

'Yeah. That didn't work out. Hang on a sec.'

She heard some rustling, the sound of muffled words in the background, and then silence.

'Hello? Okay. Right to talk now.'

Kate smiled to herself, picturing her brother extracting himself from whatever bed he was spending the night in to move to a more private space.

'Where are you?'

'At my place. Why, where are you?'

She caught the warning in his voice and let it rest.

'So, why the midnight call? All well in Blue Heeler land? How's the Arch-monster and Mr Geoffrey?'

'They're both fine. Everything's good.'

'And the baby?' The slight tinge of concern was back in his voice.

'All good. Getting massive. But everything's fine.'

'What, then? What's going on, sis? Open up to your little brother.'

She hesitated for a second, but then plunged in. 'I saw Dad today at the cottage.'

'Oh yeah? And how's the Little House on the Prairie going?'

She ignored his derision. 'We talked. Really talked. About Martin and Mum.'

Silence on the line. It wasn't a good sign.

She stumbled on into the dead air. 'Mum knew. She knew about Martin and Dad. He didn't betray her. She accepted it.'

'What? And you bought that, did you? That's bloody convenient, isn't it? Just what you wanted to hear.' He snorted loudly down the phone. 'How do you think Mum felt all through their marriage? He was in love with the man all his life. They were best friends at high school, for fuck's sake. It's been going on that long.'

Kate closed her eyes, flinching at his words. 'It doesn't mean he didn't care for her. They both made choices, Luke. It wasn't easy or clear-cut for either of them.'

'C'mon, Kit. If he had any guts at all he would have let Mum go rather than keeping her tied to him. Don't you get it? She was his cover while he rose up the ranks.' His voice rose in frustration. 'You need to grow up and stop automatically taking his side all the time.'

While you take Mum's side all the time, she lamented silently. The age-old drawing of teams. In their family, they had picked early and stayed true.

They lapsed into silence, each raking through the past in their minds.

She cleared her throat and started again. 'So, when did you break up with Ellie?'

Luke accepted the truce and responded in kind, keeping his tone determinedly light-hearted. 'You're well behind the times, sis. She was only three … No, four chicks ago.'

'That many? I am behind. Is this one someone we're likely to meet?'

'Hmm. Not sure. I'm still evaluating.'

'Ah. Of course.'

They sparred lightly for another couple of minutes before hanging up, dissatisfied on both sides, but still on speaking terms, which was something.

'Who was that?'

'Shit! You scared the crap out of me.'

Geoff was standing in his boxers in the middle of the room, fully awake. 'I scared *you*? What about me? Katie, you weren't in bed when I woke up. I thought something was wrong again.'

She heard the concern behind the sharpness of his tone. After all, she had been in hospital not two nights ago. 'Sorry, I didn't mean to worry you. Couldn't sleep. Thought I'd come out here and see if the box could send me off.'

'Who was on the phone?' Geoff tried again, his tone softening slightly.

'Oh, just Luke.'

'Did you try talking to him about Gray?'

She nodded. She had told Geoff what had passed at her father's when she got home.

Geoff joined her on the couch, pulling half of the blanket over his legs. 'And how did he take it?' His voice was gentle.

She looked away, laughing ruefully. 'It was stupid. I shouldn't have called him.'

He reached for her hand and squeezed. 'It wasn't stupid. Irrational and pointless, but not stupid.' He smiled as he spoke, willing her to cheer up.

She rolled her eyes and smiled back. 'You should go back to bed. I won't be long.'

'Too late. I'm awake now. Do you want a tea or a hot chocolate or something?'

'Yeah, go on.'

She slid down the couch and settled herself more comfortably as Geoff pottered in the kitchen. By the time he sat back down beside her, lifting her feet up to lay them on his lap, she had her eyes half closed and was lost in thought.

She accepted the steaming cup of milky comfort he offered her and took a sip. The hot liquid warmed her and she sank further into the cushions. She spoke quietly, her eyes barely open, her voice dreamy. 'Geoff, I want to run something past you. Don't say anything. Just listen and tell me if you think it sounds realistic or likely.'

'Okay, shoot.'

'I've been thinking about the flood—'

'Is this your Marshall thing? Sorry. Sorry. Continue.' He slurped his drink and lapsed into silence.

'I was thinking how easy it would be to hide a crime during a flood. The floodwaters would go through your house and remove any trace evidence, or contaminate it so badly, we wouldn't have a chance of finding anything. A body in floodwaters would get so bashed and bruised that it may be impossible to distinguish between debris injuries and blunt-force trauma, particularly if the body's been in the water for a while.'

'Well, this is certainly giving me ideas.'

She ignored the interruption and continued, speaking more to herself. 'If someone was, say, pushed into floodwaters by force, there's a fair chance that debris injuries could cover up or muck up any original injury, so it wouldn't necessarily be picked up by the autopsy. Without anything else to indicate a crime, it would just be assumed to be accidental, just someone who got washed away and drowned.'

'So, you're thinking that the woman on telly bashed her husband before pushing him in the water? But because of his flood injuries, you can't prove it?'

'Does it sound that far-fetched?'

He didn't answer, instead asking, 'But wasn't she in the water with him? Why would she put herself at risk?'

'I don't know. Maybe something went wrong and she didn't actually mean to be in the water with him.' She sighed in frustration. 'I'm still trying to work it out.'

Her husband was silent for a moment. 'Did the postmortem identify anything? Any injuries that could go either way.'

Kate shook her head in answer, silently impressed that Geoff had considered the possibility.

Geoff shrugged. 'I don't know, Katie. Maybe it was just an accident.'

'Yeah. You're probably right.' Abruptly, she didn't want to speak to Geoff about it anymore. She wished she could discuss the case with Josh. She needed the perspective of another detective, someone with experience of the inconsistencies of human nature. But Skinner had made his instructions clear on that front.

'Anyway, shall we call it a night, do you think?' Geoff heaved himself off the couch.

There was no criticism in his voice, but she could guess what he was thinking: she was doing too much, staying up too late and not taking care of herself, putting her job before her own health and the welfare of their unborn baby. The guilt reared up once more. It wasn't anything she hadn't berated herself about already.

She caught her husband's outstretched hand and didn't argue.

25

Wednesday

Kate pulled up to the kerb parking behind a battered and unwashed station wagon. The street was quiet and empty, basking in the mild, late-morning sunshine. No stray mums jogging past with their strollers. No dog walkers.

Kate glanced up at number fifteen. It was a substantial Queenslander, obviously renovated, situated on an incline. The blinds were drawn and there was no car in the driveway.

She drummed the wheel with her fingers, debating what to do. She shouldn't be here. This was a bad idea. She wasn't sure herself why she had driven here. Except that she was itching for a rematch. After last night, she was unsettled and frustrated and feeling slightly reckless. She wanted to take Gabby on again.

The song on the radio ended and was replaced by the over-excited prattle of the two radio announcers. She turned down the radio and sipped her takeaway energy-boost juice, her professed reason for stepping out of the station, disappointingly ordinary for the price.

Fuck it, she thought. She might as well since she was here.

The electric roller door of the garage whirred into life just as she made to get out of the car. She stayed put and watched. The slowly rising door revealed a well-muscled man, blond hair shaved down to fashionable stubble, in a collared T-shirt, cargo pants and joggers, throwing a gym bag into the back of a new-looking, grey-green Subaru Impreza. He turned and spoke to someone outside Kate's line of vision. As he climbed into the car, the person came into view.

The woman was dressed in a three-quarter-length nightshirt and not much else. She leaned into the open window of the car to exchange a kiss with the man, her long hair curtaining the side of her face. But not before Kate had caught a glimpse of Gabby's features.

With a small wave, she stepped back out of view and the car reversed neatly out of the driveway and onto the street. Kate looked down, feigning absorption in her mobile but he sped away without a glance in her direction.

So that theory, at least, has been proven, she thought. Regardless of when it may have begun, there was no doubt Gabby Marshall was currently in a relationship with Cameron Archer, her ex-colleague from the aquatic centre. It hadn't hit the news. Yet. That meant they were being fairly discreet about it. Engaging in a public relationship so soon after her husband's death, an ex-work colleague at that, wouldn't fit with the image of the grief-stricken widow. It didn't necessarily mean she wasn't grieving for her husband. Human relationships and emotions were rarely that clear-cut.

Nevertheless, the relationship would no doubt have serious consequences for her image and her media-generated income. If found out, the tabloids would not hesitate to immediately and gleefully tear down the media darling they had created.

The purr of her mobile, still in her hand, brought her back to the present. It was Josh.

'Kate, where are you? We've got them!'

Her thoughts cleared, all considerations of Gabby Marshall instantly secondary. 'Tell me. What's happened?'

'We got a call from Esserton High. They've had some petty theft and two kids were named. The form teacher got them to open their lockers and guess what they found?'

Kate clicked her tongue impatiently, waiting for Josh to reveal what he knew.

'Superhero masks. Specifically, the Hulk and Iron Man.'

She felt a rivulet of excitement course through her. 'I'm on my way back. Where are you now?'

'I'm with Roby heading to the school. Going to pick them up.'

'All right, I'll meet you at the station.'

She glanced back at the silent Queenslander. It was probably for the best, she reflected.

* * *

'Okay, so we've got Matthew Henshaw and Kaden Coppersmith, both sixteen years. No priors. So far, neither have said a word.

We've got parents from both sides in the interview rooms. The Henshaws have brought in the family lawyer. It's just the mother on Kaden's side.'

Kate sat with Josh in the incident room. She knew he wanted to get started on the interviews – his anticipation was palpable – but she wanted to make certain they had everything covered.

Josh rattled off what they had, emphasising each piece of information with a stab of his finger. 'Matthew's the leader. Cocky as hell. I reckon he's the Hulk. He's got the right build for it.'

A memory of muscle pinning down flesh flashed through Kate's mind.

'When we picked them up at school, he piped up straight away, claiming to know nothing. The other kid – Kaden – just took his lead and they haven't spoken a word since. I reckon we should start with Kaden. He'll talk without Matthew in the room.'

'What about the warehouse footage?' queried Kate. 'Is Darnley back yet?'

'I don't think so. But we have enough without it.' Josh's tone was impatient. 'We've got the masks, which match the Macca's footage. Plus, we've got the Rose Street intersection footage as backup. That's plenty.'

Kate nodded, but didn't answer. The warehouse-security footage was a sore point with her. It hadn't arrived at the station first thing in the morning, as had been promised by the security firm. Evidently, they were having issues with their server and couldn't access the backup files, whatever that meant. In frustration, she had dispatched Darnley to their offices with clear instructions to not come back until he had possession of the footage. Now, the arrests of the boys had accelerated matters.

'Okay, and the Toyota? Have we linked this Margaret Henshaw with Matthew?'

Josh grinned broadly. 'Indeed we have. It turns out Margaret Henshaw is Matthew's grandmother, currently on a six-week holiday in Europe with a friend. We spoke briefly with the Henshaws before the lawyer showed up. Matthew's mother confirmed that they've been minding her place and her keys while she's been away.'

'So, Matthew had access to the car.'

'Absolutely. The car's parked at the grandmother's place. No doubt it'll be news to the parents that he's been taking it for joy rides. Unlicensed, I might add. He's only on his Ls.'

Josh met Kate's eyes. She nodded her head, satisfied. 'All right. Let's start with Kaden. Set up interview room two and I'll see you in there.'

Josh sprang to his feet. 'Thank fuck for that,' she heard him mutter.

She stood up and made for the open window. The baby was kicking furiously and she held her hand to her belly to try and still its frantic movements. She rested her head against the cool glass for a second, concentrating on the thrumming within her body.

There was a sound of hurried footsteps and she turned to find Darnley making straight for her, a USB stick held high in the air, his face alight with a broad smile. 'Got it!'

'Finally!' Kate walked to the door and directed Harris to find Josh and call him back in. She sat with Darnley as he inserted the USB stick into the nearest laptop and brought up the footage.

'It's all here, Sarge, just as we thought. And their cameras are the latest gear, the footage is clear as.'

They both leaned close, taking in the crisp, night-vision images; footage captured from the camera installed on the building abutting the front boundary. As Kate had hoped, it provided uninterrupted views of the entrance road. The time stamp read 3.56 am and a car, a dark-coloured Toyota hatchback, could be seen clearly driving up along the access road. It parked a few metres before reaching the boundary fence.

'Can we get the licence from that?'

'Already done.' Darnley beamed. 'The techies at GuardSafe got me enlarged stills. They were only too happy to help, given the delay they caused. It's still blurry, but enough to get a match. It's the Henshaw Toyota all right.'

'Bloody brilliant.' Kate turned back to the footage. There were definitely figures within the vehicle, but the car was parked too far away to discern their faces.

'Do they get any closer?'

'It gets better, Sarge, I promise you.' Darnley grabbed the mouse and fast-forwarded the footage – 3.59 am, 4.02 am, 4.06 am. She saw a flurry of movement outside the car. Darnley paused and rewound the footage back slightly to 4.05 am. The doors of the car opened and two figures could be seen getting out. Even at a distance, she could make out Matthew Henshaw and Kaden Coppersmith. What looked to be a plastic shopping bag trailed from Matthew's hand. He bent over the back window and spoke to someone who had remained behind in the back seat. Seemingly unable to convince his friend, Matthew gestured to Kaden and they moved away from the car. As they moved closer to the fenceline, their identities became unmistakable.

Kate marvelled that the boys hadn't been more careful of the cameras at the location. Or had they scoped out the site in advance, and like her, assumed the place was unoccupied?

In the footage, Matthew motioned to his right and the two appeared to confer for a minute.

'He's pointing to the back of the Macca's carpark,' Darnley noted. Kate nodded. She remembered the site well from her excursion the previous day.

In the footage, the boys moved out of view, leaving their friend alone in the car.

Darnley turned to Kate. 'I reckon you were right to bag the stuff you did, Sarge. Bet you anything, that's what Matthew's carrying in that bag of his and that's what they were doing to pass the time.'

Kate agreed, thinking back to the longnecks and discarded bong she had found on site. Liquid and chemical courage before the main event. Fingerprint and DNA matches would mean another link in the evidence chain.

Turning back to the screen, Darnley fast-forwarded the footage once more. The minutes ticked by. At 4.16 am, they saw the back door of the car open and a single leg stick out, although the occupant still didn't fully emerge.

'He's a reluctant one, isn't he?' Kate remarked, observing the leg jiggling with nervous energy, as puffs of what looked like cigarette smoke rose from the open car door into the air.

At 4.26 am, Matthew and Kaden were back on screen, walking with purpose towards the car.

'This is it, Sarge.' Darnley's voice was charged with triumph.

As Kate watched, Matthew headed for the boot with Kaden in tow. When they emerged from behind the car boot, their faces were no longer visible, entirely concealed by rubber masks. The Hulk and Iron Man. Through the back door of the car, a third figure now emerged, already disguised. Captain America.

The three masked figures moved along the fence line in single file until they disappeared from view. The time stamp read 4.28 am.

'Do we have any footage of Captain America without his mask?' Kate asked sharply.

'We do indeed.' Darnley was quick to manipulate the footage, speaking as he worked. 'The camera has the boys coming back at 4.43 am, without their masks. They get into the car and wait around till 5.16 am before heading back down the road. Here we go,' he said, pausing the footage. 'Captain America unmasked.'

She concentrated on the image of the teenager, hurrying behind his companions, a canvas bag clutched to his chest. A memory stirred in the back of her mind of a boy in a photo with tightly curled, fair hair; several years younger than the version on screen, but the similarity was striking. *Could it be?*

She turned to Darnley. 'I think I know this boy. I know who Captain America is.'

THEN

Eamon lounged on his bicycle and slurped his petrol station slushy. He was parked under the shade of a huge strangler fig tree that marked the entrance to the local playground and skate park. Its gnarled bark like an ancient many-limbed creature, spread across the ground carving its territory; its roots reaching for the ground like hairy feelers, creating shadows on the sun-baked footpath.

The park was filling up with people, the usual weekend crowd. He watched as skaters honed their tricks on the concrete ramp. Further away, parents with their strollers supervised squealing, excited toddlers at the playground. A toned pack of twenty-somethings in tight Lycra jogged past him in perfect step. A handful of middle-aged stragglers lurched behind, struggling to keep up, while a golden-skinned, muscle-bound trainer ran beside them, bellowing out empty motivational phrases.

Eamon watched them shuffle past, puffing heavily, waiting for their straining figures to turn the corner before checking his watch. Almost 10.30 am. He turned his bike around on the pavement in a wide, lazy arc, and picked his moment to dart across the road, perfectly timing his crossing between two passing cars. On the opposite side of the road, he mounted the footpath and rode on, supremely unconcerned at the screeching of brakes and shouted expletives thrown his way. Grinning, he held out his middle finger at the disappearing back of the car that had beeped him.

A block on, he had reached the Sunshine Shopping Plaza, a sundry collection of shops clustered around an aging Big W store. Padlocking his bike to a vacant bus shelter seat at the front of the centre, he entered its air-conditioned confines. Past a greengrocer, bakery, chemist and sushi shop, beyond the Coles supermarket and Liquorland, he paused momentarily in front of the Big W storefront. A quick scan of the area and the checkout tills. Nothing.

He could feel the eyes of the store security guy, a middle-aged Indian man stationed at the entrance next to the security scanners. His job was to check people's bags as they exited the store. Eamon met his gaze and the man turned away.

Eamon walked into the store and disappeared into the aisles. Through the stationery aisle, the confectionary section, plus-size women's, children's and babies' wear, toys, electronics, outdoor and camping, party supplies, linen. He walked the store from end to end. Nothing. The taut sense of anticipation that had carried him through the morning dissolved instantly into despair, the day stretching out in front of him without purpose. He had not made any plans beyond this point, not thought beyond the moment when he would see her, when he would make her face him – make her speak to him. She always worked the Sunday shift for the weekend rates. He had been sure she would be here.

He began slowly making his way back out of the store. In the homewares section, he found his path blocked by a thick-set man in skinny jeans and a fedora hat bending over to compare the prices of cutlery sets in the bottom row. As the man moved his bulk out of the way, Eamon's view of the next aisle – electric kettles and toasters – opened up and suddenly there she was: Anika.

He hadn't been close to her since they had broken up two months ago, and yet she hadn't changed, her hair maybe a little longer, a new shade of polish on her nails. Even in the cheap blue polyester of her staff shirt, she still looked fresh and tailored. She hadn't seen him. She was facing away to the side, talking to a colleague, a gangly redhead with a raw patch of sunburnt skin at the back of his neck just visible above his shirt collar.

Eamon felt a stab of irrational jealousy. He knew this guy was a nobody. He knew she hadn't been seeing anyone since their breakup. He was certain. He had been keeping tabs on her. This was just someone she worked with, a friend at most, yet he hated him. He wanted to be the one she was talking to and laughing with, using her hands animatedly to make a point. He should be the one at the receiving end of her stories, of her smiles, not this fucking sunburnt ginger.

She finished her chat and was walking away. Quietly, and at a distance, he followed. She made her way to one of the checkout counters and set up her till. From the men's section, behind a rack of polo shirts, he watched her serving a line of customers. Chatting politely. Making small talk. Smiling. Efficient.

Grabbing a pair of men's socks at random from the sales bin, Eamon joined the queue behind a family of four with a heaving trolley. Skulking strategically behind the dad, a large, beefy unit bringing up the rear of the group, Eamon waited his turn, heart beating furiously and sick with nerves. After an interminable wait, where it felt like half the stock in the kids' wear and toy sections were put through the counter, it was finally his chance.

Operating on autopilot, Anika didn't notice him until she had already passed his hastily chosen socks through the scanner and glanced up to recite the price. Laying eyes on his face, her mouth formed a perfect comical O of surprise and his heart skipped a beat. As recognition dawned, she paled and he could see her eyes harden and grow blank. His half-smile and strangled greeting froze on his lips as she averted her eyes, busying herself picking out the correct change for his ten-dollar note to cover her confusion. Within seconds, it was all over and she had turned to the customer behind him.

He was left standing, four dollars poorer with a pair of socks two sizes too large that he didn't need. And they hadn't exchanged a single word. *Fucking pussy*, his mind screamed at him. *Why didn't you say something? Anything.* He walked out of the store, his hands trembling. Reaching a rubbish bin, he flung the newly bought socks inside.

At the sushi store opposite, he spied the redhead who had been speaking to Anika standing in line, waiting to order. He must have finished his shift or was on his break. Eamon strode towards him and slammed his shoulder into the guy's back on his way past. Caught by surprise and taken off balance, the redhead fell to the floor.

'Watch it, mate!' Eamon said as he stepped over the prone figure. The redhead stared at him without a word, seemingly inured to casual cruelty by a lifetime of schoolyard bullying. Eamon heard murmurs of outrage from people in line who had witnessed the attack, but no one confronted him. He didn't care and he didn't look back. It felt good to hurt someone.

26

In the incident room, Kate reviewed the footage of Kaden and Matthew's interviews, concluded over an hour ago. In the end, the case had resolved quickly. Kaden had relented almost immediately upon viewing the evidence of the warehouse-security footage, confessing to both holdups and giving up the identity of the third assailant from the McDonald's robbery: Eamon Roper, a friend and classmate who also attended Esserton High.

Matthew had held out for longer, at first confessing only to the McDonald's holdup before finally ceding to the earlier bakery incident upon being informed of Kaden's confession. But he had remained true to his friend and refused to give up the identity of the third accomplice from the McDonald's robbery. Not that his misguided loyalty had been of any use at that point.

A quick call to the principal of Esserton High had confirmed that Eamon was indeed the son of a Carlie Roper, who worked at the Esserton Aquatic Centre, as Kate had guessed. The photo that Carlie had shown Kate on the weekend was clearly an old favourite and not reflective of her son's current age, but it had been enough for Kate to make the connection. Darnley and Harris had been dispatched to the high school to bring Eamon in. Josh had tracked down Mrs Roper at the centre and she was on her way to the station.

Josh entered the room and met her gaze.

'How is he?' she asked.

'As expected. Apparently, he spotted Harris and Darnley in the school grounds and made a run for it. They had to give chase for a couple of blocks before bringing him down near Comber Street Park.'

'Is he hurt?' Kate asked. The last thing they needed at this late stage was an injury to the suspect and accusations of undue force.

Josh shook his head, unconcerned. 'Nothing that I could see. It sounds like he ran himself into a corner before finally giving in.' He grinned at Kate. 'Just processed him. He refused to remove his leather bracelets. Got quite aggressive about it, actually, but I managed to convince him that it would be in his best interest to do what I asked,' he finished with a wink.

Kate remained impassive. She wasn't about to congratulate him on intimidating a teenager.

'Want to guess what I found?' Josh continued, unperturbed by Kate's lack of reaction.

'Cutting?' Kate asked. She had expected it, but the confirmation was more distressing than exhilarating.

'Yep, under a layer of medical tape. Harris is happy. Her theory got proven. The cut on his right wrist is definitely a good fit for the footage. So, we've got him. All photographed and documented.'

Kate nodded and turned away, needing some space from Josh. She flicked through the files on her desk at random. The baby had gone quiet and she rubbed her belly, wishing for movement, missing the comforting kicks that confirmed all was well.

The door swung open and Roby ducked his head in. 'Mrs Roper's arrived.'

Kate nodded to Josh and they followed Roby out of the room. As they reached reception, a woman in a denim skirt and an Esserton Aquatic Centre pullover jumped up from her seat and came towards them, hands clenched at her sides.

Automatically addressing the men in the group, she accosted Josh, who was slightly ahead of Kate and the tallest of them. Roby stood apologetically at Kate's side.

'Where is he? Where's Eamon? They said you've brought him in for questioning? What's this about? He's done nothing wrong. Where is he?'

'Are you Mrs Carlie Roper? Eamon Roper's mother and legal guardian?'

'Yes. Yes. Of course I am. Now what's this about?'

'Mrs Roper, I'm sorry, but Eamon's been brought in for questioning about the holdups that have been on the news, specifically the McDonald's incident last week.'

'What? What do you mean? My Eamon's not involved in that.' Her eyes finally landed on Kate and widened in surprise and confusion. 'You! What are you doing here?'

'Hello, Carlie. I'm Detective Kate Miles. I'm the officer in charge of the investigation.'

Taking in Kate's title and her changed manner of speaking, the confusion on Carlie's face deepened. 'But you didn't mention anything about Eamon on Sunday.'

Josh looked between Carlie and Kate in surprise.

'What I spoke to you about on Sunday was something else, Mrs Roper.' Kate's voice was gentle. 'We only identified Eamon as a person of interest in this case today. I had no idea Eamon was involved in anything when we spoke.'

Carlie lapsed into a bewildered silence, digesting this.

Josh looked quizzically at Kate, but she shook her head slightly, motioning that she would explain later. Josh turned back to Carlie.

'Mrs Roper, does Eamon have any legal representation? Do you have a lawyer that you can call?'

Carlie's eyes widened in shock. 'What do you mean? This is all a mistake. Whatever it is, he'll be able to explain.' She closed her eyes and took two deep breaths, loudly dispelling air through clenched teeth. When she opened her eyes, she spoke with feigned calm. 'He doesn't need a lawyer. He's done nothing wrong. Now, I've answered your questions. I want to see my son.'

'Mrs Roper, at this stage, we would strongly advise legal representation for your son.'

Her expression hardened into mulish stubbornness. 'Where is my son? Where are you keeping him? I want to see Eamon.'

Josh opened his mouth to speak, but Kate raised her hand to stave him off. 'We'll take you to see him right now, Carlie. Come through.'

* * *

Twenty minutes later, they were seated in an interview room, Kate and Josh facing Eamon and his mother. Eamon had yet to speak more than a handful of words. Apart from confirming his identity, he had not answered a single question put to him.

He had stared at Kate when she had first come into the room, but hadn't looked at either police officer since, sitting slumped in his chair, his face turned away. His hands lay on the table, the sleeves of his jumper pulled down as far as possible and his fingers playing incessantly with the sleeve ends. He had not addressed his mother at all and had flinched and refused to be touched when she had tried to hug him. Stills from the warehouse-security footage were spread across the table.

Carlie was staring at the photos in shock. She snapped her head back to her son. 'Is this true? This is what you've been doing? Stealing money from McDonald's? Why would you do that, you stupid boy? Why?' Her question rang out and she struck him. A swift slap across the side of his head, more in frustration than aggression. Eamon remained silent and expressionless, barely reacting to his mother's blow.

'Mrs Roper. You need to calm down and restrain yourself. Otherwise, you will be asked to leave.' Josh's voice was sharp and irritated.

'All right. Okay.' Carlie exhaled deeply and held up her palms.

Josh returned to his recital of the evidence. 'As I was saying, Mrs Roper, the security footage puts Eamon's involvement beyond doubt. The other two boys have also confessed and named Eamon as their accomplice.'

'Hang on. No. Hang on.' Carlie was pointing to the warehouse-footage stills. 'This might be Eamon here, but it doesn't prove he was inside the restaurant. I don't care what the other two are saying. The news said that Captain America was a kid with a mark on his wrist. That's not Eamon. He's never had any birthmarks or scars or anything. So it can't be him.' She stared at them, her face triumphant: she had got one over the police, beaten them on a technicality.

'Mrs Roper, Eamon's injuries were photographed when he was brought in. We have no doubts about Eamon being the person in the McDonald's footage.'

'What do you mean *injuries*? What have you been doing to him? There's nothing wrong with him.'

Kate reached for the digital camera to bring up the relevant photos, but Carlie waved her away. 'That's not my Eamon. I'm not looking at that. C'mon mate, we're going home.' She half rose from her chair, reaching for Eamon's wrist to pull him up. At his mother's touch, Eamon jerked away as if he had been burned.

'Mrs Roper, your son's been charged. He can't just walk out of here.'

'What do you mean? This is ridiculous. This is police harassment. Eamon, just show them your bloody wrists so we can get out of here.' She was almost pleading now, panic rising into hysteria.

Eamon's grip on his jumper sleeves tightened and he refused to meet his mother's gaze. He looked agitated and close to tears.

Kate bit her tongue. She knew getting Eamon to reveal his cutting, evidence of his secret shame, was going to be nigh on impossible in this situation. She felt Josh stir beside her but made a swift movement to dissuade him. The last thing Eamon needed was more intervention from Josh.

'Mrs Roper, I think we're done here. I think we can all use a break.'

'No. Show them your wrists, Eamon. Just listen to me for one bloody minute.' She was on him, tearing at his sleeves; a battle of wills between mother and son fuelled by years of built-up anger. Josh was up and rushing towards Carlie Roper, dragging her off her son, but not before she had caught a glimpse of what Eamon had been at pains to hide.

'Get her off me!' Eamon was hysterical and in tears, rushing to cover up his wrists and retreating to the furthest corner of the room. 'I hate you. Get away from me!' The screamed insults of a scared little boy.

Carlie made no reply. She stared at her son as if he was a stranger, confusion and fear running across her face.

Kate understood the shock she must be feeling. Eamon's taped wrists said it all and his mother hadn't even seen his actual injuries. They were not an easy sight. Kate had seen the digital photos documenting each savage cut in detail. Eamon's right wrist was clear apart from a long, straight cut, the end of which they had caught on the security footage, and a few superficial scars. His left wrist, though, was a battlefield of ragged skin, scarred and red raw with line after line of cut marks, some drawn over barely healed wounds. He was clearly right-handed and the left wrist had borne the brunt of the torture.

Kate waited until Josh had led Carlie out of the room, subdued and deflated, before turning to Eamon.

'I'm sorry about that, Eamon. Are you all right? Would you like a drink of something?'

He shook his head without meeting her eyes, sniffling softly, still wedged into the corner of the room.

'Is there anyone else you'd like us to call?'

At receiving no answer, Kate rose. 'Okay, Eamon, I'm just going to go and see your mother. I'll be back in a few minutes, all right?' She could tell that he needed time to compose himself. Also, despite his refusal, she felt the kid could do with a cold drink.

'Why were you asking Mum about Gabby Marshall?' Eamon's voice was strained and hoarse. He cleared his throat.

'I'm sorry?' The change in conversation had thrown her.

'On Sunday. You spoke to Mum about Gabby Marshall at the pool café.'

'How'd you know about that, Eamon?'

'She was talking about it at home. That's what she does. Drones on about every tiny thing that happens in her day,' he said, motioning to the door where his mother had just left. 'She said she spoke to a pregnant lady from another country.' He nodded at her, half embarrassed. 'That's you, isn't it?'

Kate gazed at Eamon thoughtfully. 'As it happens, it was me. I did speak to your mother on Sunday. Why are you so interested, Eamon? Do you know Gabby?'

He brushed off her enquiries, responding with questions of his own. 'Why were you asking about her? Is it something to do with Joel? About his death?'

'Why would it make any difference to you, Eamon?'

'Because I could tell you about it. Stuff you don't know.'

'And how would you know anything about Joel Marshall's death?'

'I was there.' Eamon shook his head in frustration. 'You don't get it.'

A finger of ice along her spine. *What did he mean, he'd been there?*

'No, I don't get it, Eamon. Help me understand.'

'If I tell you, will it help me with this? Will you drop the charges?'

'I can't do that, Eamon. You were involved in an indictable offence. We can't just overlook that.'

Eamon dropped his head, his shoulders and body slumping in despair.

'However, depending on the information you give us, we can provide a letter of assistance to the court. You're a first-time offender, you weren't involved in the first holdup, and you didn't take part in any of the violence at the McDonald's holdup. There are a lot of extenuating circumstances.'

Eamon's head rose, renewed hope on his face.

'There are no guarantees. It all depends on the quality of information you have to give. We can consider it.'

Eamon nodded. 'But I don't want her in here with me.'

'You mean your mother?'

'Yes. And I want a lawyer. Then I'll speak.'

'Okay. We can arrange that.'

She left the interview room, almost colliding with Josh standing in the corridor outside.

He met her gaze. 'Do you mind telling me what the fuck's going on?'

THEN

He was running through the backyard, stumbling and slipping along the wet pebbles and slick grass.

'Wait for me, Eamon. Slow down.'

Eamon turned at the sound of Anika's voice and waited for her to catch up, before starting off almost immediately with Anika hurrying to keep up.

Panic and guilt surged through his body, making him feel almost faint. He tripped over a tree root and felt Anika's hand reach out to steady him. He looked back and could just make out her face in the dark, glistening in the rain, a single lick of wet hair plastered to her cheek. He squeezed her hand and felt her returning pressure.

They had reached the back fence. His eyes scanned the creek bank beyond, searching desperately. When he looked at Anika, he could see the rising worry in her eyes.

'I can't see him. Can you?'

He didn't answer, frantically scouring the darkened bush beyond. Suddenly, Eamon could see him. Exactly where he had feared he would be. 'Shit!'

In an instant, he was over the back fence, a needle of loose chicken wire grazing his palm. He rushed along the bank, slipping and sliding on the wet ground and fallen leaves, pushing through the dripping, overhanging scrub, the pounding of the swollen, swirling waters beyond, loud in his ears.

He could see him now. Just a little bit closer and he would be there.

Hang on, mate. I'm coming. Just hang on.

27

'Just tell us what happened in your own words, Eamon. Take your time.'

Josh was trying to engage with the boy, but Eamon's return expression was one of utter disdain. Kate could guess what he was thinking. *Who else's words would I be using, wanker?* Josh was still fuming over being kept out of the loop on the Marshall case and he was yet to build a rapport with Eamon after their interaction following his arrest. It wasn't a good start.

Eamon sat beside his Legal Aid lawyer, Coraline Meehnan, overweight, middle-aged, and in a faded pantsuit and worn-out flats. Kate had faced her before and knew better than to be deceived by appearances. She was a dedicated and fierce defender of her clients when the need arose.

Kate caught Eamon's eye and nodded at him encouragingly. The seriousness of the moment seemed to be getting to him. He picked once more at his jumper sleeves, avoiding looking at them. All eyes were on him. It was now up to him to deliver.

'We're waiting, mate. If you have something to say, you need to say it or this is all a waste of time.' Josh's voice dripped with impatience.

'Detective, my client has agreed to answer your questions. If he needs some time to tell his story, then he shouldn't be rushed.'

A snort from Josh and Kate gave him a look of silent warning. 'Eamon, why don't you tell us how you met Anika? When did you two start going out?'

Eamon glanced gratefully at Kate and grasped at the lifeline offered. 'We met at the aquatic centre. I help Mum out at the café there, and Anika used to come in sometimes with Mrs Pavić to watch her brother's swimming lessons. After Noa – that's her brother – after he'd finished, they used to come into the café to buy him a lolly bag, and we got chatting. Later, Anika would come in during Noa's lesson so we would have more time together, and we just started hanging out. Sundays at ten-thirty. Every week.'

His voice faltered for a moment, overwhelmed by unexpected emotion. Clearing his throat, he continued. 'Yeah, so anyway, Noa, he's nine and he's autistic. I mean, on the spectrum. That's why they did the ten-thirty class with Gabby Marshall. It's for kids who need more support—'

Kate interrupted him. 'So, the Pavićs knew Gabby Marshall?'

Eamon nodded confirmation. 'Yeah, I think Gabby had been teaching Noa for about a year when I met Anika.'

Kate digested this in silence. 'Okay, Eamon, can we move on to the night of the flood itself?'

'No. I mean not yet. You've got to understand about Noa first. About Noa and me.'

At Kate's questioning glance, Eamon hurried on, trying to get his meaning across. 'It wasn't anything weird. It was just … Noa trusted me.'

Kate waited silently as Eamon visibly struggled to put his thoughts together.

'Anika and I … that was one of the reasons her parents put up with me. I mean, they didn't really approve of her having a boyfriend and her grandmother pretty much hated me because I'm not Croatian. But I got on with Noa. So, they tolerated me.'

Eamon held Kate's gaze.

'Noa's into Minecraft and coding. Same stuff that I was into when I was his age. So we had things to talk about and I could watch what he was doing on the computer and we could discuss it. He just really clicked with me and he didn't mind me being around. And Anika started teaching me the kind of things Noa finds hard to deal with: crowds and bright lights and certain noises and things. Like when people eat too loudly near him or wear really strong perfume, or get right in his space. He hates all that. People doing things that he's not expecting, and too much going on. That's when he tries to run away to find a safe spot or kind of rocks his body to soothe himself and drown out all the noise and information he can't process. That's how Anika explained it to me, anyway.'

'Okay?' Kate's tone was patient, but the question mark was clear. *What did all this have to do with Joel Marshall's death?*

Eamon dropped his eyes. Now they had come to the crux of it: the night of the flood. When he continued, his voice was tense and strained. Gone was the animation and lightness when he had recounted meeting his ex-girlfriend.

'So, that night, I was over at Anika's. Her parents had gone out to dinner. It was their anniversary or something. And Anika's grandmother had gone inside her granny flat at the back of the house to watch her cooking shows. Anika and I, we were meant to be watching Noa. But, we …'

'You were what, Eamon?' prompted Kate, her tone gentle.

'We went up to her room. We were only going to be quick. Noa was busy building some kind of machine with his Lego. He's always got these aircraft builds on the go… like replicas of Star Wars vehicles but cooler.' He licked his lips. Kate could tell he was trying to find the nerve to keep going, focusing on unconnected details to delay the moment for as long as possible.

Eamon continued, his voice becoming hurried and jerky. 'We were in her bed. She hadn't closed the door properly and Noa sort of walked in on us. Anika didn't see him. Her back was turned to the door. She was … I was getting her to … You know …' He gestured towards his groin, embarrassed, and turned towards his lawyer, pleading for her to find the right words.

Coraline obliged. 'I believe what Eamon is trying to say is that at the time his girlfriend was performing fellatio on him. Is that right, Eamon?'

'Yep,' Eamon mumbled, 'Anika … She was right in the middle of it and I didn't want her to stop. Noa sort of watched for a second and then ran off without making a sound.'

An angry red blush had crept up his neck and ears. He avoided everyone's eyes as he doggedly continued.

'I should have said something. Stopped and gone after him. I know it scared him. Maybe he thought I was hurting his sister or something. I don't know. But I didn't want to spoil things with Anika. We hadn't been doing that stuff for long. It was all new and I didn't want her to feel bad about anything. I don't know. I don't know what I was thinking.'

He paused once more to collect himself. Kate didn't interject. He was now entirely immersed in the events of that night and she didn't want to interrupt his flow. When he resumed, his voice was calmer, less jerky. He had obviously got through the part he was most uncomfortable with.

'When we had finished, Anika went to the bathroom to get cleaned up and I went down to check on Noa. But he didn't want anything to do with me. He cried out when I came near him. I didn't want Anika to hear or start asking any questions, and I didn't want him getting more upset. So, I just left him in the telly room and went to the kitchen. I figured if I just left him alone for a little while, he'd come around. Anika came straight to the kitchen and we started doing a sudoku puzzle. I was sure Noa was right there in the next room.'

His voice cracked and he reached for the jug of water on the interview table. Kate watched as he fumbled with it, refusing help from his lawyer. He gulped down the water and reached immediately for a second glass, drinking it down more slowly. He placed his empty glass on the table and moved it around, watching the wet mark grow.

'Are you okay to go on, Eamon?'

He nodded. 'We had only been sitting in the kitchen about ten minutes when Anika's parents got home. Mr Pavić went straight inside to see Noa and we were just talking to Anika's mum. Then

Mr Pavić was back and shouting that Noa wasn't anywhere in the house, and Anika was screaming that he had been in the telly room just a minute ago, and Mrs Pavić just stood there all pale like she was about to faint. I've never seen her like that before. Everyone was panicking, trying to think where to look first. I just remember feeling sick.'

Eamon paused. Kate noticed his hands. They were balled into fists, knuckles clenched tight. His was clearly back there in the Pavićs' kitchen, reliving the events as they unfolded. Kate's mind flew to the evening at her father's house when Noa had disappeared. She remembered the terror on Ester's face and her own panic. She had an inkling of what the family must have experienced that rain-soaked night.

Eamon bit his lip. 'Mrs Pavić, I think, went out the back to see if Noa was in the granny flat. Mr Pavić was trying to find a torch to search outside. Anika and I headed down to the creek.'

'Why the creek? Why did you decide to head straight there?'

Eamon looked up again to meet Kate's eyes. 'It's where he goes when he gets really stressed. Their yard backs onto the creek and Noa always played down there because it's quiet and peaceful and he liked sitting by the water. That's where he went when he got upset and wanted to get away from everyone and feel safe. The water was only ever ankle-deep and Noa knew to be careful. But since the rains began and the water started rising, Mrs Pavić had been onto him and onto him about not going anywhere near there.'

His speech had started to quicken again, trying to tear past the painful memories.

'It was my fault that he ran. He was trying to get away from me. What he saw. He didn't know how to process it. He wanted to get to the creek to hide from me. He knew about the rains, but he didn't understand how the creek would be.'

Eamon paused again. He ran his hands over his face and exhaled. When he spoke, it was through fingers covering his face.

'When we got there … we found Noa. He was right on the edge of the bank. He was screaming and kicking at something on the other side. I swear, he didn't understand what was happening. He probably thought Joel was trying to grab him or something, even though he was just trying to hold on. Noa … He thinks the creek is his own special place, and when he saw Gabby and Joel hanging there, it was just too much. He was trying to get them away from his space. He didn't mean to push Joel into the water. It was all an accident.'

'You're saying Gabby and Joel Marshall were clinging onto the bank when you got there and Noa Pavić accidentally pushed Joel Marshall back into the water? Did you see it happen? Did you see them on the bank?'

'We didn't see it happen. The ground falls away into the water and you can't see down to the creek unless you're standing at the top of the embankment. We didn't even realise there was anyone there until later, after I had managed to pull Noa back. All we saw was Noa at the top kicking down, screaming. We had no idea he was kicking at a person. It was only later, and by that time it was too late.'

'So, you moved Noa from the bank?'

'Yeah, he was pretty much hysterical by that point, screaming and crying. It was a nightmare. He was trying to get away the whole time, kicking and hitting me. It was raining and slippery and I almost fell. I basically just dragged him with me.'

'When did you realise about Joel Marshall, Eamon?'

'It was after I had got Noa away. By that time, Anika's parents and grandmother were there, too, and they were trying to calm Noa down. Anika's mum and grandmother managed to walk him back to the house between them. It was after they had gone and it was a bit quieter … that's when we realised we could hear screams from the creek. Mr Pavić and I went back to have a look over the embankment. And that's when we saw Gabby. I mean, well, we didn't know it was Gabby at the time. We could just see it was a woman and she was hanging there on some rocks, still sort of half in the water. She pulled herself up a bit and Mr Pavić managed to grab her arm, and we both dragged her out.'

There was a pause. The interview room was completely still, entirely absorbed, no one daring to interrupt.

'When we got her out, she started going on and on about her husband, and a child on the bank kicking and knocking him back into the water. That was when we realised what had happened, what Noa had done.'

'What happened afterwards, Eamon?' Kate prompted as Eamon once more paused. She could tell he was running out of steam, but she needed to know the whole story, all of the details before he wound down.

Eamon resumed, his voice slow and weary. 'Mr Pavić sent Anika back to the house to call an ambulance for Gabby and to raise the alarm about Joel. We thought there might still be a chance to save him. Mr Pavić helped Gabby back to the house.

'They all went into the sitting room to wait for the ambulance. Mr Pavić found Gabby a chair and Anika had got her mum and they were finding her blankets and stuff. I think that's when they all recognised each other and Gabby realised who the child was on the bank. I saw them in there. Mrs Pavić was crying. I remember Gabby was trying to comfort her. I don't know where Noa was. I think Anika's grandmother had taken him upstairs.'

'So, while they were waiting for the ambulance, Gabby Marshall, along with the Pavićs, came up with their own version of events to keep Noa out of it.' It was a statement more than a question.

Eamon shrugged. 'Gabby knows Noa. She knows he didn't mean to hurt anyone.'

Kate watched him in silence. 'The police attended the scene that night. Can I ask where you were, Eamon?'

'I stayed in the kitchen. Mr Pavić came in before the police and ambulance got there and told me I could go home. He said he would deal with the police so I wouldn't need to make a statement. That suited me. I just waited until I could say goodbye to Anika and then left them to it.'

Eamon lapsed into silence. He had obviously come to the end of his story.

'Is there anything else you need from my client, Detectives? I think he's told you all he knows about these events.'

Kate made a brief sign to Coraline, indicating an extra five minutes, and turned back to Eamon. 'Just a few more questions, Eamon. Did the Pavićs own a cat at the time that all this happened?'

'Sorry?' Eamon stared at Kate, confused.

'Just answer the question, Eamon.'

'They've never owned a cat. Mrs Pavić is allergic.'

Kate nodded her head, satisfied. She glanced at Josh and then back at Eamon. 'Why didn't you come forward earlier, Eamon? Why have you held all this back until now?'

Eamon covered his face with his hands. When he spoke, his voice was almost entirely muffled.

'Eamon, you need to remove your hands from your face and speak clearly. Can you please repeat that?'

'Because I love her and she told me not to say anything.' His voice was barely above a whisper.

'Do you mean Anika?'

He nodded in reply.

Kate stayed silent, waiting for him to regain composure before continuing. 'Is there anything else you would like to add, Eamon?' Her voice was kind.

'I know it doesn't mean much, but I'm sorry about what I did.' He caught her eyes, willing her to understand. 'Anika and I, we broke up a couple of days after all that happened. Because I was stupid enough to tell her about Noa seeing us and Anika just couldn't get over that. After I told her, she just blamed me for everything that happened. With Noa and Joel Marshall. Everything.'

Eamon's voice rose, his face again suffused with colour. 'After that, she refused to see me or talk to me. She wouldn't even look at me if she saw me at the shops or wherever. I was so angry at her. I just couldn't think.'

'And robbing a McDonald's dressed as an Avenger seemed like the next logical step, did it?' The dig was unfair, but Josh had clearly sat in silence for too long.

'You don't understand what it was like!' Eamon's voice had almost risen to a shout. 'I couldn't stand it. I needed to get out of my head. To do something. I knew Matt and Kade were into some stuff, and one day Matt asked me to go with them. I thought, what the hell? There's nothing else going on. I swear, I didn't know that's what they were going to do. I thought we would just be fooling around. Then Matt pulled a knife on that girl. And the other one – Abigail – I recognised her from Anika's school. They're friends. I don't know … It just all got out of hand. And now I'm here and everything's fucked.'

28

Skinner observed Kate in silence as she took him through Eamon's
statement. His office was in shadow apart from a single desk lamp
that threw his face into harsh focus. The sharp line of his jaw
hardened as her recital progressed. Dusk had fallen outside and
the wind was quickening. Through the window behind Skinner's
head, Kate caught a glimpse of Coraline Meehnan in the carpark
shepherding Carlie Roper and Eamon towards Carlie's vehicle.
Eamon had been released on bail, while Matthew and Kaden
were on remand pending a court appearance, accounting for their
more serious roles in the holdups. She observed Coraline speaking
with emphasis to Eamon, before standing aside and watching the
vehicle drive away.

'So, you don't think it's Gabby Marshall anymore.'

Kate dragged her attention from the window to meet
Skinner's gaze. 'Well, Eamon's statement changes things. It's put
a completely different spin on everything.' To Kate, it had been
akin to an illusionist's trick. What she thought she knew had been
flipped before her eyes. She had been so sure of the direction of

her enquiries; all of her doubts and niggles had centred around Gabby, the obvious and prosaic suspect. Until Eamon's statement had slammed the entire case sideways.

Skinner sighed deeply, his frustration clear. This was not how he had wanted the review to play out. Kate could see it in his face. He had wanted a quick and clean outcome. A full stop rather than the opening up of a new set of complications. His next words proved her right.

'You couldn't just leave it alone, could you? Just do something simple for once. Just bloody write a report and forget about it.'

She waited him out.

'How reliable is this Roper kid?'

'I believe him,' she replied simply. Everything Eamon had said tied in with Kate's own observations of the Pavićs, before she had any notion of their involvement. From Noa's apparent newfound fear of water, which she had witnessed at the aquatic centre and which made sense given what he had gone through; to the family's fabrication of a lost cat in their police statement to cover up for their presence at the creek bank on the night.

Skinner exhaled loudly and grimaced at Kate. 'You know this statement is worth nothing, don't you? By his own admittance, he didn't actually see Joel being kicked.'

He raised a palm, forestalling Kate from interrupting him, waving Eamon's statement in the air as he spoke. 'Plus, it sounds like he's been obsessed with his girlfriend for a while. It says here, doesn't it, he began cutting himself after he broke up with her? So, who's to say he's not making this up to get back at her or the family 'cause she dumped him? After Coraline Meehnan puts him through a psych evaluation to argue leniency with the judge, that'll be the end of his credibility. The DPP are not going to go anywhere near this,' he said referring to the office of the Director of Public Prosecutions. 'Do you really think they'll support the Pavićs being charged with concealing a serious offence based on this? Eamon's not a reliable witness.'

'So what, you're saying we should ignore his statement? Bury it?'

Skinner caught her gaze and they glared at each other, a silent battle of wills, neither willing to concede.

Skinner relented first. 'Talk to the Pavićs and to Gabby Marshall. See what they say about Eamon's version. Do not even think about speaking to the child unless the parents agree.'

Kate bristled at Skinner's words. As if she needed telling, like she was some first-year probationary constable.

'If either of their stories change, then we can talk about pursuing it. But I can tell you right now, you're wasting your time.'

* * *

Kate returned to her desk, seething. She wasn't sure what to think. The satisfaction that had carried her through the afternoon following the arrest of the boys had drained away. The excitement that had sparked through her upon stumbling on the solution to the Marshall case, had similarly fizzled out. Her encounter with Skinner had seen to that. Now, she was left with doubt and anti-climax.

Kate bit her lip hard. She would not let Skinner get to her like this. She felt certain that Eamon was telling the truth. He couldn't have made up that story.

There was a discreet cough and she turned to find Darnley at her shoulder.

'What is it, Constable?' She tried to keep the irritation from her voice. It wasn't Darnley's fault that she was out of sorts.

He hesitated, checking the room to make sure they were alone. He had chosen a quiet moment. 'It's about Joel Marshall's insurance, Sarge. I know it probably doesn't matter anymore, but I've got you the details.'

Kate sat up straighter. After her interview with Neil Marshall over the weekend, she had tasked Darnley with sequestering the Marshalls' financial records to confirm the details of Joel's life-insurance policy and cross-checking it against donations to the RFS.

'You're right, but tell me, anyway.'

'It was just like you said, Sarge. A payment for a hundred and twenty-seven grand was made to Mrs Marshall's Westpac account from Metro Super, just on three weeks ago. I checked with the RFS for donations received since that time and they confirmed an anonymous donation for eighty thousand dollars made two weeks ago, which corresponds with a similar sum transferred from Mrs Marshall's Westpac account.'

'Great. Thanks for checking that, Greg. Just leave the details with me.'

'Actually, Sarge. There's something else.'

Kate could feel a headache coming on as she waited for Darnley to explain. She was too tired for long-winded discussions.

'The bank gave me a heads-up that the account's been internally flagged for a security check because it's been the subject of a number of large transactions recently. It seems that, in addition to the hundred and twenty-seven thousand payout three weeks ago from Metro Super and Ms Marshall's eighty thousand dollar transfer to the RFS, there was also a one-million-dollar deposit into the account five weeks ago from an insurance company: InsureCare.'

'Two payouts?' Kate was all ears now, the pain in her head forgotten.

Darnley nodded. 'Exactly. I checked it out and it turns out that Joel Marshall took out a stand-alone life-insurance policy over four years ago, just after their marriage. The sole beneficiary was Gabby Marshall.'

'When was the claim lodged? Do you know?'

Darnley referred to his notepad. 'Yeah, I wrote that down. Hang on. It was the ninth of February.'

Just on a month after her husband's death, Kate mused. 'Was there a corresponding policy on her life?'

'If there was, it wasn't with InsureCare.' He placed a folder of notes on her desk. 'It's all in here, if you need it. I'm still waiting on the bank records. I'll pass it on when it comes through.'

'Thanks, Greg. I appreciate it.'

Darnley walked away and Kate flicked through the neatly typed notes and insurance details he had left behind, her mind scrabbling around the possibilities.

So, Gabby had gone out of her way to create the impression that she had not greatly benefited from Joel's money. With a sleight of hand, she had convinced her father-in-law that she had donated the majority of Joel's payout to charity to honour his memory. To Neil, she was the selfless and desolate widow. Kate now understood the easy bequest of such a large sum. What was eighty thousand dollars, after all, when you had over a million dollars sitting in your bank account?

Kate shook her head. She had to stop obsessing over Gabby. She was reading too much into the insurance policies. For all her deception, the woman had done nothing illegal. She recalled Neil's observations about Gabby's background. She hadn't come from money like the Marshalls. It made sense that Joel would want to provide for his wife's financial security in the case of an emergency. Well, that circumstance had come to pass. Who Gabby slept with or what lies she told to her in-laws were no longer her concern. Eamon's story had seen to that.

'Detective Miles.'

She glanced up to find Josh accompanying Roman Allen through the office space. She hadn't realised he was at the station. Josh must have called him about the arrests to brief him ahead of the press release that would go out to the news stations.

'I wanted to say thank you, Detective, for finding the boys who did this. My wife and I are very grateful.' He held out his hand and Kate shook it.

'Do you think we could have a word? We can walk to my car.'

Rising up warily and with a glance at Josh, she followed Allen out of the station. They walked in silence until the gloom of the carpark had overtaken them.

'I remember you now, Detective. I thought I knew you from somewhere. It was in Glenugie, wasn't it?'

'Grafton,' Kate corrected him.

'That's right, Grafton. It was a long time ago, Detective. I'm a different man now. People change. They grow up.'

Kate didn't respond, her mind flying back to that summer evening fifteen years ago, to the sights and smells of the Grafton Show, to the copse of eucalypts at the back of the showground hidden from view. She had been a newbie, a probationary constable on patrol. She and her partner had stopped a brawl. A group of alcohol-soaked meatheads taking it in turns to kick a semi-conscious man curled into a ball facedown on the bone-dry dirt. His face had been mashed to a pulp and he had wet himself. She could still remember the group's raucous laughter and cat-calling, smell their sweat and testosterone-fuelled excitement. They had run away at the sight of the cops. She and her partner had only managed to nab two of the perpetrators. The star full-back of the local footy team, too drunk to run far, and Roman Allen, the son of the local state MP.

The victim had been an interstate backpacker who had spent a week in hospital and refused to cooperate, wanting only to put it all behind him. He had never explained what had led to the altercation, though Kate had her suspicions. This wasn't the first time a lone, vulnerable young man had been the subject of a brutal pack bashing in a rural town.

Both the young men had got off without a mark on their records with the help of their parents' connections and expensive lawyers. More than that, the whole thing had been hushed up. Not a word had appeared in the papers or anywhere else. Thinking about it now all these years later, Kate could still feel a bitterness at the back of her tongue.

Roman Allen cleared his throat. 'Look, I need your word that the past will remain in the past. I am very grateful for what you did for Josephine. I'd like our family to be able to move on with our lives. There's no need for things to get ugly.'

She almost laughed out loud. Nothing had changed. Roman could just as well be his father from fifteen years ago. Making deals, sweeping dirt, making inconvenient facts disappear. But the pendulum had swung the other way, she realised. For all his bluster, she could tell he was nervous. With her knowledge, she held his political reputation in her hand. It was hard to see how he would survive a scandal of that nature.

Good, she thought. Let him stew. Let him always be wondering. 'Good night, Mr Allen. Josh will be in touch regarding the case when it goes to court.'

29

The moment the front door opened, Kate had no doubt they knew.

Eamon. His bail conditions strictly prohibited any communication with the Pavićs, but it was clear to her that he had made contact last night. Kate could see it in Ester's pinched, worried face and her daughter's set and resolute expression.

There was none of the ease of two nights ago. It was like Ester had never laid eyes on her before. A couple of evenings ago, their sons had played together and Kate had been making plans for a play date between the boys. Today, she was greeted like the police officer she was. Kate took her cue from Ester and addressed her with polite formality.

She observed Anika standing at her mother's shoulder. So, this was the girl Eamon had fallen for and who had set him down the path he found himself on. She was definitely pretty, holding herself tall and straight. Kate could understand the attraction. Glancing at the mother and daughter, so strikingly similar in appearance, Kate couldn't help but wonder at the age difference between Ester's kids. Had the second pregnancy been unplanned, an unexpected addition late in life? Or was Noa the longed-for second child who had not eventuated until late in the day? How much sadness had Ester and her husband endured in between?

Following the two figures inside the house, Kate was shown into a shabby, lived-in family room furnished with well-worn but cared-for furniture covered in colourful, hand-knitted throws and mismatched cushions. An old and much-used piano stood against the wall near the window, its cover open, a thick wad of music sheets stuck to the stand. Multiple photo frames secured family scenes, almost all unposed and natural, capturing moments of genuine family togetherness. The room was neat but scattered with the minutiae of daily life. An odd Lego piece pushed under the TV cabinet and forgotten. A set of ironed clothes left on the arm of the couch, ready to be taken up to their owners' rooms. A pile of unread grocery catalogues on the sideboard. The overall effect was one of family and warmth, a million miles away from the self-conscious grandeur of the Marshall house. Kate knew which one she preferred.

An older woman with short, thinning hair and a brightly patterned house dress sat knitting on the couch. Her expression was wooden and she didn't look up when Kate followed Ester and Anika into the room.

'My mother,' Ester introduced shortly.

Kate nodded to the woman, without receiving any acknowledgement in return. She addressed Ester. 'Is your husband home, Ester?'

'Dad's at work and Noa's at school.' It was Anika who answered, inserting the additional detail about her brother. The message was clear. The family already knew that Noa was the reason Kate had called by and she would not be allowed access to him.

Kate switched her attention to the girl. 'No school for you today, Anika?'

She saw Ester move to speak, but Anika got in first. 'I had a migraine this morning. I'm feeling better now.'

'I see.' Kate turned back to address her mother. 'Ester, I'm not sure if you're aware, but yesterday we arrested three youths in connection with the armed holdup at the Tweed Valley Way McDonald's. One of the boys arrested was Eamon Roper. I understand he went out with Anika for a number of months earlier this year and late last year?'

Ester's eyes flicked nervously towards Anika before replying, 'Yes, that's right.'

'Ester, in the course of our interview with Eamon, he volunteered some information regarding a separate case: the death of Joel Marshall. He mentioned that he was actually present at the time of Gabby Marshall's rescue from your property. The circumstances he described are substantially different from those you and your husband presented at the time, and which were submitted as evidence to the coroner. Is there anything you wish to clarify about what happened that night?'

The grandmother's knitting needles had come to a halt as Kate spoke. She didn't look up, but Kate knew she was listening.

'Everything happened exactly the way Mum and Dad said. You can't believe a word Eamon says. He's a liar. He's got himself into trouble, and now he's saying anything to try to get himself out of it.' It was Anika again doing the talking.

Kate returned her gaze to Anika. The teenager's eyes were blazing and hot colour tinted her cheeks.

'The additional information Eamon gave us was voluntary. This information doesn't change his charges. He was involved in a felony. It will be up to his lawyer to argue his case.'

Anika chewed her lip and looked away.

Kate turned back to the mother and repeated her question. 'Ester? Is there anything you would like to add regarding what happened that night?' She noticed that nobody had bothered to ask her what Eamon had actually told the police.

'It's like Anika says. We've already told the police everything. There's nothing more to add. It's over. Why are you opening this all up again?'

Kate didn't reply straight away, allowing the silence to lengthen. The grandmother was now focusing directly on her, her knitting set aside, deep dislike etched on her face, all pretence of not listening abandoned.

'Can you remind me what your cat is called, Ester?'

The utter confusion on her face was almost comical. Kate could almost hear the frantic scrabbling in her head. *What cat?*

'Kiki. The cat's name is Kiki.' It was Anika again coming to the rescue.

'Is it around today?'

'No. He's gone. He never came back that night. We lost Kiki that night.'

'Do you have any photos of Kiki?' Kate gestured towards the

iPhone lying on the couch. 'I'd like to see what he looked like.'

Anika stepped in and scooped up her phone, shoving it deep into her jeans pocket. 'No. We didn't have him long enough to take any photos.'

Kate smiled inwardly. They both knew how incongruous that sounded in this day and age of instantaneous images. Still, she couldn't help admiring Anika's determination to stick it out.

'I understand your mother is allergic to cat hair? Aren't you, Ester?'

She noticed the exchange of glances between mother and daughter, Ester's eyes wide with panic.

Anika paused for a second before replying, 'Kiki lived with my grandma out the back, so Mum didn't get affected.'

Kate nodded and accepted defeat for the moment. She handed Ester her card. 'I understand that it was an accident, Ester. But Joel's parents still deserve to know how their son died. If you change your mind.'

For a second, Kate felt she had got through. Ester's expression when she regarded Kate was uncertain. She hesitated, about to speak, but Anika laid a warning hand on her arm and the moment was lost.

Kate left mother and daughter standing at the front door watching her leave.

* * *

'So, what do you think?'

Kate faced Josh across a quiet corner table. They were ensconced in a café down the street from the station: a cheerful, hole-in-the-wall eatery that featured murals from local artists on its interiors, and an ever-changing carousel of backpacker waitstaff. The remains of a burger with the lot and a side of chips lay between them, the detritus of Josh's elevenses. The meal of an overgrown high-school teen.

He slurped on a large milkshake, taking his time before answering her question. It had been Kate's idea to take Josh out of the office to discuss the case. She had felt his displeasure at being kept out of the loop yesterday. Her visit to the Pavićs alone this morning hadn't helped matters. She felt she needed to make amends.

Kate had recounted her meeting with Ester and Anika that morning and she knew he was weighing up his reply. The Marshall case was still her baby and she knew he was trying to tread carefully.

'Are you asking me if I believe Eamon's story?'

Kate nodded, impatient now.

He didn't answer her directly. 'Why would the Pavićs lie about it, though?'

'What do you mean?'

'I mean, it's a nine-year-old boy. It's not like we'd charge them. It's clearly an accidental death. Why the deception? What's the point?'

Kate regarded her partner. She suddenly realised how young he was. How do you explain to a young, single, childless man the overwhelming desire to protect a child – your flesh and blood – from the dangers of the world and sometimes even from their own mistakes? Kate understood the Pavićs' motivation. She had seen the conflict play out in Ester's eyes that morning. She didn't condone their actions, but she understood them.

Kate had witnessed firsthand the intensity of Ester's feelings towards her son. It made perfect sense to Kate that the Pavićs didn't want someone's death on their son's record, regardless of the circumstances. They knew only too well the extra challenges Noa would have to face in life. Kate could see why they wouldn't want this hanging over him, a perpetual shadow blighting his life before it really started. Trying to outrun the inevitable whispers and judgement that would follow Noa and his family in a town like Esserton. The Pavićs were flat-out keeping their heads down, earning a living and making a life for themselves. They didn't need anything to mark them out and single out their son. Kate tried to explain her reasoning to Josh. He listened to her, but she could tell that he didn't really understand.

'I guess,' he responded finally. 'Still, Eamon's version is not enough. If the Pavićs are not going to change their story, you'll need confirmation from Gabby Marshall.'

Kate nodded. It would be almost impossible to get the Pavićs to change their minds. She had realised that this morning. They were in too deep and had too much to lose.

'Do you really think it's worth pursuing?'

Kate eyed him sharply. 'Excuse me?'

'Well, you said it yourself. They're trying to protect Noa and this is only going to expose what happened. And it'll be worse for them if we show they've been lying. So what's the point? Joel's death is still going to be classed as accidental. Is there anything to be gained?'

Kate baulked for a second, feeling the strength of Josh's words. Why was she pushing the matter, apart from her own innate instinct to find the truth? She had been presented with a different version of events. Should she just look away? And what about Annette Marshall? Didn't she deserve to know what had happened? It would stop her fixating on Gabby. Maybe give her some peace. A small sigh escaped her. Whatever she did, she would be hurting someone.

Josh was finished and ready to leave. He stood up, brushing crumbs from his clothes, and waited for Kate to manoeuvre her way from the table.

'Gabby Marshall's side of it is interesting, don't you think?'

'What do you mean?' she asked, joining him.

'Well, she's got nothing to lose really by telling the truth about Noa. At the moment, she's got a mother-in-law who's hellbent on painting her as a murderer. Why doesn't she just tell the truth and close out the issue?'

'I guess she feels loyalty to the family who saved her life. Plus, she knows the family and Noa.'

Josh shrugged again. 'Yeah, but wouldn't her reputation take a hit if Annette's version goes public? If Annette's as bitter as you say, it's a big risk to stay silent. I would have thought it'd be easier to tell the truth and be the conflicted heroine who forgives the family who saved her life but was responsible for her husband's death. That would play much better to the gallery.'

Kate stopped, struck by Josh's words. Her phone beeped and she read the incoming text message, her eyes widening in surprise.

'Speak of the devil. That was Skinner,' she said, holding up her phone screen to Josh. 'Gabby Marshall is at the station.'

30

Kate followed Josh into Skinner's office, observing that Gabby was already ensconced in one of the chairs grouped around a tiny coffee table, set up at the back of the room. A seating arrangement that Skinner reserved exclusively for conversations with families.

'I believe you have already met Detective Miles.' Skinner nodded to Josh. 'This is Detective Josh Ellis.'

'Call me Gabby, please.' Gabby's warm smile was directed squarely at Josh. Kate noticed that she had barely glanced her way.

Compared to their last meeting, Gabby looked poised and in control. Her hair hung lush and luxurious down her shoulders, back to its accustomed position.

Kate met Skinner's eyes. If he was as surprised as she was at Gabby's sudden appearance, he wasn't showing it. For a moment, Kate wondered if Gabby's visit had anything to do with her own visit to the Pavićs that morning. Had they contacted Gabby to apprise her of Kate dropping by? To discuss and align their stories?

Kate joined Josh and Skinner around the coffee table, and Skinner took the lead.

'Mrs Marshall came in today, Kate, because she has some additional information she wanted us to see. Gabby, did you want to talk about the emails you showed me?'

Gabby placed a folder on the coffee table and pushed it towards Kate. 'I should have mentioned these the other day, Detective, when we met. But I guess I was too upset about the whole thing. I know that Annette initiated this whole review and everything. But I think you should look at these so you understand her state of mind.'

Kate opened up the folder and glanced through the papers. They were printouts of emails from Annette to Gabby. She recognised Annette's email address from the many messages in her own inbox. The emails were raving, hateful, expletive-filled missives accusing Gabby of much of what she had already complained of to Kate. She flicked through the pile, noting that the earliest message was dated not three weeks after Joel's passing.

'I've stopped reading them now,' Gabby remarked, her tone matter-of-fact. 'I've diverted her messages straight to the spam folder. I've never done anything about it, though, because I know she's hurting. She just needs someone to blame and I get that. But I brought it along today so you can understand just how she is. She's obsessed with me and there's nothing I can say or do to change her mind.'

'I'm sorry, Mrs Marshall. We had no idea you were being subjected to this. Is Neil aware of this? I can also speak to Annette to ask her to stop,' Kate offered.

'It doesn't matter. Honestly, it doesn't bother me anymore. And no, I haven't told Neil. He's a sweetie and I don't want to upset him more than necessary. He already does his best for me with Annette. I don't want to add to his worries.'

Skinner nodded, clearly impressed by Gabby's attitude.

'Can I ask how it's all going? I mean, have you reviewed everything? Have you found anything new?'

Kate exchanged glances with Skinner and spoke first. 'Actually, Mrs Marshall, there has been a development and it's lucky that you came in today because I was hoping to meet with you, anyway.'

'Oh?' Her expression was a picture of innocent surprise.

Clearly and succinctly, Kate spelled out the gist of Eamon's story. Throughout her recital, she noticed Gabby's expression did not change: not at the mention of Eamon, whom she clearly knew, or of Noa, or any of the Pavićs.

Gabby remained silent for a moment after Kate had finished. Then, ignoring Kate, she turned to Skinner. 'Can I ask what Eamon has been charged with?'

'It's not relevant, Mrs Marshall,' Kate cut in before Skinner had a chance to reply.

'It is relevant.' Gabby's head snapped back to face her inquisitor. Her calm façade had cracked. Her eyes sparked with anger as she spoke. 'He's obviously got himself into some real trouble. Why would he be making something like this up if he's not trying to get his charges reduced or something?'

'You believe he's making it up?' It was Josh, his voice mild.

'Of course!' Gabby glanced at Josh and made an effort to regain control, then turned once more to Skinner, the senior officer. 'You're not taking this seriously, are you? If this was true, why didn't Eamon say anything before? Why bring this up now? What's the point? None of this is going to bring Joel back.'

Skinner spoke, trying to calm the situation. 'Mrs Marshall, we have a duty to check on matters that are brought to our attention. All these enquiries are routine.'

Gabby nodded and resumed in a quieter voice. 'Look, I don't know why Eamon is choosing to do this. I know him, of course. He's the son of the woman who runs the café at the aquatic centre where I used to work. She and I didn't always see eye to eye. I thought she was a shameless gossip, to be honest. Maybe he's got a grudge against me because I didn't like his mum. I don't know. Maybe he wants to get back at his girlfriend by making up stories about her family. I heard Anika broke up with him ...'

Kate could see Skinner raising his eyebrows at her significantly, but she ignored him, concentrating on Gabby.

'... but why he would pick on Noa, I have no idea. Noa's just a kid. I used to teach him swimming. You know he's autistic, right? The Pavićs don't need this, okay? I mean, they saved my life that night. They don't need stories made up about them by a delinquent teenager who's trying to get back at his girlfriend. It's just wrong.'

'Have any of the Pavićs been in touch with you recently, Mrs Marshall?' Kate interjected.

'No. Why should they? I lost touch with the family after I left the centre. This probably doesn't sound very nice, but I find it hard to be around them. It brings back too many memories of that night.' Her voice wavered.

There was a silence as they waited for her to regain her composure.

Finally, Gabby looked up and faced Skinner, speaking to him directly. 'Have you spoken to the Pavićs about Eamon's story? Did they say anything?'

Skinner glanced over at Kate. He knew of her interview with the Pavićs that morning and what had come of it. His expression was telling her that it was over.

'Yes, actually, we have spoken to the Pavićs and they agree with you. They deny Eamon's story categorically and haven't changed their version of the events.'

Kate sagged in her seat.

'There. You see.' Gabby pounced on his words. She looked from Kate and Josh to Skinner. 'So, is that it? You're not going to pursue this anymore?'

'I think the coroner's findings stand, Mrs Marshall. I haven't seen anything that would justify reopening the investigation.'

Kate felt the door shut with finality on the case. The meeting ended soon afterwards, with Kate watching from the sidelines as Gabby spoke warmly to Skinner, shaking his hand and holding onto it for a touch longer than necessary. Josh was also bestowed with a smile while she was pointedly passed over. The charm offensive felt tired and performed by rote. Kate suspected that Gabby interacted in much the same way with almost all men, an automatic role she stepped into around the opposite sex.

Josh murmured under his breath to Kate, 'She really doesn't want us to pursue the Pavić angle, does she?'

At Skinner's behest, Kate accompanied Gabby out. They walked in silence, each focused on their own thoughts. The click-clack of Gabby's heels wavered momentarily as they passed Darnley at the photocopier. He nodded at the women and Kate felt Gabby glance his way.

At the station exit, Gabby paused. 'That officer. He's wearing the same cologne that Joel used to.' A small catch to her voice.

She turned to Kate, uncertainty marking her face as if she was debating something, trying to make up her mind. The moment stretched and Kate saw something flicker across Gabby's face. An expression Kate could not place. A momentary desperation that did not gel with Kate's general impression of her. For a second, it felt to Kate as if Gabby's mask had slipped.

Gabby's mobile rang – a sudden loud burst of pop music – interrupting them. She turned away automatically to take the call, the moment lost. Kate stared after Gabby's departing figure with the distinct impression that she had been on the verge of saying something, but had changed her mind.

* * *

By the time Kate pulled into her driveway, a brisk wind was whipping up the unswept leaves on the footpath. Before leaving the station for the day, she had placed a printout of the Marshall report, revised and undoctored by any unsupported personal theories, on Skinner's desk. Further argument was pointless. He had hardly glanced up at her entrance.

The closure of the case meant that Annette Marshall would be left to flounder without resolution. Next week, or the week after that, someone from the station would no doubt call the Marshalls and give them the news. By that time, Kate would be on maternity leave and it would no longer matter. At some point, she would make the effort to call on the Marshalls herself to explain in her own words.

Kate cut the engine and slumped in the car for a second, feeling the exhaustion of the day fill her body. A weariness that seemed to dig deep into her bones. *One more shift*, she told herself. *Just get through one more day.*

Shouldering her backpack, she struggled out of her seat and locked the car. She heard the ping of a message on her phone just as she reached for her house keys. She could hear the sound of cartoons coming from the inside of the house. Archie was apparently still awake.

She glanced at her phone screen, more out of habit than curiosity. A text from an unknown number with an accompanying image file. She clicked open the message.

> I think it might have been the one at the end of the table wearing the grey shirt. She always had a thing for older men.

Curious, Kate tapped open the image, expanding it on her screen. It was a group photo of people seated along a table littered with food and drink. It was clearly a footy function. Most of the men sported purple-and-red Esserton Raiders jerseys, showing their support for the local football club. She recognised Joel at the front, beaming and holding up a beer to the camera. Gabby sat to his left, also smiling, although less enthusiastically than her husband. Towards the back of the table, partially obscured by an arm raising a wineglass, Kate could make out another face in the act of lifting a Crown Lager to his lips, the only person in grey.

Ice slithered into her stomach as she recognised the unsmiling profile of Constable Murchison.

Kate realised who had sent her the message and photo: Melanie Chen, and she was showing Kate whom she had suspected of carrying on an affair with Gabby.

31

Kate lay in bed watching the half-light of dawn bleed into day.
She was moulded across various pillows and cushions, and for the
first time in weeks, her body felt no discomfort. Geoff lay beside
her beneath layers of blankets, the occasional snuffling snore
indicating his location. The baby was active and she concentrated
on its comforting movements, delaying the moment when she
would have to get out of bed.

She felt an overwhelming sense of inertia. It was her last day at
work. She should be enjoying the satisfaction of making it to the
end. In theory, she had concluded both her active cases and there
was nothing major requiring her attention. She had an easy day
ahead of her. Finishing off paperwork, a final handover with Josh
and a pub send-off in the afternoon organised by Harris, although
she would be the only one there not able to enjoy a drink.

And yet, she was plagued by a deep unease. Her sleep had
been punctured by strange dreams involving Gabby Marshall,

Noa and Murchison. Violent and horror-filled imaginings, where Gabby had rescued Noa from torrents of mud-filled floodwaters only to kill him by bashing his head in with a rock. Gabby and Murchison had then conspired to hide the body, digging and burying him in a shallow grave by the river in the pouring rain. Oozing mud had sucked Noa into its depths face-first. Kate had woken up in a panic in the middle of the night and had only drifted back into unconsciousness in the early hours.

Now awake and thinking of the Marshall case, she had the overwhelming feeling that she had missed something. Something vital. That despite all her efforts, she was no closer to the full story.

The image file she had received from Melanie Chen the previous evening was gnawing at her, burned into her mind. She couldn't decide what it meant and whether it was even true. After all, it was only something Melanie suspected. She had no actual proof that a relationship had ever existed between Murchison and Gabby Marshall. The fact that they were both members of the same local football club meant next to nothing, and certainly wasn't reason enough to suspect a conflict of interest in Murchison's investigation of the Marshall case. At its heart, Esserton remained an overgrown regional town. It was expanding, yes, but people had all sorts of connections to each other, stretching out like root tendrils under the surface. Murchison had lived in Esserton for years before transferring to Tweed Heads. There was no reason why he wouldn't continue to support his old footy club.

And yet ... What if? What if Melanie's instincts about her friend were correct? What did that mean? Did Murchison know or suspect more than what he had detailed in his investigation? Had Gabby confided in him? Had he been happy to look the other way at Gabby's behest? It certainly put a different spin on Murchison's marked interest in Kate's review of the case.

She felt herself go cold. She thought briefly about taking her concerns to Skinner today, but dismissed the idea almost instantly. It would smack of nothing but desperation on her part. A last-ditch attempt to cast doubt on the Marshall case, by smearing another officer's reputation, no less. She had zero doubt how that conversation would go down.

Geoff stirred beside her and she heard a plaintive cry from the room next door.

'Mummmyyyy.' Archie was awake.

It was time to get up.

* * *

Kate waited outside Esserton Primary, checking the time on her mobile. It was a cold and unsettled kind of day and she shivered under her cardigan, wishing she hadn't left her overcoat behind in the car. She could hear the laughter and chatter of uniformed children as they mingled in the school playground waiting for the morning bell. Parents herded their children across the zebra crossing manned by a lollipop man resplendent in hi-vis gear, and said their goodbye at the gate. A line of cars were banked around the corner for the morning drop-off.

She had been waiting by the gates for close to twenty minutes, ignoring the quizzical glances of several of the parents. She hoped she hadn't somehow missed Ester. She had spoken to Coraline Meehnan and checked with Eamon to confirm which primary school Noa attended.

She once again glanced at the clock digits on her phone, unable to decide whether she was wasting her time.

A car drove past and Kate recognised Ester's ancient Celica. It slowed, looking for a park, finding a spot a few metres up the street as another vehicle pulled away. Kate saw Ester exit the car with Noa. They chatted as they walked towards the school, Noa carrying his school bag slung over his shoulder. She waited until they had reached the school's entrance gate before detaching herself from the fence line to make her presence known.

Ester stared at her, shock and dismay playing across her features. 'What are you doing here? You can't be here.'

'Ester, I'd like to speak to you and Noa if I could. Just for a few minutes. Hi, Noa,' she added, smiling at him.

'Hello,' Noa replied, glancing her way. 'How are the chickens going?'

Kate blinked and then caught on. 'I think they're good, matey. I haven't seen them since the other night when we were all together.'

'We used the eggs that Gray gave us to make a cheese omelette. Three eggs, a dash of cream and a sprinkling of grated cheese. Delicious.' He made a chef's kiss with his thumb and forefingers over his lips and grinned. Kate laughed and Ester's face softened.

'That sounds yummy, Noa. I look forward to tasting your recipe one day.'

'Yes, maybe when I come over for a play date with Archie.'

Ester cut in, waving her hands before Kate could reply.

'Stop this. We're not talking to you. Noa will be late for school. You have to leave. You shouldn't be following us. This is harassment.' A dad leading a tiny girl in pigtails who looked too young to be at school glanced at them with curiosity as he passed.

'You're making a scene,' Ester whispered fiercely. 'You shouldn't be here.' She moved past Kate, guiding Noa ahead of her.

'Ester, please. Just ten minutes. I promise you. Ten minutes only and I'll leave you alone.' Kate waited as indecision played on Ester's face.

'You can speak to Kate, Mum. I'm fine.'

'I know you are, my beautiful boy.' Ester pressed her face to her son's forehead murmuring something in Croatian.

She turned back to Kate.

'Ten minutes. But just with me. Noa has school.'

Minutes later, after waving goodbye to Noa, they walked in silence to a café up the road. They sat opposite each other, Kate nursing a decaf coffee, Ester fussing with the napkins and cutlery on the table, unable to still her hands. She had refused to order anything.

On the table beside them, a range of complimentary newspapers lay fanned out. The three boys arrested for the holdups were featured across the front page of the local rag. She watched as Ester glanced over and quickly turned away. Like the other two boys, Eamon's face was blacked out, but Kate had no doubt that Ester had recognised the subject.

Kate had perused the article online while waiting for Ester at the school entrance. It was a follow-up article to the arrests reported on the previous day. A special-interest story, analysing the factors that could drive teenagers, especially young boys, into crime. The article quoted a psychologist specialising in the mental health of teenage boys and included an exclusive interview with Coraline Meehnan, who painted a suitably tragic picture of the many young clients she had represented battling mental health issues. There was no direct reference to Eamon, of course, but Coraline was clearly laying the groundwork for her client. The article, Kate knew, was designed to generate public sympathy, though whether the tactic would work was another matter.

Kate met Ester's eyes. 'How are you, Ester?'

'Don't …' She held out a hand, grimacing. 'Let's not do this. Just ask me what you need to so I can leave.'

Kate nodded and tried again, not knowing quite how to begin. 'Ester, the story that Eamon told us—'

'It's lies. We already told you this. It's all lies.'

'Ester. I believe Eamon. I know what he said did happen.'

'No. No—'

'Wait.' Kate held out her hand, trying to calm her. 'Ester, let me finish. I think Eamon told us everything he saw, but I don't think he saw everything. Only Noa knows exactly what happened that night. He was the only one at the creek bank. He's the only one who saw Gabby and Joel.'

She waited, letting the significance of her words sink in.

'I know what Gabby told you happened on the bank that night. What she said Noa did. But I would like to hear it from

Noa, as well. To understand things from his point of view. It could be that Gabby misinterpreted what she saw. It was dark and raining after all. Has Noa ever talked about that night?'

Ester stared at Kate, her expression full of confusion and distress. 'Nothing happened,' she whispered. 'Noa wasn't on the creek bank. Nothing happened.'

'Ester, please talk to Noa. Ask him what he remembers. It could be really important.'

'No. I told you already. He doesn't know anything.' Ester blinked away tears and scraped back her chair. 'Just stay away from us.' Without a backward glance, she disappeared out the door.

Kate remained in her seat, the aborted conversation replaying in her head. She could have handled that better. Sighing, she manoeuvred herself to her feet and made her way out. Ester was nowhere in sight. Slowly, she walked the short distance to where she had parked, at a council lot around the block. Her mobile rang as she reached her car and she answered without glancing at the caller ID.

'You couldn't just call us yourself, could you? After all your bloody promises of keeping in touch and keeping us informed and pretending to care, you couldn't make one phone call? Just left it to some lackey from Preston's office to do the dirty work for you.' A voice, almost incoherent with rage, was screaming down the line. Neil Marshall.

'Do you know what you've done to her? You've bloody broken her. Do you understand me? She trusted you and you've broken her. I mean, what kind of police officer are you? All you had to do was come and see us. Explain it to her properly. She's got nothing now. Do you understand? She's been living on hope, the hope that you bloody fed her, and now she's got nothing.'

The line went dead, leaving her standing in the wind-swept carpark, the silent mobile still pressed to her ear.

32

Kate's hands shook as she navigated her car through Esserton's busy, town centre back to the station. She swore as the car crawled along at a snail's pace as pedestrians flocked the shared traffic zone. Stuck behind a tour bus emptying out passengers, she waited for a dozen or so tourists to disperse before driving on.

She shouldn't have come this way, but she hadn't been concentrating. She had unheedingly followed the traffic, her mind on the phone call she had received, only realising she was in the wrong lane when it was too late. She felt sick thinking over Neil's words, her gut churning with acid. She had tried his number repeatedly, but he wasn't answering. She had finally left a desperately inadequate message on his voicemail, apologising for what had occurred and asking him to call her back.

Kate still couldn't believe it. *Stupid! Stupid!* She had once again underestimated Skinner. She had not thought that he would send the file on so quickly. Next week maybe. After someone from the station had first informed the Marshalls of the outcome. Of course Skinner had passed the report on as soon as he was able to. He couldn't wait to absolve himself of all responsibility for the case. The AC's office had clearly called the Marshalls as a good-faith follow-up. They weren't to know that no one from Esserton had yet made contact with the family.

Neil was right. She should have been the one to have visited the Marshalls and explained properly. She pictured Annette's face and guilt flooded her. She gritted her teeth, her anger rising.

Back at the station, she extricated herself from the car, feeling the full weight of her pregnancy. Her hips and ligaments protested, the skin around her pelvis overstretched and hypersensitive. It was like she couldn't take a single step without some part of her over-taxed body complaining. She grunted and collected her bag.

She entered the station via the back entrance, walking into a squad room, which was empty apart from a couple of officers changing shifts. Constable Grant was on duty at reception, manning the front desk. She nodded at him. 'Where is everyone?'

'There was an accident on Kyogle Road. A truck and a couple of cars. They're all at the scene.'

'And the chief?'

'He's left for the day.'

'Left? What do you mean?'

'A lady friend pulled up in a flash car about half an hour ago and he left with her.' Grant's knowing grin faded as he saw the expression on Kate's face. 'He said he'll be on his mobile,' Grant mumbled.

'Right.' Kate turned to leave.

'Sarge. Hang on.' Grant disappeared under the counter and reappeared with a garishly wrapped cellophane concoction. 'The chief asked me to give this to you.'

She accepted the gift in silence and walked straight back to her car, throwing the bulky package into the back seat without a care. It looked to her to be a nappy bouquet, of all things! Skinner must have picked the first gift he saw in whatever online baby-shower catalogue he had clicked on. She couldn't see him putting the thing together himself.

She breathed deeply, trying to control her frustration. Of course, he had managed to dodge her. She punched in his number on her mobile and waited for the inevitable voicemail message. At the sound of his hearty voice recording, she hung up. She pictured his suave, self-satisfied face and wanted to punch something. She put the car into gear and drove out again.

When she pulled up at the Marshall residence, it was silent and drawn, without any sign of habitation. The wind had picked up and the day was rapidly closing in. Low, heavy clouds had amassed in the horizon like a leaden blanket. Kate drew her overcoat tighter around her shoulders.

She knocked on the front door and pressed the doorbell, calling out Neil and Annette's names. There was no response. She tried their mobiles once more. Still nothing. She glanced up at the high windows, trying to discern if any were open. Was that a flicker at one of the blinds? It had been so quick, she couldn't be sure. She had the feeling Annette was in the house, listening to her banging on the door.

'I'm sorry, Annette,' she called out. 'Truly, I am. You shouldn't have found out this way. Could you please open the door so we can talk?'

The blind on the upstairs window remained determinedly still. She gave it another few minutes and accepted defeat.

* * *

Kate examined the accumulated detritus of her two-and-a-half years at Esserton Station: a stationery drawer full of note pads, chewed out pens, half-eaten packets of crackers, roll-on sunblock and a congealing tube of moisturiser. It was late afternoon and she had spent the last few hours cleaning out her desk and finalising her handover notes to Josh and Skinner. She had debated driving straight home, to plead illness for the remainder of the day. What did it matter if she started her leave a few hours earlier? Instead, she had made herself return. Tossing items indiscriminately into the bin, she heard Grant walk up behind her.

'There are some people here to see you, Sarge. A Mr and Mrs Pavić and their son.'

Kate stilled and felt a charge of electricity spike through her as she rose to follow the constable.

At the front counter, she found Ester looking scared but determined, and Noa, seated on the plastic seats in the waiting area. She smiled and waved at Noa who managed a tiny smile in return. He was still in his school uniform and looked flat and subdued compared to when they had spoken that morning.

He had a click pen in his hand and was clicking it continuously near his ear, humming a low tune to himself.

A man sat close beside Noa, his body trained towards him, protective and gentle. He was heavyset and balding, wearing dark blue cargo pants and a collared T-shirt with a mechanic logo. This had to be Marin, Noa's father, whose name she had come across on file but had never met. At Kate's approach, he rose with his wife and extended his hand. Rough and careworn, his fingertips stained with years of working with oil and grease. Kind grey eyes, framed by spectacles, regarded her as they shook hands.

'Thanks for coming, Ester. Marin, it's nice to meet you.'

'I spoke to Noa like you said,' Ester rushed in, her voice high and anxious. 'I took him out of school early and we had an ice-cream at the park. I asked him and he told me everything … And it's all wrong. What I thought. What we thought.' Her voice cracked. Marin squeezed her shoulder, an ineffectual gesture of comfort.

Kate regarded Ester. She was the perfect fodder for questioning: upset and angry, searching for absolution. She itched to take her to an interview room and let her run. But she had to consider Noa. Kate glanced over to him. Reliving his memories earlier with his mother had clearly cost him. Would he be willing to do it all again, with her? Or would it prove too distressing?

She nodded to Grant, who swiped the security card for the internal door and ushered the family through.

* * *

Over two hours later, Kate faced the Pavićs in the family interview room, seated on opposing couches, across a low coffee table adorned with the obligatory box of tissues and glasses of water. Beside the couple sat their lawyer, a crisply tailored young man, picked by the Pavićs from a list of local firms that she had made available to them. He conferred quietly with his clients.

The back half of the room was set up as a kids' play area with boxes of donated toys, a shelf filled with children's books, and a low table and chairs with a range of drawing pads, textas and crayons. Kate had suggested that Noa and his family wait in the room until they were ready to begin, so that Noa could become comfortable with his surrounds and less nervous. She had organised for a late lunch to be brought in for the family, ensuring that Noa's favourite foods were included: crumbed chicken and cucumber maki rolls and chocolate milk. Noa had spent the time exploring the room and watching a Star Wars movie on his iPad. Kate could see that the time had helped. He appeared calmer and not put out by the multiple adults in the room.

He was currently sitting cross-legged in one of the armchairs in the kids' area, headphones on, busy on his iPad. A middle-aged counsellor, with laugh lines crisscrossing her face and intelligent eyes behind red-rimmed spectacles sat beside Noa, unobtrusive while he concentrated on his tablet. It had taken some work to run down a counsellor at short notice on a Friday afternoon, but Kate had succeeded by going through her contacts and arguing her case. And she seemed to have built a rapport with Noa, which was important. Earlier Kate had noticed them in conversation about the movie Noa had been watching: *Rogue One*. A film Noa had apparently seen over a dozen times and, in his opinion, one of the best movies in the Star Wars universe.

Kate sat silently observing Marin and Ester. She had gone through the preliminaries, advising them that the interview would be recorded. They were clearly anxious and jumpy, Ester in particular, who sat at the extreme edge of the couch. She ran her hand nervously across the coffee table, picking up stray grains of sushi rice from their earlier meal and crushing them into a tissue.

Kate knew their experience so far had been difficult. She had briefed both the lawyer and the counsellor on the contents of Eamon's statement, in particular the matters that could prove upsetting to Noa, so they could prepare Ester and Marin ahead of the interview. She had no doubt that the details in Eamon's statement regarding Anika had not been an easy read for the Pavićs. She didn't want the interview to be hijacked by the issue, but it was necessary for everyone to be clear on the events for Noa's sake, to support him if the discussions proved to be triggering.

Noa giggled suddenly, a snort of laughter bursting into the silence. He pointed something out on his screen to the counsellor and they both laughed. Ester smiled, the tension in the room easing slightly.

'Ester and Marin, I understand you are here today to revise your statement about what occurred on the night of the sixth of January at your property with regards to the rescue of Gabby Marshall from Red Cedar Creek. Is that correct?'

They nodded and Kate asked them to speak for the purposes of the recording.

'Yes. That's correct.' Marin spoke for them.

'Thank you. I have provided you both with a copy of the statement made to us on the eleventh of April by Eamon Roper regarding that night, and I understand you've both had the chance to read it.' Kate didn't miss the tightening of Marin's jaw and the blanching of Ester's face at the mention of Eamon. 'For the purposes of this interview, I want to focus specifically on the events that Eamon states occurred at the creek bank,' she resumed, eager to move on from the circumstances at the house relating to their daughter.

'Do you agree that the events of the night at Red Cedar Creek occurred substantially as Eamon describes them, or is there anything you would like to add to his account?'

'Eamon's statement is correct. That's what happened at the creek bank.' Ester's voice was cracked and pained. Kate could barely catch her words.

'As you can tell from his statement, Eamon didn't actually see what occurred at the creek bank with Noa. He only asserts Gabby's version of what happened between Noa and Joel, which he took to be the truth. Today, with your permission, I would like to ask Noa about what he remembers from that night to see if his memory tallies with Gabby's account. Are you both comfortable with that?'

They assented and Kate continued.

'I understand, Ester, that you spoke to Noa today about what he remembers from that night?'

Ester glanced at Marin, who nodded encouragingly.

'Yes, that's right. I went back to the school, after you …

after we met at the café.' Ester's voice shook as she spoke, tears threatening to spill. 'I needed to find out what happened. That's why we're here. So he can tell you.' She gritted her teeth. 'She lied to us. About Noa, about everything.'

'Do you mean Gabby Marshall, Ester?'

Anger and distress flared across her face. 'Yes,' she whispered, apparently not trusting herself to say any more.

'Is there a reason why you never spoke to Noa before today?' Kate asked, her voice gentle.

'We tried. We really did. In those first few days, both me and Marin tried asking him if he wanted to talk about anything that happened that night. We wanted to reassure him. Make sure he didn't think any of it was his fault. But it was just too upsetting for him. He just clammed up, so we left it.' Ester's eyes filled with tears.

'Those first few weeks were awful. He was so withdrawn. Didn't want to go to school and he got upset over the slightest thing. He stopped swimming. He still refuses to enter the water, even though I did try taking him back a few times. It's only really been in the last month or so, where it's felt like we're seeing the old Noa back again. He's always been such a happy child. Always laughing. It was awful seeing him like that. We thought it best to just leave it. We wanted him to forget. It was an accident, that's what we thought. There was no point dredging it all up and making him feel guilty about something that we couldn't change.'

She met Kate's eyes, pleading for understanding. 'That night when Gabby told us what happened ... we believed her. We had no reason not to. She was wet and bloody and covered in mud and hysterical. It was like a nightmare.' She turned to Marin, tears streaming down her face.

Marin took over. 'Noa has reacted before, when he was younger. Just when kids got too close to him. Nothing serious, just a little push or shove if they really got into his space. I mean, he's not aggressive at all.' Marin's voice rose in an effort to explain. 'He's lovely and gentle, but the kids, they don't know how to leave him be sometimes. They're in his face all the time and really loud and he just has enough. Last year, one of his classmates fell over when Noa pushed him away and the kid hurt his hand. So when Gabby told us what he'd done… it felt like something that could happen—'

'It's because she knew him,' Ester broke in, interrupting her husband. 'I had spoken to Gabby about Noa's triggers, so she could keep an eye on how other kids interacted with him in the pool. That's the only reason I told her. So, she knew exactly what to say to make us believe her. She lied to us and we fell for it.' She clutched her hands tightly together, the knuckles turning white. Marin's hands closed over his wife's, trying to calm her.

'We believed her rather than checking with him.' Ester was speaking directly to Marin. 'What does that say about us? About me? I'm his mother. I should have questioned her more. I should have stuck up for him.' Ester dissolved into tears, sobbing into Marin's shoulder. He held her without speaking.

Kate didn't hurry Ester, waiting until her crying had subsided. Ester blew her nose and accepted a glass of water.

When she resumed her voice was scratchy. She glanced over at her son. Noa remained absorbed, a smile playing on his lips and his feet tapping softly in time with what he was watching.

'When I spoke to him today I was so nervous. So afraid of how he might react. But he's stronger than I give him credit for.' Ester smiled. 'I'm always underestimating him. He just needed some time. His own time to process everything. You'll see when you speak to him. He'll be brilliant.'

33

The Royal Hotel was buzzing, awash with bodies escaping the cold and toasting the weekend. Tradies, farm hands and office workers mingled at the bar and congregated around tables. Kate negotiated her way past a group of laughing, well-dressed women farewelling the work week in style, to the back of the room, where she could see Josh and Harris standing together alongside a couple of junior constables.

'Kate. You made it.'

She grinned. 'I couldn't miss my own send-off, could I?'

'Can I get you a drink, Sarge?' Vickie motioned at everyone's glasses. 'They do mocktails here.' She thrust a drinks menu at Kate.

'Ah. The hard stuff. Well, it is my last day, after all.' Kate grinned and perused the lengthy list of non-alcoholic options. 'I think I'll have a Naked Caprioska, thanks, Vickie.' She reached for her purse but was forestalled by the constable.

'It's my shout,' Vickie said.

Kate nodded at the two other officers in quiet conversation together and glanced at Josh. He looked exhausted. She knew he must have made a supreme effort to make it here for her, or possibly for Vickie. Either way, she was glad he had come. She had no doubt the accident scene hadn't been easy.

Kate gestured at Josh's glass of lemonade set next to Vickie's. The fact that they weren't drinking alcohol meant their workday wasn't over. 'You're heading back, then, after this?' she asked.

'To the hospital. We're doing a combined press conference with the doctors in a couple of hours.' He checked the time as he sipped his drink. 'Darnley and Roby and a few others are still at the scene, clearing the remainder of the traffic.'

'How many dead?'

'A mother and her two boys, two and five. The father's in surgery, critical. Took a while to remove him from the wreckage. The truck jack-knifed and the container overturned. There's fertiliser shit all over the road. The driver's lucky to survive.'

Kate nodded. There was nothing to say. They sat together in silence.

Kate made no mention of her interview with the Pavićs. This was not the right time. She would come into the station and speak to Josh tomorrow, after he'd had the chance to rest. They would tackle Skinner together. She was certain Josh would back her up, once he'd had the chance to hear Noa's statement. The trick would be convincing Skinner, but she was determined to make him listen.

Vickie returned with her drink, a fluoro-green concoction complete with a pineapple piece stuck to the rim and a jaunty cocktail umbrella. Kate sipped it cautiously. Sweet, sharp and minty, and surprisingly good.

There was a loud slap on Kate's shoulder, making her almost spill her drink. 'Miles, what the hell are you drinking? It looks like green dishwashing liquid.'

She turned to find Skinner at her side, beer in hand. A heavily made-up woman, dressed in a wraparound dress and heels, stood beside him holding a wineglass. She appeared younger than Skinner by several decades, and bored.

'Sir. I thought you had left for the day?'

'Couldn't miss the party of the century, eh? Constable Harris here would never forgive me, would you, Vickie?'

Vickie coloured and didn't answer, concentrating on downing her glass. It was an unnecessary swipe, Kate felt. It wasn't the constable's fault that many of the team were stuck at the accident site and had not been able to attend. Kate took in the flushed face of her boss. Clearly, the drink he was holding was not his first. He was in a belligerent mood. There were things they needed to discuss, but it was obvious now was not the time.

The woman beside him pulled at his sleeve and Skinner remembered her presence. 'Anyway, kids, got to run. Be good, won't you? Kate, good luck with everything.' Kate watched as he rubbed at his tummy, just in case she didn't know what he was referring to. With a wave, they were off. Skinner hadn't bothered to introduce his companion.

Kate exchanged glances with Josh. 'Right. I think I'm going to find something to eat. Anyone want anything?' Kate waved off Vickie's offer to go up to the bar again and headed there herself, taking her place among the waiting throng.

Kate mulled over the blackboard offerings, trying to decide what to order. She was feeling lightheaded and sore, exhaustion creeping in. She needed food and a lie-down. Abruptly, the idea of home, TV on the couch with Archie and Geoff, and a takeaway curry, filled her with longing. Maybe just a bowl of chips to share around, she figured. Then she could give it another half an hour and make her exit.

She felt someone move behind her, and suddenly there was hot alcohol breath on her neck and a harsh guttural voice was whispering in her ear.

'So, you didn't find anything, after all, stupid bitch.'

She stood frozen, unable to move. The press of flesh against her body, a clear threat of violence.

'Too bad, I was almost starting to enjoy myself, following your fat arse around.' The rank smell of sweat and beery fumes swamped her. Something pushed on the small of her back. The hard muzzle of a service pistol or something else to give her that impression? A shot of stomach-clenching fear thudded through her. There was a shout of laughter and the pressure released.

A group of twenty-somethings, lost in their own conversation, shouldered past her, forcing her to turn around. There was no one behind her, but she had recognised that voice. *Darryl Murchison.* She scanned the crowd quickly, cold sweat prickling her skin but there was no sign of him.

'Changed my mind. Do they do wedges here?' Josh had caught up with her and was scanning the bar-snacks menu.

'Actually, Josh, I think I'm going to take off. I'm not feeling very well. I think I'll just head home.'

'You sure? Everything okay?'

'All good. Just tired, I think. It's all caught up with me, finally.' She smiled weakly. 'If you have time tomorrow, we should meet for coffee. There's a couple of final things I need to go through.'

Josh eyed her quizzically. 'Yeah sure. That's fine.'

'Tomorrow.' She waved off his unspoken query. 'Thank Vickie for me, will you?'

'Will do, Kate. Take care.'

She jostled her way past the crowds and exited the pub into the cold sharpness of the cheerless evening. She breathed in the cool air, regaining her composure. So, the news had already reached Tweed Station. She wasn't surprised. She assumed Skinner had briefed Superintendent Wright after passing on the Marshall file to the AC's office, and Wright had naturally passed on the news to Murchison.

She peered into the darkness of the carpark, searching for Murchison's distinctive blue Ford Falcon, but could see nothing.

Her mobile rang as she crossed to her car. She recognised the number and felt her stomach drop. It was the last person she wanted to speak to right now.

'Neil. Thank you for returning my call. I just wanted to say, about this morning—'

'Annette's gone. I don't know where she is. She's not answering her phone and her car's gone.' Neil's voice was rushed and panicked.

'Slow down, Neil. What do you mean, Annette's gone? How long has she been away?'

'I don't know. I mean maybe since this morning. After the call from Preston's office, I had to get out of the house. Be by myself for a while. That was around eleven o'clock, I think. I've been out all day. I only got back about half an hour ago.'

'And when you got back, Annette wasn't at home? Could she have stepped out somewhere? To the shops or some sort of an appointment, or to visit a friend?'

'No, you don't understand.' His voice was impatient. 'Annette hasn't left the house since the funeral. She refuses to step out of the front door. She hasn't driven in months. I've called all the friends that she could be with and I even called Esserton and Murwillumbah hospitals, you know, just in case.'

'You've done all the right things, Neil. Can you remember what she was wearing this morning? Maybe look in her wardrobe and see if she might have changed into something?'

'Leggings and a grey jumper. One of Joel's old gym jumpers,' he replied without hesitation. 'It's what she was wearing this morning. That's all she wears now. Joel's old clothes. Nothing in the wardrobe's been touched. Everything in the house is exactly the same as when I left it this morning. She's just locked the house and driven off.'

'What does Annette drive and what's her number plate?'

'It's a silver BMW five-series sedan. Licence plate K-A-5-2-B-E.'

'Is her bag in the house? Do you know if she took her purse with her?'

'Her bag? Hang on. I'll check.' There was the sound of muffled scuffling.

Kate climbed into her car as she waited. From her rear-view mirror, she saw someone in an oversized jacket, his cap pulled low over his face, walk quickly to a vehicle a couple of rows back from her. *Was that Murchison?* She saw its headlights turn on and her adrenaline skipped and then ebbed as the car – a blue sedan, not a ute – pulled out of the carpark.

'I've found her bag. It was in the dining room. Her purse is here and all her bank cards. She must have only taken her mobile and keys.'

Kate dragged her attention back to the call. 'If she's left her purse behind, it's likely that she hasn't driven far and is intending on coming back.' She made no mention of the alternative possibility. 'Are there any favourite spots that Annette liked to visit, before Joel died?' Kate asked. 'Places that she went to when she was stressed out. One of the beaches, maybe? Places of significance. Maybe somewhere that she associated with Joel?'

'I don't know,' replied Neil, obviously thinking hard. 'She isn't a beach person. Maybe the oval where Joel played footy?' he suggested doubtfully. 'Or the cemetery. Maybe she's gone to the cemetery? She's never wanted to come with me when I visited. She always said it would be too much for her. But maybe she went there today? It closes at six, so maybe she's on her way home?' His voice held desperate hope.

'You're probably right, Neil. I think the best thing you can do is to wait for her to come home. I'm sure wherever she's gone, she'll be back soon. I want you to stay there and give me a call in an hour. If she hasn't returned by then, we'll make things official, okay? In the meantime, I'll make some enquiries at my end.'

He mumbled his thanks.

'Also, have you spoken to Gabby?'

'Gabby? No. Why? Annette hasn't spoken to her in months. Gabby wouldn't know where she is.'

Kate didn't respond, but a separate idea was forming. A memory of hateful emails, pages and pages worth over weeks and months, came to her mind.

'One last question, Neil.' She hesitated hating having to ask and to put the image in his head. 'Do you keep any weapons in the house? Any licensed or unlicensed firearms?'

'No. Of course not. Nothing like that.' Neil's tone was unequivocal, but he didn't enquire why she had asked the question.

She hung up the phone and closed her eyes, her plan for getting home to Archie and Geoff in tatters. She could palm this off to Josh, but she knew he would be stuck at the hospital for most of the night. Technically she was already on leave, but she knew she owed Neil.

She checked the time. There was a chance Grant was still at the station. She phoned and caught him on his way out. She gave him Annette's car details with instructions for patrol officers to cruise past some of the known suicide spots in the area that were within driving distance of Esserton.

She hesitated and then tapped her phone, scrolling through for Gabby's contact details, saved from earlier in the week.

She tried the landline first. It rang five times before being answered by a generic, automated message. She hung up and tried the mobile. On the eleventh ring it was answered by a breathless voice.

'Hello?' She recognised Gabby's voice. She could hear soft music in the background. It sounded like she was somewhere intimate. Kate swallowed the unexpected anger that whipped through her, her mind flicking to her afternoon with the Pavićs.

'Mrs Marshall. It's Detective Kate Miles.'

There was a silence. When Gabby replied, her tone was clipped and wary. 'Detective Miles. What can I do for you?'

'Mrs Marshall. Where are you at the moment? Are you at home?'

'What? No. I'm … I've been out all day.' A hint of defiance had crept into her voice. 'What's this about?'

'I am trying to locate Annette Marshall. She's not at the house and she's not answering her mobile. Neil was out all day and doesn't know where she's gone. She's taken her car. We think she left the house before midday. Has she contacted you today?'

'Today? No. I haven't spoken to Annette since the funeral. I have no idea where she could be.'

'Mrs Marshall, your in-laws were informed this morning about the closure of Joel's case.' Kate paused infinitesimally, acid snagging at her throat. 'I understand Annette didn't take it well.'

Gabby snorted down the phone. 'I'm not surprised. She would have completely flipped.'

Kate forced herself to remain calm. 'Gabby,' she reverted to her first name somewhat sharply, 'with your permission, I would like to visit your house to have a look around.' She didn't need to put it into words. If she was right in her thinking, Kate wanted to find Annette first, before anyone else, and certainly before Gabby. She owed her that much. The guilt she would have to learn to live with.

There was silence as Gabby digested Kate's words, and what had been left unsaid. 'Yes. Okay. That's fine.'

'I would like you to stay away from the house for now. Just until I call you back. I shouldn't be longer than half an hour.'

Gabby agreed and the line went dead.

34

The drive to Gabby Marshall's tree-lined street didn't take long. The entire ride, Kate had repeatedly tried Annette's mobile on her hands-free without luck. When she arrived, the street was choked with parked cars. There was obviously some kind of function or play at the local high school up the street, and all available car spots had been snapped up. The kerb in front of Gabby's house was completely blocked.

Past a heavily treed front yard, she almost missed it: a badly parked silver BMW, its back slightly jutting out onto the road. She slowed down to get a better view: licence plate KA52BE. She drove on, finally finding a free space on a side street.

Trudging back slowly on foot, she stopped to get a better view of the BMW. It was empty and the doors were locked. On a hunch, she rang Annette's mobile once more. The muted strains of a phone jingle could be heard from inside the car. Through the window, she saw the light of a mobile phone glowing on the floor of the passenger side.

Out the front of number fifteen, she peered up at the still house. It looked to be hunkering down in the darkness. The blinds were drawn across all the windows and the garage door was closed. The driveway was steep and she traversed it slowly, one hand supporting her belly. Reaching the top, she stopped for a second to catch her breath. A slow, dull ache was radiating from deep within her. Breathing with the pain, she waited for the cramping to pass like a wave rolling over her, rubbing her belly gently.

'Not the best timing, little one,' she whispered softly.

She thought of the last time she had experienced the very same tremors. Fizzling out to nothing. Was it the same or something more? She couldn't tell. Just a quick squiz around, she told herself.

A sensor light had turned on and she glanced around her. The front door was accessed via a verandah up a flight of steps. She would tackle that last.

She moved to the side gate. Further sensor lights came on, illuminating a gravel pathway. She clicked open the latch and made her way along the side of the house, past the council bins. An overgrown photinia hedge to her left brushed silent leaves across her face. She moved through the still backyard, the only sound – her boot heels crunching on the loose stones. A sudden scurry in the undergrowth: a nocturnal creature about its business. The glare of her phone flashlight caught nothing but leaf litter. Navigating past a glassed-in pool, an inky black lagoon encircled by dense tropical foliage, she made her way onto the vast back deck. She tried the sliding doors from the deck into the house. Locked and screened. She made a slow circuit of the house, checking any doors and ground-floor windows with access. All were locked and secured.

Finally, she returned to the front of the house. For a moment, contemplating the steep steps, she wavered, waiting for another contraction to pass. The cold night pressed in on her. Was this a wild goose chase, she questioned herself. Was this all in her head? She should be at home with Geoff. They should be getting organised to get to the hospital again. Asking Nidah to babysit Archie.

She ran through the possibilities in her mind. Annette, she assumed, still retained a key to the house. Was she in there right now? Prowling through the rooms that she thought she had a right to? Rifling through Joel's old possessions to assuage her grief?

She grimaced. She knew she was delaying the inevitable. *Let her not be dead in there*, she prayed. She took the stairs slowly, leaning heavily on the railing.

Reaching the verandah, she peered into the expansive windows. Curtained. The front door was closed, but out of habit, she checked the handle, anyway.

It swung ajar at her touch.

Instantly, her senses tingled on high alert. So, Annette was inside. Her gut churned, preparing her for the worst.

Kate pushed open the door noiselessly and stepped inside. She waited at the threshold, not calling out, but listening intently. Despite her misgivings, if Annette was still alive and well in the house, Kate didn't want to alarm her. The woman seemed fragile: like a bird. Kate didn't want to startle her into falling or injuring herself.

She could hear nothing. The house felt empty. Kate looked around, letting her eyes adjust to the gloom, taking in the layout.

Immediately to the front of her, a hallway seemed to lead to the back of the home and a staircase provided access to the second floor. To the left, the corridor opened up to a living and dining room, which appeared to give way to a kitchen around the corner to the right. She could just make out a section of wall cabinet.

She made her way into the living room. It was in shadow, the muted glow from the verandah light filtering in through the drawn curtains. The main wall to the right sported a gas fireplace, and above it an intricately painted artwork – a study in dark swirls. Directly in front of her, a grand dining table that could easily fit ten people had been positioned in front of a large framed mirror.

She turned the corner into the kitchen. A cavernous space of stainless steel, quartz and timber opened up, complete with a huge island bench and a second living area with glass sliding doors. She assumed they led out to the oversized deck she had passed earlier. She rested for a second at the island, feeling the cold stone beneath her palms as she breathed through another slow crest of pain. Were the contractions getting more frequent?

She straightened up and felt, rather than saw, a flurry of movement behind her. From the corner of her eye, she glimpsed a confused reflection of a figure in the dining-room mirror. Holding something up? Waving something?

A burst of light and she heard a deafening crack. She fell to the ground, automatically taking cover, her police training coming into effect and her body obeying without question. Adrenaline pumped through her as she moved her bulk as best she could around the side of the kitchen island. She reached for the familiar weight of her firearm, realising too late that she had handed in her Glock at the end of her shift, marking the start of her leave. *Shit!*

A wetness was spreading along the length of her trouser leg and she felt frantically for the source of the wound. It wasn't blood, she realised. Her waters had broken. She closed her eyes and pressed her hand to her belly. Her heart pounding in her ears, she risked a peek around the edge of the island base.

Another shot rang out, narrowly missing her right shoulder, and she ducked her body back out of sight.

'Come out here, you bitch.'

'Annette, you don't want to do this,' cried Kate, but her words were drowned out by another shot.

Kate could hear her soft tread getting closer. She knew she had to get Annette talking if she was to have any chance. She had to shock her out of her fury.

'Annette, my baby is coming. I need to get to hospital. You have to stop.' It was a gamble. Would Annette care about Kate's unborn child when she had lost her own? Yet the way that Annette had stared at her swollen belly when she had visited the house came back to her, clear and sharp. She had to believe that Annette would care.

The silence was absolute.

'Annette? Are you all right?'

'What? Who …? But I thought you were …' Annette's voice trailed off, trembling and uncertain, and suddenly Kate understood. In the darkness of the house, Annette had mistaken her for Gabby. It wasn't Kate she wanted to punish. It was her daughter-in-law that she wanted to hurt.

'Annette, it's Detective Kate Miles here. I came here looking for you. Neil was worried when you didn't come home and he asked for my help in finding you. He's waiting for you at home right now.'

'No!'

Kate heard the sound of muffled sobbing and whimpering; Annette realising that she had not got her woman, after all.

'Annette, it's all right. I'm coming out now, okay?' As she spoke, Kate got to her feet with difficulty and slowly moved out from behind her cover. 'Everything is going to be all right. You and I, we're going to drive back home tonight and sort this out. Everything's going to be fine.' Kate moved slowly towards Annette. She could see the other woman still held the firearm in her hand.

'Annette, how about you give me the gun and we can go home, okay?'

Annette stared at Kate through tear-filled eyes, her gaze lowering to her protruding belly. She raised her right hand, which held the weapon, slowly towards Kate.

There was a noise near the dining room and a harsh voice rang out through the stillness. 'Put the gun down right now!'

Kate yelled in protest as a ringing shot filled the air and Annette screamed.

'Down on the floor! Down on the floor, right now!'

An intense pain ripped through her body. She saw Annette collapse in a soft heap and her gun slide across the timber floor. Kate stumbled, her eyes locking onto the ashen face of Constable Murchison staring down at her in horror.

On the floor, she lay disorientated and unmoving. She heard the sound of keening like an animal in pain and realised it was coming from her. A puddle, the colour of rich red wine, was spreading underneath her. She could smell its metallic scent. Hands, rough and scrabbling, were pressing on her shoulder. And pain. Waves of pain were shuddering through her body. Darkness pressed and she closed her eyes, surrendering herself to it.

THEN

Water swirling around her. Tearing at her. Dark and thick with mud and teeming with jagged, unseen things. Joel holding onto her, panicked and terrified. Her shoulder screaming with the strain of holding him up, of not letting go. His ineffectual strokes struggling against the fast-flowing water. He was dragging her down.

'Don't let me go, Gabby!'

Shut up, shut up, her mind screamed at him. She was doing her best to keep them both alive, trying frantically to hold on to Joel while clinging to the rocky outcrop jutting from the creek bank, their only tether to safety. Her feet had no foothold and she was treading water, trying to keep afloat. Joel was a dead weight, barely keeping his head above the water.

She gritted her teeth and heaved with all her strength against the force of the torrent, trying to edge him closer to the rocks so he could grab hold. Except he hardly moved, maybe snagged on something, and the water surged against her efforts. He wasn't even trying to help. Just clinging onto her, expecting her to do all the work.

A wave of resentment flooded her. They wouldn't even be here if it wasn't for him. Why had he tried to drive through the causeway? He wouldn't listen. Bloody pig-headed male. Wanting to prove his ute was good enough.

She could feel him tiring. He was giving up. He slipped lower into the swirling soup, almost wrenching her off the rocks. She strained to not lose her grip. She could tell he was almost done. If she didn't do something soon, he would take her down with him.

She closed her eyes and loosened her grip on his shoulder. She could feel his surprise as his ineffectual fingers tried to maintain his grasp onto her arm.

'No! Gabby! No!' Joel's half-choked cry of panic was swallowed in a rush of water. He surfaced, spluttering, his outstretched hand scrabbling to find purchase, finding her wrist and holding on.

She felt herself being sucked into the water. He had rotated his body to grab at her arm with both of his hands. Their eyes met.

'No, Gabby! What are you doing?'

Holding his gaze, she twisted her arm, shaking him loose and watching him fall back under. This time she pressed against his scalp, pushing with force and holding him down. She could feel the vibration of his futile struggles pulsate up her arm.

The swell of the water had him in its wake and in a second he was gone.

All she felt was relief. She was finally able to secure herself to the rocks with her entire body. The spot where he had slipped under, writhed and moved until she couldn't pick it anymore. The liquid merging into a single, fast-moving slick.

She clung onto the rock face for a minute, exhausted. Something large and sharp rushed through the water, snagging her hip and almost hauling her in again. She held on, her fingertips rigid on the wet stone. The debris pulled free and was washed away. She remained in place, her body and arms gripped to the rock, her eyes closed, hardly aware of the new pain in her leg where the object had bruised her. She was still in danger. She needed to get to safety.

From above, faint shouts floated down to her. She gazed at the bank, eyes squinting through the falling drizzle. A figure, a boy, was sitting on the top of the embankment in the rain, staring down at her.

If there was a child, that meant there were people. She didn't hesitate. Gathering up the remaining reserves of her strength, she began to haul herself from the rocks, reaching up for a foothold on the weed and scrub-choked bank. Immediately, the boy let out a high-pitched wail and began kicking at the bank's edge, trying to kick at her hands. The soil above her head crumbled in little avalanches as his feet stamped at the dirt. His skinny legs were at full stretch, almost scraping the top of her fingers. The little shit was trying to prevent her from getting up the bank.

She stared up at him and his face, long, black hair plastered to his temples and dark, wet eyes, came into focus. She knew this boy.

She heard someone shout out again. Someone was looking for him. His name registered in her ear with deafening clarity.

Noa. His name was Noa.

35

Saturday, eight weeks later

Kate entered the North Arm cemetery with her family and stopped to get her bearings. The cemetery was one of the oldest in the area, a vast, labyrinthine tract of treed avenues and landscaped grounds that had sprung into existence in the early 1900s and expanded over the years to encompass over forty hectares.

The cemetery lay shaded and still in the mid-morning sun. A crisp and jewel-bright winter morning with fine wisps of cloud streaking the sky. They chose the path to the left, following the sign that pointed to the Rose Garden. Archie ran ahead, zig-zagging his way among the gravestones. Geoff hurried after him, calling out.

Kate followed them at a slower pace. A small path led away to her right across to a section of flourishing ground cover, shaded by massive eucalypts and a single gnarled boab tree. There was no sign marking the garden, but Kate knew it was in remembrance of the many dozens of stillborn babies that had been disposed of without proper funerals in decades gone past. Babies whisked away from their mothers shortly after their delivery as part of the standard birthing practice of hospitals at the time.

Kate shivered, despite the sunshine, hugging the tiny body strapped to her chest in a carry swaddle. A tiny head, round and perfect, with the barest hint of whispery-fine hair peeked through the top of her carrier. She kissed her sleeping daughter lightly, feeling the powder-soft sensation of her skin. Amy. Beautiful Amy.

Without warning, Kate felt her body flood with ice as her mind flew back to Gabby's house. How close she had come to losing her baby. She stopped for a minute, breathing deeply, using the techniques she had been taught to calm her mind. She was getting used to the flashbacks and the anxiety attacks that followed, slowly learning how to move past the crippling fear for her family that gripped her, constricting her chest and making it hard to breathe. Exercise helped, and so did the counselling. She was learning to let the flashbacks wash over her and not allow them to take over.

Geoff looked back, as if sensing something was wrong. 'You all right?' he asked.

She smiled, giving him a thumbs-up sign. 'All good.'

He waited for her to catch up and put his arm through hers. She pressed in close.

She had been lucky. The final shot, fired off accidentally by Annette after being startled by Murchison, had missed her torso entirely. She had escaped with a flesh wound to her left shoulder. It could have been so much worse, and the thought of what could have happened to Amy mired her in guilt on a daily basis. Geoff had not said much, but she knew he too struggled at times, fighting through his own what-if scenarios. Their family was intact, but they were still trying to process the enormity of what they had survived.

Josh had taken it upon himself to keep her in the loop about the fall-out from the shooting. He had become a regular fixture in their lives, visiting every week. She knew Josh had started texting Geoff almost daily while she was in hospital to check on her progress, and the habit had continued even after she'd been discharged. To her surprise, she had learned that Skinner had been doing much the same, keeping tabs on her via Geoff. She accepted now that it had been a good thing. Geoff needed to feel in control of something after what had happened, and she had needed something to pull her out of herself. To keep her from slipping over the edge.

Through Josh, she had learned of the gun that Annette had used to fire at her: a revolver that Joel had purchased years before, during a brief stint when he'd joined a shooting range. Annette had found it after rooting around in Joel's wardrobe that day. Apparently, she had arrived at her son's home with no fixed intentions apart from retrieving his belongings without Gabby's permission. After finding the weapon and stewing in the house for hours, a different plan had presented itself.

The entire mess had developed into a critical-incident investigation, with the events of the night, including Murchison's presence at Gabby's house, under scrutiny. Kate had already fronted the investigation team five weeks ago, and had been informed only in the last week that she had been cleared by the Professional Standards Command.

Rounding a corner, Kate saw her father waiting for them on an adjoining path.

Archie spotted Gray and raced ahead. 'Grandpaaa!' Within seconds, Archie was squealing in delight as Gray swung him into the air.

Placing Archie on the ground, he turned to greet his daughter and son-in-law. Kate kissed him and shifted her body so Gray could catch a glimpse of Amy. Gray smiled, transfixed by the tiny, snuggled figure, two minuscule frown lines visible on her forehead as she concentrated on sleep.

Gray switched his scrutiny to Kate, studying her until she looked away. He squeezed her arm.

'I heard the Marshall brief is going back to the coroner next week.' She knew Gray had taken a keen interest in the case, getting in Josh's ear when he needed to.

'That was good work, Kit. Josh reckons it wouldn't have happened if you hadn't got the Pavićs' statement.'

Kate smiled lightly, acknowledging the compliment. She thought back to her interview with Ester and Marin. It seemed like a year ago, rather than a mere handful of weeks.

Kate remembered the brightly lit family room in which Noa had finally divulged what he had seen that night. It had taken the counsellor some time to coax him to speak. He had been hesitant and would not meet their eyes, but his account had been lucid and straightforward, exceeding all her expectations. Noa had been brilliant, just like Ester had promised.

Noa's simple retelling belied the horror of what he had witnessed. He had recounted seeing a woman clinging onto rocks, her body half swallowed by raging waters, a man desperately holding onto her shoulder, trying to prevent himself from being swept away. As Noa watched, the woman had, without warning, relinquished her grip on her companion. He had slid under the water, spluttering and screaming and trying to find purchase. He had resurfaced and managed to catch hold of her arm. According to Noa, they had struggled and he had seen the woman pressing the man's head under the water. In a few seconds, the man had washed away around the bend of the creek, his body disappearing almost instantly beneath the surge. The woman had then proceeded to pull herself up onto the bank. In fear for his own safety, Noa had described how he had desperately tried to kick at her to prevent her from climbing any closer to him.

Based on Noa's evidence and the Pavićs' and Eamon's statements, a new coronial investigation had been launched, with Gabby at its centre, unleashing the inevitable storm of media coverage. The DPP was still on the fence on whether to pursue manslaughter charges against Gabby, preferring to wait for any referral or findings arising from the inquest. Kate knew that Noa's recollections of the night, given the length of time that had lapsed and his age would be subject to challenge by Gabby's legal representatives. It was only Noa's word against Gabby's in the end. The inquest findings, Kate knew, could go either way.

According to Josh, Gabby had not said a word since it had all erupted, and Kate was still undecided on what had led her to this point. Had her marriage been that unbearable? Or had it been an opportunistic moment of weakness, the instinct for survival even at the expense of a loved one, that she had regretted ever since? Kate suspected they were unlikely to ever find out, but her mind had flicked back on more than one occasion to the last time she had seen Gabby at Esserton Station, that impression she'd received from Gabby of something akin to remorse.

For Neil and Annette, it had been a mixed victory. Annette had been charged with being armed with the intent to murder, as a result of her actions at Gabby's house, her intended victim being her daughter-in-law. From Josh, Kate understood that Annette's mental state was not good, spiralling into deep depression. Kate had no doubt she would be treated with leniency by the courts, given the circumstances. The woman needed counselling more than jail time.

'How's Murchison doing?' Gray broke into her thoughts, enquiring how the constable had fared under the PSC investigation.

'Fine, I think. He's back working, as far as I know.'

Kate and Geoff exchanged glances. Geoff was the only one Kate had divulged the whole story to, but neither made a comment.

Kate had not spoken to Murchison since the shooting, apart from a single visit he had made to her hospital bed, days after the incident. He had apologised, white-faced and contrite, shocked out of his bluster by the implications of the incident on his career and livelihood. Against her better judgement, she had omitted reporting his behaviour to the investigation team. To explain his presence on the night, she knew he had fed the investigating team a story about visiting a friend in the area when he had heard Annette's shots. He had been lucky not to be tested over the limit, but his alcohol readings must have complied. She figured Murchison owed her now, and that would no doubt come in handy in the future.

'How lucky were you that he turned up that night,' exclaimed Gray. 'I still can't believe how it all worked out.'

The feel of Murchison's hot breath on her neck flashed into Kate's mind and she bit back a retort. Yep, definitely a stroke of luck. She grimaced. Sensing her reluctance to be drawn on the issue, Gray dropped the subject.

They walked on, making their way along a row of graves to arrive at Kate's mother's gravestone. Aneesha Grayling: 1950–2012. From the shopping bag he was carrying, Gray removed two simple bouquets. He handed one to Kate and they laid the flowers on the grave. They stood side by side, not speaking, both busy with their own thoughts. Kate's eyes rose to Geoff and Archie, who were examining gravestones further down the row.

She turned to her father, noticing the more pronounced worry lines on his face. The last few weeks had taken their toll on him, too, she realised. She hesitated, and then spoke. 'Luke came up for a visit last week,' she said finally. 'Did he—'

Gray shook his head, not bothering to reply.

Kate bit her lip. Luke had promised her that he would see Gray before flying back to Sydney, but he had obviously chickened out.

They lapsed into silence once more.

Kate surveyed the gravestones beyond. She could see Geoff trying to corral Archie out of a newly landscaped area, a sign saying, *Keep Off the Plants*. She could tell Archie wasn't going to last much longer. They would need to get going soon.

A couple of rows away, a woman in jeans and a T-shirt was attending to what looked like four new gravesites all set together. It took Kate a moment to realise that the woman was Rosalyn Adderton, the mother of the dairy farmer who had killed his family before taking his own life. The graves must be that of her son's family. The woman glanced up and caught Kate's eye. Although Kate was sure she had been recognised, Rosalyn turned away, pretending she hadn't seen her. Kate followed suit, leaving her in peace. It was time to go, anyway.

They parted at the reflection pond situated right at the heart of the cemetery. Kate knew Gray would be staying on to visit Martin's grave. She kissed her father goodbye and joined her family walking towards the exit.

THEN

She plunged, seal-like, into the crashing surf, feeling the energy of the waves surge over her. She kicked hard and propelled herself forward with ease, impervious to the cold, determined to not come up for air until she had reached the sand bar. Her feet scraped sand grains and she delayed coming up for another few seconds, feeling her lungs strain, enjoying the discipline of taking her body to the edge. Finally, when she felt her lungs couldn't take any more, she burst out of the water, breathing in air in rapid gulps.

Resting for a few minutes on the sand bar, she gazed around. Apart from a few stray swimmers and families dotted along the beach, the bay was empty, the cloudless skies and emerald blue waters for once left to the locals to enjoy. A group of seagulls circled each other overhead, squawking half-heartedly. She floated on her back, her eyes half closed, enjoying the sun's warmth on her skin, letting her body gently move with the waves. A stray wave washed over her and she dipped below the surface, lazily treading water.

'Gabby!'

The sound of someone calling her name floated through the air and she surfaced. A figure was standing on the beach, waving at her. His face was in shadow, but she knew immediately who it was. A surge of adrenaline flooded her and she felt a rush of happiness.

Joel had made it, after all. Standing on the sand bank, she half rose out of the water and waved back, beckoning him in. She watched as he removed his shirt and plunged into the water in his boardies. She could see his head bobbing in the water as he swam towards her. She had swum out a distance and he had to rest halfway. She waited for him, laughing and refusing to swim back and meet him. He reached her finally, out of breath and gasping for air. His arms were around her and they were laughing. His body was warm next to her. They kissed, the stubble on his cheeks gently grazing her skin. She tasted the saltwater on his lips. The water lapped at her body and the gulls squawked overhead.

Gabby's eyes opened and she was instantly alert. The luminous digits on her bedside clock blinked *Thurs 5 April, 2.52 am*. She turned around, automatically reaching out for Joel, her hand stopping just short of waking the immobile figure lying next to her. She crept her hand back and lay with her eyes open, staring at the ceiling, waiting for the emotion to pass. The sudden, intense physical hunger for her husband would fade, as it always did, to be replaced by emptiness.

She hadn't dreamed of him in weeks. She had hoped the dreams had finally passed, that she could close her eyes and no longer have to relive his face. The weight of his body. The sound of his laughter.

It was easy during the day, when memories of Joel barely grazed her thoughts. On occasion a stranger's expression or the smell of Joel's aftershave on someone else's skin could leave her breathless, slipping through her guard. But those moments were few and far between. Joel was fading and she preferred it that way. She could serve up her carefully crafted blank self to the media without fear of disturbing the subsoil below. Only at night did Joel come back to her in technicolour reality.

Her companion moved beside her, grunting softly in his sleep. Gabby turned her head, her expression softening. She watched him sleep, his chest moving gently up and down, his mouth slightly open, the blanket rumpled halfway down his torso. She moved closer to him and closed her eyes, waiting for sleep to come.

AUTHOR'S NOTE

The events and characters in this novel are fictional, but were inspired by real-life flooding events and stories of survival and rescue that I came across while writing this story.

To the many thousands of dedicated police officers who juggle family life with one of the most challenging and heart-breaking jobs in the world, I suspect I haven't come close to scratching the surface. I know I have taken liberties with Kate being on active duty so late in her pregnancy. This and all other procedural liberties, remain my own.

To the people of Northern Rivers New South Wales on Bundjalung Country, please forgive the great cheek of plonking an entirely fictional town in your midst. All errors and failures of description, are my own.

This novel was written on the traditional lands of the Dharawal nation.

ACKNOWLEDGEMENTS

To the incredible team at HarperCollins Australia, for the gift of the Banjo Prize and everything that has come afterwards. I still can't quite believe you picked me! Thank you to my publisher, Anna Valdinger for *getting* Kate Miles straight away, and for *that* phone call, which began this whole fantastic ride. Thank you for all the laughs and each of our 'ten-minute' chats. You are an absolute gun to work with!

Thank you to the wordsmiths who worked on this novel to ensure that it made it out into the world in the best possible state, particularly Alexandra Nahlous, Abigail Nathan and Lachlan McLaine. To Darren Holt for the stunning cover art. Got it in one. Thank you! To the entire HarperCollins Australia marketing, sales and publicity teams, especially Dave Cain, for cheering this novel on.

To Alex Adsett, for always making time to listen and having my back every step of the way. I'm so lucky to have you in my corner. Thank you!

To my very first readers, who gave me feedback when I was first starting out and dipping my toes into writing: Tom Flood of Flood Manuscripts, Ruby Ashby-Orr and Cosima McGrath of Affirm Press and the bloody brilliant Emma Viskic. The draft that I entered into the Banjo Prize is the direct result of your generosity, time and feedback and I will be forever in your debt for my apprenticeship.

To all my early readers for your insights and for gently nudging me to do better: the Wilson family, Frank & Co Readers, the Queensland Writers' Centre Publishable Program, Baz Radburn and the incomparable Cass Moriarty. The manuscript is a much better read for your input.

I relied heavily on the generous advice and feedback of barrister, Les Nicholls and Sergeant Andrew Dante for police procedural matters. All errors and bending of facts to fit the story, are entirely of my own making.

I owe a huge debt to the generous feedback of my sensitivity readers including Lee Valentine and Sam Wren Quan Sing of Frank & Co Readers, and Emma Stergio, Kristen Watts and Virginia Grant, especially in relation to my depiction of Noa. A huge thank you for your advocacy and advice, always guiding me in the direction of positive representation.

To all my friends in the writing community who have helped me on my way, with encouragement, friendship, feedback, advice and plain old understanding of the work that goes into writing and trying to find a home for your words. Especially to all the established authors who go out of their way to make time for emerging writers. I have been overwhelmed by the generosity of the Australian writing community, who have welcomed and held so many doors open for me.

A very special shout-out to all the friends I have made through my local writers' group run by the Fellowship of Australian Writers, especially to the crew behind the Writers Unleashed Festival, who have kept this local event running for over a decade entirely through volunteer power. Here's to many more years!

To all the legends at BOOK CLUB, for your friendship and support and all the laughs!

Thank you to all the wonderful book humans who provided a cover quote for this book. No review means quite as much as those from people in the book industry and I am incredibly grateful for your generous words.

To my fellow 2022 debut writers, AKA our Twitter 'book gang'. It has been an absolute joy sharing these months with you unpacking our shared worries, insecurities and excitement about our books entering the big wide literary world. Looking forward to seeing each of your gorgeous books fly!

To the very many writing organisations, writers' centres, publications, podcasts, and festivals who support the book industry and emerging writers. I have constantly benefitted from the resources, events, workshops, opportunities and content – so much of it for free – that you make available to readers and writers. It has made a huge difference to my writing and publishing trajectory and I am enormously grateful. To bookstores and libraries who connect readers with books, none of this would work without you.

To my friends and especially to my family – the McKenzie and Wijesekera/Wickramasinghe clans – for your unwavering support, and for not missing a beat when I suddenly announced I had written a novel. To *grandma* who would have loved to have been here for this moment. To my work colleagues for your support and for granting me extended leaves of absence to devote to writing. A massive thank you to Shaw Fire Arts for the never-ending printing requests!

To my husband and children, who bear the brunt of my frequent mental flights of absence as I spend time in my parallel made-up-world. Thank you. I couldn't have done this without you and wouldn't want to. To Scott for supporting and believing in me, every single time. Love you, always.

And finally, dear reader, to you for choosing this book and for giving me your time.

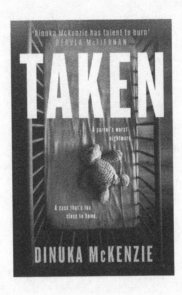

'Dinuka McKenzie has talent to burn'
DERVLA McTIERNAN

TAKEN

A parent's worst nightmare.

A case that's too close to home.

DINUKA McKENZIE

Detective Sergeant Kate Miles is back from maternity leave and struggling on multiple fronts – the pressures of a second child, financial strain from her husband losing his job, and a corruption scandal that may involve her father.

When an infant goes missing, Kate finds herself fronting a high-profile and emotionally fraught case. Was baby Sienna removed from her bassinet by an unknown abductor or is the answer much closer to home?

Amidst a frenzied media demanding answers, and a station chief looking for any reason to remove her from the investigation, Kate is pushed to her limits, pulled between the competing demands of the family at the centre of the case and her own spiralling personal life.

'A masterclass in crimes that are too close to home …
Prepare yourself for another fast-paced thrill-ride with heart.'
Hayley Scrivenor